Love, Ava

Love, Ava

Alton Rivers

ST. MARTIN'S PRESS

NEW YORK

This is a work of fiction. All of the characters, organizations, and events portrayed in this novel are either products of the author's imagination or are used fictitiously.

www.stmartins.com

Design by Maggie Goodman

ISBN-13: 978-0-312-36279-9
ISBN-10: 0-312-36279-X

First Edition: February 2007

10   9   8   7   6   5   4   3   2   1

Dedicated to the memory of my son, John Alan,
who brought so much joy and laughter to the world,
and asked for so little in return.

Acknowledgments

Many thanks to my literary agent, Tom Colchie.

My special thanks to Bob Wyatt, friend and editor, who did his magic in turning a badly flawed manuscript into a novel.

Many thanks to Charles Spicer, Joseph Cleemann, and others at St. Martin's Press. It was a great pleasure to work with such a helpful and professional group.

And most of all, gratitude to my best friend and wife, Conni, for her support and patience.

Love, Ava

Prologue

I t was the hottest day of the summer—everybody was saying so—and the twelve-year-old boy felt the heat of the cement through the soles of his shoes as he hurried along North Tryon Street toward the inviting shade of the Carolina Theater marquee. There was no line at the ticket window, and he had his coins ready. He clutched his ticket as he stepped into the elaborate lobby. The soft lighting and air-conditioned chill were relief from the blinding whiteness and blistering heat of the August sun. He entered the theater, and after several eye-blinking moments adjusting to the darkness he hurried carefully down the aisle lined by small, shielded lights. He chose a seat in a nearly empty middle row and settled into the comfort of the soft upholstery and the dark solitude.

He ran his fingers through his dark hair, brushing it from his eyes, and looked up at the images on the giant screen as the feature movie began.

Warm colors flooded the scene: a small Parisian bistro filled with accordion music. The glow of lights above the dance floor reflected brightly in the mirrors and glittered in the glasses shelved behind the bar. It was

Paris nightlife taken from "The Snows of Kilimanjaro," Hemingway's
story of American expatriates in the twenties.

The boy sat quietly, his eyes fixed upon the screen.

*A tall, handsome man wearing a gray suit enters the bistro and orders a
drink at the bar, exchanging cordial greetings with the middle-aged woman
who serves him and who calls him Harry. He accepts the drink and turns toward the dance floor, drawn to the sound of a woman's laughter. A dozen
couples fill the floor. Again, there is the laughter, and through the crowd of
dancers he sees her. She is wearing a red dress, and she is brunette and beautiful. He knows the man dancing with her. It is Compton of the* Chicago
Tribune *Paris desk, a friend. He watches them a few moments and then
carefully makes his way across the floor.*

He taps his friend on the shoulder. "Hello, Compton."

"Harry!" Compton and the woman stop dancing. "How's the book?"

*"How's anybody's book? It isn't finished." He steps toward the woman,
offering his hand to her. "Mind if I cut in?"*

"Oh no, my friend," Compton replies. "No, no."

"Perhaps you'll allow the lady to decide."

*"Sorry, Harry. She's with me." They dance away and the woman looks
back at him, her smile teasingly sympathetic. As they disappear among the
other dancers, he again hears her pleasant, throaty laughter.*

*Unhurriedly, Harry makes his way to the front door. The owner of the
bistro, a small man wearing an apron and garters on his sleeves, stops him
and asks, "You are leaving so soon, Harry? Is something wrong?"*

*"A case of avoiding a broken nose, Emile—either mine or Compton's."
He looks back at the dance floor and grins wryly. "Because a laugh like hers
would just have to lead to a lousy fight. Good night, my friend."*

The boy was riveted to the screen, mesmerized by the dark-haired actress. He thought of the recent *Time* magazine article about her. It had described her high cheekbones, the slight dimples when she smiled, the cleft
in her chin. The article said she had green catlike eyes, and that part of her

attraction was her mischievous nature, her devil-may-care attitude. It said she was headstrong. He didn't know about that, but he now knew that she was just as pretty as the article had said.

And there was something else about her. He didn't know what, but *something*.

Now the scene changed to a crowded, fashionable club. It was a larger room than the bistro, and it was dimly lit, candlelight flickering on table-tops. Well-dressed men and women sat at tables, or on the floor, or stood along the walls, quietly listening to black musicians playing slow, plaintive jazz.

At the side of the room the tall man leans against the wall in a slight slouch, an unlit cigarette in his mouth, listening closely to the mournful sounds of a saxophone. He holds a drink in one hand, searching his suit pocket for a match with the other. A soft, sultry voice comes from the shadows beside him. "Would you, please?"

It is the woman he had seen dancing at the bistro an hour earlier, the woman in the red dress. She leans forward, holding a cigarette. "Well, hello," the man says.

He strikes the match and holds it to her cigarette, the glow of the small flame illuminating her face. He studies her closely during the brief life of the flame. Sensuous eyes are languid in the soft light. Her skin is luminous, with soft shadows at the high cheekbones and the distinctive cleft of her chin.

The boy had been transported. The dark theater was another world, and he was carried away by her face, her voice. He was entranced.

The woman turns toward the music. For several moments she listens quietly, thoughtfully. Watching the saxophone player, she asks, "Hasn't that African any piety at all?"

The man doesn't answer. He sees Compton across the room. He is looking for her. The tall man straightens from his slouch. "I must remember my manners. Are you, ah . . . are you particularly Compton's lady?"

"No. I'm not particularly Compton's lady. I'm not Compton's lady at all." She turns back to him. "I'm my own lady."

"Then how would you like it if you and I were to just piety right out of here?"

She pauses, her eyes searching his. For the briefest moment she seems almost afraid, as if her answer will change her life forever. Then, smiling, she answers, "I suspect I would like it very much."

Harry couldn't take his eyes from her.

Neither could the twelve-year-old boy.

He shifted in his seat, his elbow on the armrest and his hand cupping his chin. He gazed at the actress as though trying to memorize her every feature and wanting to remember forever the sound of her voice. She was from North Carolina, too, and he had read the *Time* article about her again and again in his room. There were times he lay in bed for hours, looking at her photograph on the magazine's cover.

He felt magically drawn to her, and he sat quietly in the darkness, looking intently at the shadows and light forming the image of Ava Gardner on the screen.

One

C aptain Russell Jefferson ran his fingers through his dark hair and shifted his weight impatiently in the deep, soft chair. He glanced at his wristwatch. Two minutes since he had last checked. He felt the waiting room closing in on him. He was the only person in the room except for the receptionist, who was typing and seemed to have forgotten he was there. She seemed also unaware that time no longer moved. He started to say something to her, then changed his mind. He looked at his watch again and stood.

The United States Air Force uniform, its insignias and silver wings gleaming, fit Russ Jefferson's six-foot frame perfectly. Although he couldn't have been much more than thirty, his expression, hardened by conflict or pain, made him seem older.

He moved about uncertainly. He rubbed the back of his neck. His eyes darted back and forth at every small noise. Now he turned squarely toward the receptionist and said, "This appointment was for three. Are you sure he wants to see me again?"

She stopped typing, looked at him, and said, "It's only five after, Captain. The doctor will see you in a moment." She gave him a brief, understanding smile and then quickly turned away, perhaps to avoid staring at the scars. They were ugly, covering the cheek and temple at his left eye and extending above his eyebrow.

Her fingers had become a blur over the Selectric typewriter when the intercom buzzed. She picked up the phone, pushed the lit intercom button, and answered, looking at him. "You may go in now," she said as she returned the receiver to its cradle.

He thanked her, crossed the room, and opened the wide door of the office. A heavy, balding man rose from behind a cluttered desk. His thick glasses reflected light from the overhead fluorescents. "Come in, Captain," the psychiatrist said. "It's good to see you again."

The younger man didn't answer, taking the chair indicated by the doctor.

"And it's soon to be *Major* Jefferson, isn't it?" A perfunctory smile appeared. "Congratulations on your promotion."

"Thanks."

"When do you pin on the gold leafs?"

"A couple of weeks."

The psychiatrist sat down and began a search of his desktop. The smile didn't last long. "Things been going okay since we last talked?"

"I guess so. No problems."

"You look tanned and fit."

"A few rays at the pool. Not much else to do."

"Ah, yes, I *am* your last hurdle, aren't I?" the doctor said, as if they were old friends. He found the file he was looking for and opened it.

The friendly tone didn't work. Russ remained edgy. "Yes, you are," he said.

"You've come a long way. Shoulder and back surgery. Burn treatment at Wilford Hall." He turned a page, glanced at it, and put the file down. "I'm impressed."

"Impressed?"

"Yes. Yes, I am."

"Don't be impressed with me. I just lay there. The docs did the work."

"I'm told you were very cooperative." The doctor removed a pipe from an ashtray and began filling it with tobacco from a leather pouch.

"Did I have a choice?"

The laugh was an abrupt snort. "I suppose it seemed that you didn't. But you did well in physical therapy. That was a lot of painful work, Captain."

Russ said nothing.

"I see in your file that Dr. Pendleton recommended further plastic surgery. He said that your scars could be minimized. Perhaps two more procedures." With a pudgy index finger, he gently tamped the tobacco in the bowl. "Why didn't you let him do that?" he asked.

"I got tired of wearing bandages. Tired of stitches and staples." The pilot shrugged. "Besides, the eye works."

"You're very fortunate, you know. No permanent damage to your vision."

"Yeah. That was my lucky day, all right."

Casually, the doctor jotted a note as he asked, "How are you feeling about things now?"

"Things? What things?"

"Things we've talked about before."

Russ shifted restlessly. "Fine," he said. "Really terrific."

"You seem a bit agitated. Something happen?"

"No. I just don't think this is necessary."

"Don't you?" The doctor struck a match. He held the match just above the bowl and began puffing slowly.

"I don't know why I'm here."

"Nothing sinister. Nothing mysterious." The doctor's round face was half hidden behind the smoke. "We need to talk about your capture, Captain. Just routine."

"For you maybe. Not for me."

"We're completing our interviews with you now. All of you."

"Interviews?" A cynical smile appeared briefly on the captain's face.

"Yes. There's always much to learn from the human experience." The man behind the desk puffed again. "You and the others experienced a lot of pain during the time you were POWs."

Russ's expression did not change.

"Self-discipline, Captain. When you were released, every one of you wore a somber face until you were on the plane because you didn't want the North Vietnamese to see any expression of emotion. That's amazing control. Yes, there's a great deal we can learn from you."

"Fighter pilots have a reputation for being loose, but we *do* know about discipline," Russ started to explain, then wondered why he was bothering. No need getting into a useless exercise. "Doctor, is there some particular reason I'm here?"

"You've been physically treated. Your back. Your shoulders. The burns."

"And so?"

"And so the Air Force decided you should spend some time with guys like me."

"To see if we've become a bunch of psychotic cripples?"

"It could be useful. You've known a lot of mental and emotional turmoil, Captain. There may be things you want to get off your chest, things you might not want to say to a friend or a relative."

"I really don't need this." Russ stood abruptly and walked over to the window. He stared out into the glare of the Texas sun. An enlisted man in a work uniform was mowing grass.

"Perhaps you're right, but I don't think it can do any harm. Do you?" The doctor sounded nonthreatening, speaking slowly and softly. "We can finish up today."

The pilot stood silently for several moments, still looking out the window. Then he said, "Your job really sucks."

"Let's try it for a few minutes."

Russ hesitated, shrugged a reluctant agreement, and returned to his chair. He tried to find a comfortable position. "Okay. Go."

"Are you hanging out with your friends?"

"A couple of guys are still here."

"Do you spend much time with them?"

"We get together for dinner once in a while."

"How are they?"

"Okay, I guess."

"Are they feeling all right about things?"

"Yeah, except for being bugged by you guys."

"Have they received their assignments?"

"We all have."

"Your friends are returning to the cockpit, aren't they? They're going back to fighter squadrons."

"Yeah."

"But you're not?"

"That's right." Russ's tone became more defensive.

The doctor leaned forward, his chin jutting. Behind the thick lenses, his eyes were penetrating. "Have you called on Noonan's family yet?"

"Yeah. Flew up to Kansas City. Went to their home Wednesday night."

"Did you have a long visit?"

"With his mother. An hour, I guess."

"Was it difficult?"

"Of course. Don't you think it'd be *difficult* to talk to her after you've killed her son?"

"You didn't kill her son."

"He was my backseater. It was my responsibility to get him back from the mission."

"How did you feel after talking to her?"

"I don't know."

"Of course you do," said the doctor. "You felt better. Or worse."

"She was nice. It was hard."

"Did you feel less guilty after you talked to her?"

"No."

The doctor paused thoughtfully, and Russ knew the line of questioning was about to change. "Tell me," the heavy man finally said, "how do you feel about having been sent to Vietnam and made to fight?"

"Better than if I had been sent into the war and *not* allowed to fight."

"Shooting down the two MiGs. Killing two pilots. How do you feel about that?"

"Pretty damned good. They were trying to shoot me down at the time."

"And the bombing missions? Killing civilians?"

"Better them than me."

The doctor studied his pipe bowl, then looked at the younger man closely. Jefferson was discarding questions with cocky responses, a conditioned reflex. "What about the morality of the war, Captain?"

"That's for religious scholars and Timothy Leary to work out."

"Will history judge us favorably?"

"If we wrote it, it might. But winners write the history. This time we aren't writing it. We lost."

The sound of a lawn mower's small motor came through the closed windows. The doctor waited until it went away, then asked, "How do you feel about your future?"

"A little better than I did a year ago."

"You're single. Met any girls since you've been back?"

"No. Have you?"

"I'm not a hero flyboy," the doctor said with a smile. "Besides, I'm married."

"Congratulations."

"You were married."

"Yes."

"How long since the divorce?"

"A couple of months."

"Tough. Must've been difficult to come back to a marriage and—"

"I didn't come back to a marriage." Russ shifted his weight uncomfortably. "She left me more than two years ago. The paperwork got held up."

"What caused the breakup?"

"Who knows? Things."

"Let's talk about your marriage."

"Let's not." Russ's voice tightened as if his throat hurt. A different pain.

"Where were you when the marriage broke up?"

"Broke up?" He gave the doctor a contemptuous look. "You make it sound like a train wreck."

"Maybe it was. What caused the wreck, Captain?"

"She didn't like life on a remote Air Force base in the middle of a desert." The younger man's eyes were coldly locked to the doctor's. "She grew up in Beverly Hills."

"You were at that remote base when she married you. She must have seen something attractive about your life."

"At first she found it exciting and adventurous. But it turned out to be the wrong kind of excitement. The wrong kind of adventure." He arched an eyebrow. "Where she was from, excitement was an afternoon polo match. Adventure was sailing to Santa Catalina."

"And?"

"And she soon learned she didn't belong in a world where her husband's adventure is a war in Southeast Asia and excitement is staying alive." An emotional silence gripped the room. A long, empty silence. Finally Russ shrugged and said, "She told me it wasn't normal. She couldn't stay in it."

The doctor studied his pipe for a moment and then looked up. "Are you ready to face the world?"

"Isn't that your job?" Russ asked through a half-smile. "To get me ready?"

"I'll rephrase the question. Do you feel ready to reenter the world?"

"Doctor, I'm on my way to London. Embassy duty. Know a better way to reenter than that?"

"Think you're ready to handle the pressure?"

"It's the *embassy*. Pressure? Embassy pressure is like the pressure *you* work under. You screw up and you just stop at a bar on your way home and have a couple of fancy drinks with umbrellas in them. Fighter pilots work under a pressure that if you screw up, you're a smoking hole."

"You don't have to go to the embassy," said the doctor. It sounded like an accusation. "You had several choices, in fact. You could've had an assignment to F-4s in North Carolina. Practically at home."

Russ said nothing. He straightened in his chair.

"Isn't that right?"

The nod was almost imperceptible. "Yes," Russ said tightly.

The doctor paused to relight his pipe. After he got it going again he squinted at his patient and in a cold voice asked, "Why did you choose the embassy?"

Russ's eyes hardened. He looked at the doctor for a moment and then said, "Say again?"

"Why don't you want to fly?" Bright reflections in the thick eyeglasses obscured the doctor's eyes. "Why did you ask your General Kreeger to get you an assignment to the safe work of an embassy rather than return to the cockpit?"

Russ leapt to his feet and pounded his fist down on the desktop with a loud crash. A framed picture toppled. "That's enough!" he hissed sharply. He glared at the doctor for a long moment, then walked out of the office, slamming the door behind him.

Russ drove the rental car slowly toward the officers' club. It was early. There was time for a drink before dinner. He concentrated on his driving, not for reasons of safety but in an attempt to block out the meeting with the psychiatrist. It didn't work. The questions kept ringing in his ears. Why? *Why?* Why was he alive and why was Noonan dead?

It was hot and the Texas summer had been dry. Sprinklers were busy on both sides of the street, silently swinging their clear arcs in large circles. Water was nurturing and keeping the grass alive, and he wondered what would nurture him, what would keep him alive.

The shrink had hit a nerve. *What caused the breakup?* He didn't want to think about Jenny. He had willed his mind to not think about her. There was too much pain and he had to shut out the hurt. *Why don't you want to go back to the cockpit? Why don't you want to fly?* The one thing he had loved. The one thing he had done best. And he wouldn't return to it. Why had he chosen the embassy? He didn't know. Why didn't he *know* what he wanted?

Only a few cars were in the parking lot, and he took a space near the entrance to the officers' club. He strode into the main foyer and followed the wide hallway to the bar. It was a large, well-appointed room. He took a stool at the long L-shaped bar and looked around. The place was almost empty. Not like a fighter squadron's club. One man sat at the other end, and a couple of others shared a small table near the bar. He ordered a bourbon and water.

Russ glanced at the two officers at the table. They were wearing class B, short-sleeved uniforms and pilot wings. One was a lieutenant, the other a captain. Russ could see that the captain was describing an aerobatic maneuver by the way he was using his hand to depict an aircraft in a roll. Fighter pilots couldn't talk about flying if they couldn't use their hands. His drink was placed in front of him, and he lit a cigarette as he studied the amber liquid.

At the small table, the captain illustrating the maneuver to his friend hadn't noticed Jefferson enter the bar. He was saying, "So I was showing my student how smooth an aileron roll should be," and then he suddenly stopped talking and became quiet. "I'll be damned," he said in a lowered voice.

"What is it?" asked the lieutenant as he turned to see what had distracted his friend.

"Someone I never expected to see again."

The lieutenant turned back to the captain. "Who? The guy at the end of the bar?"

"Yeah."

"You know him?"

"Not personally. He was at Udorn when I first got there. He shot down two MiGs. We were in different squadrons and I never got to know him, but I knew who he was. Everybody knew who he was."

"Who is he?"

"That's Russ Jefferson. One hell of a fighter pilot. Maybe the best of the best. Lots of people thought he'd be wearing stars someday."

"Oh, really?" The lieutenant turned again to look at the MiG killer.

The captain sipped his drink. He remembered the day Jefferson had been shot down. He'd never forget it: May 10. Last year. The strike was one of the biggest of the war, and losses were high, but the buzz that night at the bars was about Jefferson because he was one of only a few fighter pilots who had gained celebrity status in Vietnam. Word had it that the F-4 Phantom pilot had ejected right over the target he had just bombed.

No one expected that he would ever make it back. Not ever.

"I'll be damned," the captain said again, as if he couldn't quite believe it. "Russ Jefferson."

Two

Rain had fallen steadily throughout the morning, and few, if any, of the American embassy staff had left the large building at Grosvenor Square for lunch. Rather than bothering with wraps and umbrellas, they had chosen the embassy's large cafeteria in the basement or one of its several coffee shops.

The coffee shop on the third floor was crowded. Near the corner three women sat in quiet conversation. Joanna Thompson, Irene Harrington, and Vivian Rutherford were of varying ages, but they all wore sweaters and pearls.

"We'll be a sodden mess tomorrow," said Joanna, her fingers tracing the gray streak that ran from her widow's peak through her dark hair.

"Reynolds doesn't expect you to go in the rain, does he?" asked Irene Harrington.

"My dear husband believes there is no excuse worthy of missing an Arsenal match. Not illness. Not a family funeral. Certainly not rain." Joanna shrugged helplessly.

"There's more excitement at a funeral than in my office," complained Irene, her dark-streaked blond hair swinging slightly at her shoulders as she shook her head. "Why are finance people so incredibly boring? Their only interest is endless columns of numbers. It's depressing." She picked up her purse from the floor and took out a pack of cigarettes.

"You should work for my boss," said Joanna. "God, Eads is such an ass." She watched Irene take a cigarette from the pack and braced herself for a wave of craving.

Irene turned to the third woman. "I wish your promotion to the Air Attaché's office would come soon, Viv," she said.

"I'm told the first of the year," Vivian Rutherford said softly. "We'll see."

"I want your job. You have no idea what it's like to be condemned to daily servitude with dull bureaucrats."

"Daily *servitude*?" Vivian raised an amused eyebrow.

"Well, it's true," insisted Irene, smiling mischievously.

"You'll like my office much better," Vivian assured her.

"God, I know! An office with three young military officers. Throw *me* in that briar patch."

"There goes my new guy now," said Vivian, nodding toward the wide doorway.

The other two secretaries looked and saw a slender man wearing an Air Force uniform walk past the coffee shop. "Major Jefferson?" Joanna asked.

"Yes, Major Jefferson," said Vivian.

Still looking at the door, Irene lit the cigarette held centered between pursed lips. The lighter snapped off and she released blue smoke toward the ceiling. "How is he doing, Viv?"

"He seems to be settling in."

"I'd love to settle in with him." The blonde batted her eyelashes with a mock innocence. "That dark, mysterious manner is such a turn-on."

With the longing look of a smoker attempting to quit, Joanna watched her friend exhale and said, "He seems terribly unfriendly. Almost rude, in fact."

"He's quite nice, actually," Vivian replied.

Irene pushed a strand of hair away from her face and brought the cigarette back to her mouth, hesitating before placing it between her lips to say, "I've met him in the halls three or four times, and he hasn't even spoken."

"It's just that . . . well, he's one of those intense ones," Vivian said. "He's been busy since he's been here. Today, for example: studying embassy policies all morning; a lunch meeting with a squadron commander from Spain; tied up all afternoon. He's hardly had time for chatting with the staff."

"I didn't expect him to chat," retorted Joanna. "Just to say hello or something."

"I'm sure you'll like him once you get to know him." Vivian straightened in her chair and placed both hands on the edge of the table, a signal that she was through with this conversation. "It's one-thirty. I must get back to my desk."

"Yes, me too," said Joanna.

"Yes, back to the cages to tame those wild columns of numbers," muttered Irene as she gathered her things.

They left the coffee shop together. Irene walked over to the elevator. "See you later, Viv," she said, pressing the *up* button. "You too, Joanna." The other two secretaries gave her a small wave and left her waiting for the elevator as they continued down the hallway toward their offices.

Vivian stopped at the door marked OFFICE OF MILITARY AFFAIRS and said, "Enjoy your afternoon, Joanna."

"I will. Eads will be at the Air Attaché's staff meeting most of the afternoon."

Vivian smiled at her friend and then stepped into the office. After stopping at the private bath to check her makeup, she went to the newly assigned major's office, looked about briefly, and turned out the light. She paused, her hand resting on the doorknob, then closed the door and returned to her desk in the OMA's outer office.

She sat down, unlocked the center drawer of her desk, and removed the files she had put away before lunch. It would be a quiet afternoon. Commander Graves was working with the Intelligence and Research staff this afternoon. Major Jefferson . . . well, Major Jefferson was just *out*. Her eyes returned to the door of the new major's office.

Major Russell T. Jefferson. A strange one, all right. She had implied to her friends that he was really no different from any of the other military officers assigned to the embassy, but that was far from true. Only three weeks at the embassy and he was already getting off on the wrong foot with some very important people.

There was, for example, the instance just this morning. *I won't be in this afternoon, Miss Rutherford,* he'd said. *If anyone asks for me, just tell them I'm out.* Just like that.

He was scheduled, she had reminded him, for a 2.00 P.M. briefing in the Air Attaché's conference room, mandatory for all Air Force officers assigned to the embassy.

I'll be out all afternoon, Miss Rutherford, he had repeated. *If anyone asks, I am out of the office until tomorrow morning.* And he had left.

She opened the file. Regarding the missed meeting, maybe she could smooth things over. The Air Attaché, General Elliott, still owed her a favor or two.

Major Jefferson was different, all right. He certainly turned the heads of the younger ladies, and she understood why. The black hair and dark eyes. His perfectly tailored uniforms, adorned with ribbons beneath the pilot wings. He moved with a kind of lightness on his feet that made them think he was surely a divine dancer. But there was something else about him, something that warned others to stay away.

It was something other than temperament or moodiness. Something other than rudeness. It was an anger. And, of course, those horrible scars.

Lieutenant Colonel Scott Mitchell waited in the Columbia Club, the white-columned United States Air Force officers' club in London, just off Oxford Road. He looked out the rain-streaked window. Russ Jefferson was late.

It had been three years since the former squadron mates had seen each other. A long time. A lot had happened since then. Mitchell was eager to see Russ, but he was also concerned. His friend had been through a lot.

Suddenly Russ appeared through the wide glass doors. Umbrella under his arm. Turtleneck and corduroy sports coat. Mitchell got up from the table and started toward his friend, and when he was halfway across the room Russ saw him. Mitchell grinned and said, "I was about to send out a search party." The two men embraced, and Mitchell led his old friend to the table.

"You look great, Russ. Glad you could get away." The waiter arrived and Mitchell ordered two bourbons. Straight up.

"What are you doing in this part of the world?"

"A short stopover on my way back to Spain. Had to look up my old wingman."

"How'd you know I was at the embassy?"

"I bumped into General Kreeger at the Pentagon last week, and when I told him I'd be stopping in London on my way back to Spain, he told me you were here."

"I heard they made you squadron commander at Torrejón."

"The Sixty-third Fighter Squadron. Twenty minutes from Madrid. What could be better?"

"Congratulations."

"Thanks. And congratulations to you, too. Your promotion. You must be the youngest major in the Air Force." He glanced at Russ's clothing. "Don't you wear uniforms at the embassy?"

"I went by the flat and changed."

The waiter put their drinks in front of them. Mitchell raised his glass and waited for Russ to raise his. The glasses clinked, the two men's eyes held in an unspoken toast, and after a moment's pause, they drank.

Neither spoke for a moment, and then Mitchell asked, "Where do you live? I hear prices are steep here."

"You hear right. I was lucky. A senior officer in Political Affairs has been recalled to Washington on a special assignment. He'll be gone a year. It's an upscale flat, and he doesn't want to lose it. I'm subleasing it. It's really a good deal for me."

"Close to the embassy?"

"Ten-minute drive. Chelsea, not far off Kings Road."

"Have you bought a British sports car yet?"

"No. Bought a VW from the guy who owns the flat. I don't drive it a lot, though. Parking in London is a nightmare. I usually grab a taxi to get around in the city."

"Is it true what they say about swinging London?"

"Don't know. Haven't been out much."

Mitchell nodded and looked curiously at his younger friend. He and General Kreeger had discussed at length Russ's capture and rehabilitation. Russ was Kreeger's boy. What they knew about the past year and a half of Russ's life raised lots of troubling questions and speculation. As a way of taking care of Russ, General Kreeger had gotten him this assignment to the embassy.

Rain lashed at the window now, distorting the view of the grass and hedges of the grounds and the broad street beyond. Russ lit a cigarette.

Mitchell leaned forward. "I want you to visit me at Torrejón, soon. Some of our old squadron mates are there. Lane Temple's my A-flight commander." He waited for a response and, when Jefferson only nodded, continued, "Phil Drake is also in my squadron. He's my training officer."

Russ turned toward the window and stared out at the rain.

"You remember Phil. At my promotion party in '69 he was the guy that ended up on the roof, he and Noonan, dueling with brooms." The awkward moment had happened. Mitchell tightened his jaws and cleared his throat. He hadn't intended to get into any of that—the war, Noonan, or the Hanoi Hilton.

Russ sat still, his eyes hardened.

"Hey, I'm sorry," Mitchell said. "I didn't mean to bumble into anything you don't want to talk about."

"It's okay." Still Russ stared out the window. "Noonan was killed. That's reality. Every one of us lost friends."

"Yeah, but . . ."

"You don't need to worry about me."

"I know." Then Mitchell looked closely at his friend. "But if you *ever* need to talk to someone, let me know. I can be here by sundown—or sunup, whichever the case may be."

"I know. Thanks."

"Have you seen or heard from Jenny?"

"No."

"Any chance of the two of you working things out?"

"Old news, Scott. I got divorce papers from her lawyer in May. She would've gotten them to me sooner, but she didn't know the post office box number of the Hanoi Hilton."

"You two should find a way. You're perfect together." Mitchell knew he was getting very personal, but he was also an admitted true romantic, with a calling to lost causes.

"I called her when I got out of Wilford Hall. She was with a guy. Didn't want to see me." His voice was emotionless. "It's over."

Mitchell started to say something but stopped. There was too much pain there.

"Something else, Scott?" Russ cocked his head and frowned.

"Nope." A hesitant, sheepish smile appeared and Mitchell attempted lighter conversation. "In the meantime, this town isn't a bad place to be."

"London's a beautiful city."

"Yeah, but as soon as you get your fill of the soft life and before boredom sets in, let me know. I'll get you into my squadron, strap your ass in an F-4 cockpit again, rekindle the spirit. Stir the blood."

"The embassy's a good assignment. Good staff experience."

"A staff assignment's okay, but you'll soon want an operational assignment to a fighter squadron." Russ showed no interest, but Mitchell went on. "You're ready to be a squadron operations officer. That's the best preparation for command in the Air Force. Then get your own F-4 squadron, or maybe a new F-15 squadron." Still getting no response, he added lamely, "Then go to the Air War College and a high-level staff job."

"When did you become my career planner, Scott?"

"It's just that you've got your choice. General Kreeger will get you any assignment you want. He's your sponsor, and he's got one hell of a lot of horsepower."

"Your meddling is getting tiresome, Colonel."

Mitchell ignored the remark. "He wants you to take it easy for as long as you need. When you're ready, all you have to do is say the word." He gave Russ a conspiratorial smile. "Ask him to send you to Torrejón. You can be my operations officer. We'll have the best damn fighter squadron in the Air Force."

"I don't want to go to a fighter squadron."

Mitchell frowned. This wasn't the *real* Russ Jefferson. This guy was an imposter. He tried again to create a lighter mood. "London's gonna be one hell of a blast. Auto shows at Earl's Court. Wimbledon in June, strawberries and cream. FA football at Wembley." He put on a practiced leer. "Lotsa babes working in the embassy. You'll see—"

"Knock it off, Scott!" Jefferson's eyes flashed. "I'm *not* some depressed psycho."

"I know you aren't."

"Then stop the bullshit!"

"I'm just trying to talk sense to you. You're letting yourself down. Go after what you want! You always did before!"

"Just leave it alone, Scott." He stubbed out the cigarette in the ashtray.

"Losing Jenny? Hell, go see her. Go after her. *Fight* for her!"

"Goddamn it, leave it alone. Leave *me* alone." Russ rose quickly and walked toward the restrooms.

Carly Simon sang from the bar speakers.

Nice going, Scott, thought Mitchell. *What in the hell do you think you're doing? Playing shrink? But damn it, Russ needs help. Or a kick in the ass. Something to straighten him out.*

Mitchell checked the time and ordered two drinks. These would be the last. He had to catch his flight at Heathrow in two hours. It was time to get back to his squadron. He listened to Carly and the waiter brought the two shot glasses of bourbon.

"A toast," said Mitchell when Russ returned. He rose to his feet and lifted his glass.

"A toast," repeated Russ as he held his glass toward Mitchell.

"Here's to those who didn't make it back," said the lieutenant colonel. "And God help us that did."

Two hours later, Russ stood near Alexandra Gate at Hyde Park and viewed the scene curiously. With missionary zeal, his eyes closed and his face lifted toward the heavens, an old man stood on a bench, wailing his convictions, enjoying the self-indulgence of his own rhetoric. Russ turned away and crossed the park's Carriage Road. The pavement was still wet, but the rain had stopped before he and Scott had left the Columbia Club.

He had no intention of returning to the embassy now; after struggling with policy documents all morning and then spending two troubling hours with his friend, he decided to take a long walk. Plus, he had time to kill before getting ready for Gerald Graves's dinner party.

He exited the royal park and followed the sidewalk along Kensington Road. The walk was again crowded with old people and young mothers pushing prams. Artists were setting up their paintings along the path.

He approached an older woman and her eyes held his face—the left side of his face—then she looked away self-consciously. He was becoming accustomed to reactions to the crude and unsuccessful patch job by an overreaching and poorly equipped North Vietnamese who wanted to be a doctor when he grew up. On the other hand, docs at Wilford Hall, the Air Force burn center in San Antonio, had become extraordinarily skilled in burn treatment. Plenty of opportunities to practice during an eight-year war.

He crossed the wide street and walked south through a residential area. The quiet street was lined with Regency homes nearly obscured by the rich autumn foliage of plane trees. He walked slowly, enjoying the late afternoon. He turned another corner onto another street with impressive homes behind iron-railed fences and gates. Trees grew precisely lined in long, narrow strips of grass, and there was a garden square apparently for the private use of the privileged.

The afternoon became darker. He checked his watch to see that he had walked longer than he realized. Time to return to his apartment and shower. Gerald Graves, the Navy lieutenant commander in Military Affairs, had invited him to dinner this evening. Gerald had told him the newly assigned Judge Advocate General officer would also be there.

He walked another block or so, then looked around. He had no idea where he was. No problem, plenty of time. It couldn't be more than a ten-minute taxi drive to his apartment, and finding a taxi shouldn't be difficult.

A street sign told him this was Ennismore Gardens. He turned north, back toward Hyde Park, and began walking faster. It was getting cooler. Two hours earlier the corduroy coat and the light turtleneck had been comfortable, but he'd have to wear something warmer this evening.

A taxi entered the street at the next corner, turning toward him. Instinctively he waved at it before noticing its light was out, and he chided himself for thinking the first one would be available—that never happened. But it slowed as it passed him, approaching the curb and stopping only a few yards away. Unbelievable. He turned and moved toward the black car, watching as the driver got out and hurried to the back door.

There was one passenger—a woman wearing sunglasses and a wide-brimmed hat. The taxi would be available to him after all. It was a stroke of very good luck. Russ stopped a few steps from the side of the car, waiting until the woman got out and paid her fare.

A leg appeared. Her skirt pulled up slightly as she began getting out. Her legs were long and shapely, and she wore high heels. She was holding two packages, and the driver offered to take them. Russ couldn't hear her reply, but the driver remained beside the car door, and he assumed the passenger had refused the offer. He watched as the woman stepped from the taxi to the curb. He was admiring an ankle when her foot slipped on the damp surface. Without thinking, he dropped his umbrella, sprang two steps toward her, and caught her by the arm. As she fell against him the packages slipped from her hands and tumbled to the sidewalk. Easily and surely he held her, a firm grip on her arm, his other hand at her back as she steadied herself. Hesitantly, she removed her hand from his arm and reached to the taxi's door for support. He looked down at her. The dark sunglasses and hat concealed most of her face.

"Don't put any weight on that ankle, yet," he instructed her. "You turned it. You need to give it a minute or two." He waited for her to regain control and balance, holding her gently, aware of her perfume, "That's it, take it easy. Are you all right, now?"

The woman nodded and he released her arm slowly as she held the door. He knelt, picked up the packages, and turned to her. "I'll be glad to carry these for you," he said, then fell silent, staring.

The wide brim slanted low over her face. The upturned lapels of her coat covered part of her features. The dark sunglasses concealed her eyes. *And yet he knew beyond a doubt!*

The high, distinctive cheekbones.

The unmistakable cleft in her chin.

It was her!

Stunned, he struggled to recover his manners. After what seemed long minutes staring, he finally said, "I'll carry these for you." His voice sounded like someone else's. His head was swimming. It was incredible! And yet, it was *her*.

She still held the door for support. "That won't be necessary," she replied. Even in her abruptness, he recognized the voice from the Paris bistro scene; the low, soft voice that had tantalized with its husky laughter. For the first time in his life, he experienced being dumbfounded.

Tentatively, she placed more weight on the injured ankle and immediately returned to the other foot, wincing.

"You need help," Russ said, fighting through his astonishment. "Is this where you live?" He nodded toward the wrought-iron gate fronting wide steps and a lavish doorway.

"Yes, but . . ."

"Okay, here's what we're going to do: I'll take your arm." He nodded toward the driver. "He'll carry these packages. We'll have you inside in just a moment."

As he handed the driver the packages a doorman appeared and hurried down to them, stepping to the woman's side and taking her other arm. They carefully helped her up the steps, then the doorman held the door open as the woman, the driver, and Russ entered. Across a small foyer and entry hall the open elevator waited. They got in.

The muffled sounds of old cables and pulleys became silent as the elevator stopped at the second floor. She removed a key from her purse and had it ready as they helped her from the elevator and crossed a hallway. The door unlocked with a solid click, and she pushed it open.

The room was enormous. Russ thought her flat must occupy the entire second floor. The doorman helped her to a wide wing chair near the fireplace.

Russ took the two packages from the driver and placed them on a small table and then returned to the driver, who waited at the door. Ten pounds seemed enough to include an adequate tip, he thought. The driver touched his hat and left. Russ returned to the center of the room just as a small dog appeared. It was tan and white and black, with short legs and big ears, and it looked at him suspiciously.

The room was decorated in an Oriental style, adorned with Chinese screens and tall vases. Heavy, ornate chests and mirrors occupied wide areas of walls. Green plants brought the space closer and divided the living and dining areas. Beyond the open hallway door photographs of famous faces lined the wall.

Two large wing chairs were angled before the fireplace across from a love seat. She removed her sunglasses and placed them on the table beside the chair. "Thank you, Roberts," she said as the doorman nodded respectfully, turned, and left. He closed the door behind him.

Russ said nothing. Obviously, he had been expected to leave with the doorman—and should have—but he simply stood there as she dropped the hat to the floor beside her chair. He watched, fascinated.

Suddenly he realized the two of them were alone except for the small dog that was now ignoring him. "Well," he said awkwardly, "will you be all right?"

She looked at him as if his question made no sense at all. "Of course I will." Her manner was cool, distant.

He couldn't stop studying her. She sat somewhat erectly, her legs crossed. Her brown hair was perhaps one shade lighter than he would have expected, and she tossed it casually back from her face. Her eyes were a green he had never seen before. Magnificently pouted lips. Her face was fuller than it had once been, but beautiful.

God, he was *still* staring. He tried to recover. "Can I get you anything? A glass of water?"

"I'll be just fine, thank you."

He was only vaguely aware that he had been dismissed. Everything seemed so unreal. He couldn't believe that he was actually standing in the same room with Ava Gardner, the beauty who had mesmerized him since he was a boy. "If there's nothing more I can do, I'll go," he offered, shrugging. He turned toward the door and saw that the dog was at his feet. He reached down and patted it for a moment, and then looking back at her, said, "You may want to use ice."

She appeared completely uninterested, not even listening.

"In a scotch and water, maybe," he added. It was a weak attempt at humor, and it failed miserably. He opened the door, paused, and said, "It was nice meeting you. Good-bye."

"Is this your first visit to London?"

Her question surprised him and he stopped midstride. "I'm not visiting."

"You aren't a student," she said flatly. "You're too old."

"No. I'm not a student."

"Corporate work?"

"No," he replied with a slight smile.

"Government?"

He nodded and crossed the room, removing a business card from its leather holder and handing it to her. "I've only been here three weeks," he said lamely.

She looked at the card as she unbuttoned her coat. Her eyes returned to him with a gentle interest. "You're obviously from the South."

The gentle look. The unbuttoned coat loosened at the front. Somehow she seemed softer.

She cocked her head slightly. "Could you possibly be from—"

"North Carolina."

For the first time she smiled and the dimples appeared. The cleft in her chin was a small shadow. "*I'm* from North Carolina."

"I know. Smithfield."

The moment had somehow become a friendly one. "Thank you for catching me," she said.

"Anytime." He smiled briefly, then stepped out the door, closing it behind him.

As he drove to the dinner party, Russ's thoughts were still on the experience of that afternoon, but he pushed them away as he tried to prepare for the ordeal ahead. It was only a dinner invitation from a colleague, but now even informal get-togethers with people he didn't know made him uptight. The nearer he drew to his destination, the more nervous he became.

He parked the VW in front of a brick house, one in a row of similar houses. He double-checked that the address was correct.

Gerald Graves answered the door. "Hello, Russ," he said, holding the door open. "Come in. Let me have your coat. Brenda and Raymond are in the living room."

Russ slipped out of his raincoat and Gerald took it. He followed the Navy pilot into a room where a tall, bespectacled man stood by a fireplace, his arm resting on the mantel. An attractive woman sat across from him. Gerald introduced Russ to his wife, Brenda, and to Raymond Holt, a legal officer recently assigned to the embassy staff. Russ handed Brenda the roses he had brought, then crossed the room to shake hands with Holt.

"Thank you," said Brenda, admiring the roses. "They're lovely. Perfect for our table this evening."

"Very nice," agreed Gerald. "Darling, fix Russ a drink while I hang his coat, will you? Raymond's may need freshening, too."

"What would you like?" asked Brenda. She gathered glasses and he followed her to a game room equipped with a bar. He told her a bourbon and water and then moved out of the way. She was unpretentious and direct. Nice figure. Minimal makeup. He was impressed. "I'm so pleased you could come," she said. "I was beginning to worry that you may not make it."

"Traffic."

"It can be murder in London at times. I always give myself half again the time it's supposed to take to drive somewhere."

In spite of the Graves's welcome, he still felt uncomfortable, and he would have to force conversation. And it *was* forced. "Very pretty dress," he said to Brenda.

"Thank you." She could see that he felt awkward. Gerald had told her the Air Force pilot had been a POW. She understood. Two of her best friends were Navy pilots' wives whose husbands had been captured and held captive in Hanoi. She knew what they had been through.

The next few moments were quiet as she refilled glasses and he watched. She mixed his drink and handed it to him. "Is that all right?"

He sipped and nodded. "Perfect."

"We're informal, so now that you know where the booze is, help yourself." Brenda picked up the other two glasses and returned to the living room where Gerald and Holt waited. "You guys give me a few seconds, and dinner will be ready," she said as she handed them their drinks. "I hope you're hungry." She disappeared into the kitchen and its wonderful aromas.

Jefferson took a chair and sipped his drink. Raymond Holt sat on a couch.

"People were looking for you this afternoon," Gerald said to Russ.

"Oh? Who?"

"The Air Attaché's secretary. And the Deputy Director."

"Why?"

"The Air Attaché's staff meeting. They wanted you there."

"Miss Rutherford could have told them I was out."

"She did. She just couldn't say where. But I think she took care of things with the Air Attaché."

"She could manage that? Without knowing where I was?"

"Word is they had a thing going at one time. But you did put her in a tough spot."

"I had other things to do. No big deal."

"Your boss thought it was a big deal."

"General Eads?"

"Yeah. It was a very big deal to him."

"That's surprising."

Raymond Holt spoke for the first time. "It wouldn't be if you knew him."

Brigadier General William Eads, Deputy Director for Military Affairs, was the immediate supervisor of both Graves and Russ. "Do you know him?" Russ asked Holt.

"I served with him at headquarters in Saigon."

"What's he like?"

"Classic example of a little guy with a big chip on his shoulder. You know, the kind that pushes his weight around. Makes a mountain out of a molehill every time."

"I've been around that kind," said Russ.

"I'm not sure you have," Holt said seriously. "Not like Eads. I know of three officers who had their careers ruined by him at Saigon."

"For violating regs?" asked Gerald.

"No. They submitted reports on operations. The problem was their reports didn't agree with information Eads was promoting. Cost Eads credibility. Stature. He made sure they paid."

Brenda reappeared and said to her husband, "Darling, would you start pouring the wine? C'mon in, guys." They followed her to the dining room.

Gerald poured wine, and Brenda held a long match to light the candles. Russ asked, "May I do that?"

She looked at him thoughtfully for a brief moment, then said, "Please do." She handed him the match and matchbox.

The meal was wonderful, the finest he had had in ages. "This is terrific," he said to Brenda. He thought she probably always made things turn out just right.

Dinner conversation turned to London theater. Brenda and Gerald talked about shows they had seen in the West End. Then Holt confessed doubts that he would ever learn to drive on the wrong side. Everyone complained about London weather. They discussed briefly the topic that dominated American conversation everywhere: Watergate. Out of nowhere, Holt said, "I read today that Saigon will fall within weeks." Then he pronounced, "It was all for nothing, gentlemen. A waste."

Russ's fork dropped noisily onto his plate, and he mumbled an apology.

Brenda quickly changed the direction of the conversation, making much fanfare about the dessert she would be serving. It was, she explained, her grandmother's personal recipe. As she talked, she looked at Jefferson with soft eyes and smiled understandingly. He gave her a grateful nod.

Russ knew that Holt's comment about the war should have meant nothing to him. There was no reason to react the way he did. But any conversation about the past two years made him feel disoriented. Sometimes it jolted him. It was as if he were beginning chapter ten of his life after skipping chapters eight and nine.

Russ did his best to be pleasant over dessert and during a few minutes of after-dinner conversation. When Brenda began clearing the table, he asked, "May I help? I worked at a resort one summer as a busboy." She gave him an amused smile and welcomed the offer. He helped stack the dishes.

A half hour later he excused himself. It had been a long day, he reminded them.

He said good night to Holt, then turned to Brenda. "Thanks for a terrific evening. The dinner was fantastic, especially your grandmother's cake."

"I hope you'll come back often," she said.

He knew she meant it. "I'll look forward to it."

Gerald helped him with his coat and stepped out the door with him.

"I'm envious, Gerald. Brenda's a terrific lady."

"Navy wives are a special breed."

"I hope I find someone like her someday."

"I'm a lucky man," said Gerald. "A very lucky man." He watched Russ start down the steps. "Good night," he said, then stepped back inside.

Russ stopped at the bottom of the damp steps and looked up into the sky as he took a deep breath of fresh night air. He crossed the street to his Volkswagen, thinking of what had happened that afternoon. It was just so damned *incredible*.

A one-in-a-million chance meeting.

The engine started with the first turn of the ignition, and after a quick check in his mirror he pulled away from the curb. Traffic was light. His thoughts returned to the actress and their encounter. He couldn't quite get over it still. Hard to believe. He had been simply walking along, looking for a taxi, and suddenly there *she* had been. Of all people. Impossible.

He would have scoffed at any suggestion that he was a fan of a movie star, but since he was twelve, whenever her name or photograph appeared in print, he had been drawn to it. She had always meant *something* to him, even though her glamorous and exciting world was distant and remote from his.

Across the city in Ennismore Gardens, Ava Gardner sat at her dressing table, the soft glow of the mirror's pastel lights bathing her face and highlighting the white silken sheen of her gown. She stared flatly at her image as she pulled the brush through her hair, then she stopped, closed her eyes, and remained still for a long moment.

She looked back at the mirror, picked up the glass half filled with gin, and quickly drank. Then she held the glass to her head, massaging her temple with its cold hardness. Black spots swam before her eyes like motes of dust and wouldn't go away. For several more seconds she pressed the glass against her temple, then slowly moved it over her brow.

It had happened again today.

It was getting worse, and she didn't know what she was going to do. Her fall that afternoon had not been due to slipping on the damp pavement; she had blacked out momentarily as she got out of the taxi. The same thing had happened last week. And last month. She was afraid. The damned blackouts were getting worse and the stupid spots floated insolently before her eyes and she couldn't make them disappear. She didn't mind growing old, but she hated being afraid. She had never been so scared.

There was, she thought as she sipped from the glass, a second part to that assessment: she had never before been so afraid—or so alone.

She had always been surrounded by people. Crowds were always there for stars. Fan clubs. Footprints and handprints in the sidewalk at Grauman's Chinese Theatre. Her name in a Cole Porter lyric. The whole bit. All the years in Hollywood's dizzying circles and during her highly publicized marriage to Sinatra. It had been impossible to get away from people. The years in Spain, the continuous swirl of bullfights and festive nights, always in a crowd.

Now completely alone. Of course, she could *always* be surrounded at parties, but she didn't need party crowds anymore. Only when she felt depressed or scared did she resort to them.

Hurriedly she finished her drink.

And so, she thought as she forced a smile, after so many years of stormy relationships, so many mercurial and tempestuous affairs, she was going to face this new fear alone. And she wryly acknowledged that was one hell of a thing for an old Hollywood sex symbol to admit.

She had no idea what these blackouts meant. She only knew they scared her, and there was no one to share her fears.

And she had never been so scared.

Three

"General Kreeger, this is Scott Mitchell." The connection between Spain and the Pentagon crackled with interference.

"Hello, Scott," the familiar, gruff voice answered. "How's everything with the Sixty-third?"

"Great. We've got top-notch people, General, both in ops and maintenance."

"That's what it takes, Scott."

"Sir, I hope I'm not interrupting you at a bad time, but I wanted to tell you that I saw Russ Jefferson last week." Lieutenant Colonel Scott Mitchell leaned back in his swivel chair, propping both feet on his standard government-issue, gray metal desk. His flight boots would leave black marks. A red banner with a black panther at its center adorned the wall behind him. It was the emblem of the 63rd Tactical Fighter Squadron. A cup of strong coffee sat before him, his last one of the day.

"So, how's Russ doing?" The general's voice twanged with the echoes of the Autovon line, the Air Force's long-distance telephone system. He was interested in every man who ever served under him, but only a very few gained his special favor and had been taken under his wing. Jefferson was the best example.

"Not bad," Mitchell replied. "He took some time off, and together we solved most of the world's problems. All of this was over three or four shots of bourbon, of course."

As he always did, the general got straight to the point. "How's he *really* doing, Scott?"

"He isn't his old self, sir. Nothing like his old self."

"How bad is it?"

"It's as if . . . well, he seemed completely uninterested in old squadron mates, even guys that were good friends." Mitchell's voice became more forceful. "General, he wasn't even interested in talking about flying. Didn't want to discuss returning to the cockpit." He took a sip of cold coffee and made a face. "It was the damnedest conversation I *ever* had with Russ Jefferson. It was weird."

There was a short pause at the other end of the line. "He needs time, Scott. He'll be okay. Just give him time."

"I'm sure you're right, sir. You did him a big-time favor getting him the assignment to the embassy. It's the best thing for him. He's in no shape to be in a squadron yet." *And that's an understatement,* thought Mitchell.

"Yeah," the distant voice replied, "it's the best place for him right now. A no-risk environment. At least in the embassy he can't get into trouble."

"You're in big trouble, Major."

"Sir?" Russ Jefferson said, a one-word request for clarification. He moved toward the chair at the corner of the desk.

"I didn't give you permission to sit," snapped General Eads. He was thin, with wiry gray hair and a mustache, and he looked small behind the wide desk.

Russ stopped in midstep, looked incredulously at the man, and then with a mental shrug and a wry smile retraced the two steps to stand squarely in front of the desk. *You run into this kind once in a while.*

"I expect your full military courtesy, Major. I will tell you when to be at ease." The voice was harsh, unnecessarily strident.

Russ casually reached up to the top button on his uniform coat and unbuttoned it. It was a special gesture, a custom from World War II when fighter pilots—and only fighter pilots—wore their uniform with the top button undone. It was a custom not practiced anymore, but Russ knew about it, and it still meant the same thing it always had, asserting a certain cockiness and arrogance. He had signaled his attitude, and now he waited for the general to continue.

That morning Russ had been awakened by Vivian Rutherford's telephone call at his apartment. General Eads, she had told him, had called for him first thing, and when she told Eads that he wasn't at the embassy, the general had instructed her to "have Jefferson in his office within the hour." With a touch of sarcastic humor, she reminded Russ that Brigadier General Eads *was* his boss and informed him in a very stern voice that he *was* almost an hour late for work already. Forty-five minutes later he had entered his office, greeted by an admonishing look from Rutherford that immediately softened into an expression of patient fondness.

Now the general continued in a sharp voice. "You're getting off to a very bad start in this assignment, Major. You've been here one month, and I already have complaints." Eads stared at the unbuttoned top button of Jefferson's uniform.

"Such as?" Russ shifted his weight to the other foot and slipped his right hand into his pocket.

"I've received a complaint from Political Affairs. According to the political officer, you were extremely rude in a meeting last week."

"Rude?"

The general's eyes were piercing. "He said you interrupted and contradicted him throughout the entire meeting."

"Well, not throughout the *entire* meeting," Russ said sincerely.

Eads's nostrils flared.

This isn't going well, thought Russ as he shrugged and continued. "The guy got into operational matters of the Air Force that he obviously knew nothing about. I just corrected him a couple of times on the most outrageously erroneous things he said." The general glared. "And maybe I interrupted him a couple of times . . . but only to keep the guy from saying something *really* foolish."

"That *guy,*" the general said, bristling, "is the political officer in one of the most important of all United States embassies."

"Well, I didn't say anything about his political statements."

"You also missed the Air Attaché's meeting last week." Eads's voice took on a sharper edge. The young officer was abrasive, and he didn't like it. "All Air Force personnel were directed to attend that briefing. It was a mandatory meeting, Major."

"Something came up."

"You didn't inform me. I didn't excuse you."

Russ looked innocently at the man. "I exercised my own judgment. Priorities. Something more important came up." He knew he was getting out of line. This was not the way to respond to a general, but Eads was obviously a by-the-book staff guy, and rank sometimes didn't matter between a MiG killer and a staff general. Russ's judgment of General William Eads was complete and final. Although the two men wore the same uniform with the same insignias and emblems, he viewed them as being of two different worlds. The senior officer behind the desk had fashioned a very successful career—that was not arguable. He had made general-officer grade by age forty-five or so, but he was of a particular type not respected by combat pilots. He had wings on his chest, "slick" wings with no star or wreath, meaning minimum time in the cockpit, probably a Strategic Air Command copilot. One of those who always exceeded the formal paperwork standards of SAC, probably winning a "below-the-zone" promotion in the process. But he had obviously avoided flying assignments. He wore ribbons but none earned from combat missions. Eads had been a part of the headquarters crowd of the Seventh Air Force in Saigon—SAC colonels and generals getting their tickets punched for a Vietnam tour by sitting in air-conditioned staff jobs. It was a quick judgment, a completely condemning one, and Russ had no doubt about its accuracy.

Seething, the general looked the younger officer up and down and frowned. Then his eyes were drawn back to the button. "This is not a fighter squadron, Major, but this office is a military organization with military standards."

"Could've fooled me." The remark was accompanied by a slight smile.

"I will not tolerate your insolence, Major! You were almost three hours late this morning."

"It wasn't quite two, sir."

Eads paused to control his anger, to collect his thoughts. The young pilot, given prestigious assignments by generals, was in a preferred status, and Eads backed off. He spoke with an even voice. "I'm going to give you the benefit of the doubt, Major Jefferson. I know your career is of special interest at the Pentagon, and I realize this assignment was handpicked for you." A condescending aloofness was apparent in the disparaging reference to the circumstances of Jefferson's assignment. "I will not formally reprimand you, this time."

The younger officer knew this wasn't over.

"But this is all the leniency you get. No more. I will not tolerate further negligence or disrespect. Shape up, Major!"

Russ turned and started toward the door.

"Major!" Eads's voice was sharp. "I didn't dismiss you."

Russ paused and looked back. "That's okay . . . sir," he said politely, and he walked out the door.

He returned to his office, nodding to Rutherford in response to her inquiring eyes. She said, "You've had some telephone calls," and handed him a note. "A lady has been trying to reach you, but she won't leave a number." He took the small yellow memo, retreated to his office, and closed his door behind him. He removed his uniform coat and threw it on a chair as he crossed the room to the window.

Dumb beyond belief! It was incredibly stupid to create problems with General Eads. What did he think he was doing, posturing for a personal little war? He knew better than to get caught up in something like this. God, that was dumb!

To his left a forest of antennae bristled on the embassy roof. One day he would go for a short tour and see what they had there. Probably comparable to what they had at Nakhon Phanom, on the Laos-Thailand border close to North Vietnam. Stuff that would knock your socks off.

A small flock of pigeons hovered above the window ledge in preparation for landing until they saw him and then fluttered away. He turned to his desk, still cursing his needless wiseass treatment of the general, and sank into the chair.

As if he wasn't having enough problems fitting in here at the embassy, he was now engaging in some senseless, egocentric game with a general officer who just happened to be his boss. What in the hell was he thinking?

His intercom buzzed. "There's a call for you on line two," said Miss Rutherford. "It's that same lady again."

"Okay, thanks." *A woman?* He punched the illuminated button in the row of five. "Hello," he said.

"Major Jefferson? Major Russell T. Jefferson?" The voice was low. Almost husky, almost breathy, but not quite. It had a faint hint of a southern accent.

"Yes?" *Surely it's not. It can't be.* The thought was so unreal his mind wouldn't accept it. But he knew it was! It was the voice that had always been perfectly matched to the image—sexy, mildly amused.

"Major." She hesitated for a breath, then softly announced, "this is Ava Gardner."

"Well, hello." His throat was sand. There had to be more he could say, but what? "How's the ankle?"

"As good as new, thank you." There was a soft chuckle. "And you were right about the ice, Major."

His mind was totally blank; his pulse throbbed. "Well, ah, I'm glad that it's better. The ankle, I mean." He searched for something to say. Anything.

She spoke first. "I didn't want to interfere with your work at the embassy, but it was the only number on your card."

"That's all right," he blurted. "Really, it's quite all right to call me here." He couldn't help adding, "*You* can call me here, anytime."

The throaty laugh again. It was the same laugh that Gregory Peck had said "would just have to lead to a lousy fight." "You were so helpful the other day. I really don't know what I would have done without you."

"I just happened to be there. Glad I could help."

"I want to repay your kindness. In the old-fashioned North Carolina way."

"I, uh, didn't do anything. Not really."

"Yes you did, and I want to invite you to dinner, Major."

"Oh, there's no need . . ." He paused, hoping, in fact, that she would.

"Of course there is," she insisted. "It's the least I can do. How about Friday evening? Six. A cocktail and then dinner."

"That would be great." *God, do I sound giddy?*

"Very well, Major, Friday then. Good-bye."

"Good-bye," he said. There was a click on the line and she was gone.

He swung his swivel chair around toward the window and stared blankly at the sky. Concern about his encounter with the general was forgotten. His thoughts swirled like leaves in a wind.

He had never been around many celebrities. The show-business people he had seen during the months at Las Vegas had certainly never impressed him. There were exceptions: Natalie Wood had visited his fighter squadron at George Air Force Base once, attending a reception; James Garner had once been in a group that invited Jefferson for beers following a sports-car race at Riverside. Both seemed to be genuinely nice people, pleasant and friendly. But this was different.

He had never thought he would see her again. He'd accepted the accidental meeting as a one-in-a-million shot. That was it—that was all.

God, she was unbelievably beautiful, just like in the films. Absolutely ravishing. More mature, her face slightly fuller, but she was the most beautiful thing he had ever seen.

And she had called him!

Friday. Three days away.

Admiral Frank Fleming, Director of Military Operations, looked up from his briefcase and said to General Eads, "What's on your mind, Bill? We don't have much time." The admiral was preparing to leave on a month-long assignment to the States that very day. Eads had called at the last minute and asked to meet with him before he left. Fleming closed his briefcase and pushed it aside. "Make it quick."

Eads adjusted his position in the deep chair. "I know you're very busy, Admiral, and I won't take but a few minutes. Because you're going to be gone awhile, I need to inform you of a personnel problem. If it continues, I'll be forced to take serious measures, perhaps before you return. I didn't want you to be caught cold."

"What's the problem, Bill?" Admiral Fleming's broad, plain face widened with a lopsided grin. "We don't have many military folks here to have such a big personnel problem."

"It's Major Jefferson, sir."

"Russ Jefferson?" The admiral scowled curiously. "What kind of a problem are you having with him?"

"He's insolent and irresponsible. Disrespectful and insubordinate."

"That's quite a mouthful, Bill," the rugged Navy officer said as he looked at his wristwatch. "Maybe you've just misunderstood his ways. You're accustomed to having brownnosing pencil pushers working for you. Staff types. Jefferson's a fighter pilot. He's arrogant, but that's not a personnel problem."

"He's missed meetings. He comes and goes as he pleases." Eads was frustrated by the admiral's lack of interest. "He was disrespectful to the political officer during a meeting."

"Bill, Major Jefferson's okay. You've read his Form 381."

"I will not tolerate—"

"Knock it off, Bill. That man was shot down. Spent almost a year in the Hanoi Hilton. You'll have to tolerate the few weeks it may take him to get adjusted to this sanitized puzzle palace."

"If it continues, then I must go over your head, Admiral."

"You'll *what?*"

"If he keeps on, I'll have to take the appropriate action."

"You'd better not do that, General." Fleming's voice took an authoritative tone. He didn't like armchair generals sitting in judgment of men who had put it on the line. He knew Eads's history of screwing over subordinates, of ruining young officers' careers. "Do I need to remind you that I'm in that chain of command? If you and the Air Attaché make this an Air Force deal, you'd better be ready to take me on when I get back."

"Sir, with all due respect, you don't understand how he—"

"No, *you* don't understand. You've been buried in staff work too long. That was a real war out there, General. Men flew their F-4s and F-105s north against the most extensive and sophisticated air defenses in the world. Day after day, week after week. Sound tactics were nonexistent. They weren't allowed to hit strategic targets. Rules of engagement were insane. But they kept flying north, because that was their job." The admiral leaned forward, his voice lowered. "Some of them paid the full measure, and didn't come back. Some were shot down and captured. We owe those men a hell of a lot more than we can repay."

Eads's temples throbbed. His knuckles were white.

The admiral checked the time again and said, "I'm *impressed* if Russ Jefferson is still cocky after all he's been through. We'll most assuredly allow our little tidy staff world to be inconvenienced for a few weeks, if it's necessary, for him to become accustomed to our ways."

Eads stood, starting to protest, but the admiral abruptly shut him off. "I'm busy now, General. You'll excuse me." And he picked up the telephone.

Eads paused, began to speak, then decided not to. He turned on his heel and headed for the door.

A disgusted look appeared on Fleming's face as he watched the man leave. He knew that this matter was far from finished.

Four

The taxi pulled up in front of his apartment building, and Russ asked the driver to open the door. His arms were filled with parcels, but he managed to get into the backseat without damaging them. "Thirty-four Ennismore Gardens, Knightsbridge," he instructed.

He settled into the seat and took a deep breath. It looked like he was going to be on time. For a while, he hadn't been sure. He had cut out of the embassy early, run by a wine store and to the same florist where he had gotten Brenda's roses, then hurried to the flat to shower, shave, and dress.

He laid the flowers across his lap and the wine on the seat next to him and checked the pound notes in his shirt pocket. Good. Easy to get to. He was proud of himself for this particular bit of farsightedness. Handling two fragile packages in his state of anxiety was like driving cross-country in a British sports car: just asking for trouble.

Ten minutes later the taxi turned onto the quiet, exclusive street and stopped before the converted Victorian building. Gathering the gifts, he stepped out of the car and paid the driver. Everything under control. The first obstacle hurdled.

He glanced about. This was the right place; the black iron-rail fence and gate, the wide stone steps and lavish entrance. He opened the gate and started up the steps. The doorman, recognizing him, held the door open. "Thank you, Roberts," he said as he entered. Soon the lift had him at the second floor and he was at her door. He hesitated, taking a deep breath and squaring his shoulders. *I am not going to be like some awkward, stumbling schoolboy,* he told himself.

He didn't know the exact time—because his hands were full and he couldn't check his watch—but he knew he wasn't early. He rang the doorbell. His nose itched. He waited. He adjusted the paper-covered bouquet that rested in the crook of his arm and tightened his grip on the wine. *Nothing to be nervous about. Relax.* His nose itched more than ever.

Don't act like some awkward schoolboy!

Then the door opened, and she was there.

Those eyes. That face. God, she was indescribably beautiful. But her eyebrow was slightly raised, her smile slightly puzzled. A moment's confusion, and then she recognized him. Yet she was obviously surprised to see him and hesitated before opening the door wider. "Come in," she said uncertainly.

He stepped inside and stood there. As soon as she closed the door she said, "I'll be right with you. I'm on the phone." She hurried across the room and settled into one of the armchairs by the fireplace, picking up the receiver from the small table. "I'm back, Bappie," she said. "Someone was at the door."

He stood unmoving, holding the wine and the bouquet and feeling more than slightly foolish. Looking about, he saw a heavily decorated cabinet and put the wine and roses on it. Lightly rubbing his hands on his trousers, he looked at her. She was facing the fireplace. He thought of sitting down, then decided to remain where he was. Easing his weight to the other foot, he slid his hands into his pockets and studied his surroundings.

Oriental carpets covered polished floors, and the Oriental screens were placed in just the right spaces. Ornate cabinets stood against the wall. There were scatterings of small tables and delicate silk screens. On hallway walls were photographs of Gregory Peck, Clark Gable, and other luminaries. Floor-to-ceiling French doors opened onto a balcony overlooking the gardens.

The small dog entered the room, and Russ knelt to get her to come to him. It was, he now knew, a corgi. He had looked it up in a dog book in a bookstore. The corgi came to him and Russ began petting her.

The actress half-turned toward him as she continued her conversation. She was wearing a large, sloppy earth-colored sweater and jeans turned up to the knees. She was barefoot. Her hair was slightly disheveled, and she wore no makeup.

"I have to go now, honey," she said. "Yes, I'll call you next week. Yes. Bye." She replaced the receiver and turned fully toward Russ, her eyes studying him. With a curious smile, she said, "Major . . . er . . ."

"Jefferson," he said as he stood up. *God, she has such tiny feet!*

"Major Jef-ferson," she said slowly and thoughtfully. "Yes, of course. Major Russell *T*. Jefferson."

"That's right." He rubbed the slight itch along the side of his nose.

Her smile widened. She tucked her feet under her. "I have a not unreasonable question for you, Major Russell T. Jefferson." She placed a long tapered finger beside her smile, her hand resting against her cheek. "Why are you here?"

He cocked his head as if he hadn't heard her correctly. "I beg your pardon?"

"*Why* are you here?"

"This is Friday; it's six o'clock," he said as though that explained everything. Seeing no sign of understanding, he added, "You invited me. You called me at the embassy and . . ."

"Oh God." She turned her face and laughed softly into her hand.

Shaking her head, still smiling, she stood up and came to him. "We were to have dinner, weren't we?"

"I thought so." A shy smile turned up one corner of his mouth. He picked up the roses and wine and handed them to her. "I didn't know what you like. I hope these are okay."

She took the roses and held them to her face, then went over to a vase filled with yellow flowers at the end of a long table. She emptied the vase and placed the roses in it, adding a few final touches, arranging one or two of the buds just so. Then she took the wine and studied the label. "Oh, this is wonderful." She placed it on the table with the flowers. "But, right now I'm having my double G's—Gordon's gin." She ran a hand through her uncombed hair. "Can I fix you a drink?"

"A gin and tonic would be fine."

She stepped behind the bar. He watched as she busied herself making the drinks. His mind whirled. This was unreal. That remarkable face, those unbelievably green eyes, and she wasn't an image on a screen! She was right there before him.

She handed him the drink and nodded toward the bottle of wine. "Don't you think that would go well with leftover lasagna?" Her smile revealed perfect teeth. "If Carmen were here, she could fix something more extravagant, but . . ."

"Who's Carmen?"

"My friend. Companion. She's visiting her family in the States."

"I think it will be great with leftover lasagna."

"Let's sit over here, shall we?" She gestured toward the two big chairs as she moved to the one by the telephone and curled up in it.

He took the other one. She looked so casual and comfortable, but he felt awkward in the deep, soft chair. He wished he had taken the solidly upholstered, straight-backed chair a few feet away. There was a silence. Where was that clever conversation? Those charming lines he had practiced the last three days?

"Cara approves of you," she said smiling.

"Who?"

"Cara, my darling little corgi," she said as she leaned down to scratch the dog's ears. "She doesn't approve of just anyone. She sometimes bites ankles."

"I'm glad she likes me." He wanted to be clever, but it just didn't come to him. "I didn't wear my heavy boots."

"Is your drink all right?"

"Fine," he said, and hurried to take his first sip. Just then a most peculiar sound emanated from his stomach and he hurried to say something—anything—to cover the embarrassing growl. It wouldn't stop. "How long have you lived here . . . in Europe, I mean?"

"Oh, fourteen, fifteen years." If she had heard the noise, she didn't let it show.

As he tightened his stomach muscles he thought of the many magazine articles about her, the pictures of her at bullfights. "You lived in Spain at first?"

"Yes. The first ten years."

"In Madrid?" He relaxed his stomach muscles. No noise.

"At first I lived in La Moraleja, and then I moved into Madrid."

"You must have liked it there a lot."

"Bullfights, bullfighters." She smiled as if at a memory, and when she spoke again, her voice had become breathy. "Narrow streets lined with bars that are open all night. Flamenco dancing." She looked at him. "*Sola-sombras.*" His expression was blank. "Which are," she explained, "cocktails made of absinthe and Spanish cognac, mixed in lethal proportions. Perhaps not the right reasons to like Madrid, Major, but those were a few of my favorite things."

"Do you like London?"

"Oh, yes. The people here smile and speak and then let you alone. London is very polite that way." Then she asked, "Do you like it here?"

He was enchanted, his mind hardly functioning; then he realized that she had asked a question. "Uh, yes. Yes, I do." *Come on, Russ. You've gotta do better than this.* "Are you planning another film soon?"

She shrugged a shoulder and glanced at her watch, a distracted thought creating a long pause. Finally she said, "Good parts are rare, honey." She shrugged again. "And I'm not exactly at the top of any casting director's list."

His conversation was standard interviewers' questions she had heard countless times; had grown weary of long ago. He should have recognized it. Sensed it. Normally he knew when he was nearing tiresome ground, but not this time. He was beguiled by her magnificence and unaware that he was becoming a bore.

The telephone rang. "Pardon me, Major," she said as she reached for it.

He rose from the chair. *I should give her privacy. Move to a polite distance. But where? Where would I look right? Maybe a rakish pose at the fireplace . . . an elbow on the mantel. No, that's right at her chair.* He took three aimless steps toward the center of the room. *Just don't look so uptight. Maybe unbutton the coat for a casual effect.* He went to the wall to examine a lightly brushed watercolor painting of an Oriental garden.

Suddenly she raised her voice. "No, goddamn it! I will *not* play that role! No, no, no!" She took a quick breath and still in a firm voice said, "Don't you bastards ever think you will sign me to a contract like that. Tell them I said they can go straight to hell." She slammed down the phone and glared at it.

He waited uncertainly, and then she looked at him. "That was nothing serious, Major, regardless of how it sounded." She stood. "It's just the plight of agents trying to get movie roles for washed-up old broads."

"Miss Gardner, you should get *any* role you want."

"Well, I should have put you on the phone with my agent. The best he can do for me is a role with me standing with Moses in the middle of a goddamn earthquake."

"I think you should have your choice of roles."

"Thank you, Sir Lancelot." She smiled at him and reached for his glass. "Let's freshen these." As she walked to the bar she passed a mirror above a table and glanced at it. She ran her hand through her hair in an attempt to neaten it and chuckled. "Puffy eyes, crow's-feet, and a double chin. No great demand for washed-up old movie queens, Major."

"But your latest roles have been your best. *On the Beach. Night of the Iguana.*"

"Honey, that was nine years ago."

"Oh," he said, feeling foolish.

"Today's movies are different from the kind of fluff we used to make. This generation is—" Again the telephone interrupted. With a helpless shrug and an apologetic smile she asked, "Would you finish making these?"

Her greeting to the caller was warm, and he could hear parts of her conversation. She was talking about medical prescriptions, and then she said sharply, "Damn it, Paul, I'm *taking* the goddamn pills, so stop hounding me." A moment later she laughed and said affectionately, "Tell Spoli I said hello. I'll see you two next week." Then she hung up.

As he finished making the drinks, he watched her pick up Cara. The dog sat in her mistress's lap and enjoyed the petting and rubbing.

Russ handed the glass to the actress, then made his way to the straight-backed chair. "A very busy evening. Is your drink okay?" The chair felt just right, letting him sit with both feet solidly on the floor.

She seemed distracted as she tasted the drink. "It's fine," she answered.

Finally, he accepted it. She was too preoccupied for conversation. She had forgotten inviting him and forgotten any intention of having leftover lasagna. He should have realized he was intruding, but he had been lost in his boyhood crush.

"I want to thank you for inviting me tonight." His voice was respectful. "It's been . . . well, a real pleasure." She looked up, focused on him for the first time in several minutes. The green eyes were soft, and now she seemed so vulnerable. He felt, somehow, the need to help her. "I'm imposing," he offered. "I really should go, I think."

She closed her eyes and slowly shook her head. "I'm terribly sorry, Major." There was a genuine regret in her tone. "I've been so very rude. Really, I'm sorry."

"No, you haven't been rude," he said as he got to his feet.

"Yes, I have." She put Cara down and rose from her chair. Her smile was tired, but she reached out and touched his cheek. "I promise to make up for this evening. Honest."

Her touch tingled and he started to say something, but the telephone rang, preventing him from replying with certain banality.

Wearily she reached for the phone, her eyes still on Jefferson as she answered. The caller identified himself. "Francis!" she cried excitedly. Her face came alive, her voice enthusiastic. "Where in the hell are you?" Her eyes danced as she listened.

Francis? Numbly he began to take it in. *It's Sinatra. Jeez. Ava Gardner, right here before him, in person, not four feet away. And Frank Sinatra on the telephone.*

He felt like an awkward, stumbling schoolboy.

Five

"Major Jefferson speaking."

"Russ, this is Josh Sims."

"Josh! How are you? Where are you?" Josh Sims had been in his pilot training class at Lubbock, Texas.

"I'm just fine. Maybe a step slower on the handball court, but still holding my own." He waited for a standard Jefferson put-down, but when it didn't come, he went on. "And I'm here—in England—at Upper Heyford."

"What are you doing there? F-111s?"

"That's right."

"The last I heard, you were flying the F-105."

"Still would be, but somehow we ran out of Thuds. War, you know." It was typical gallows humor. "I heard about you."

"Seems everyone has. I guess when you fly your fighter smartly into a lethal projectile, people tend to talk about you."

"Are you doing okay?"

"Yeah. I'm fine."

"I'd like for you to come up and see me."

"I'm buried here. Paperwork."

"I know. But I need to talk to you and not on the phone. We've got a problem and you're the only guy I know who can look into it for us."

"Me?" He laughed dryly. "What can *I* do for you? I'm in the *embassy,* Josh."

"I know. Exactly where we need some help."

"We?"

"The Twentieth Tactical Fighter Wing."

"Well, sure. You know I'll do what I can." He paused. "Can you tell me about it?"

"I'd rather not by phone. Let's get together. Why don't you come up here, Russ? We can talk things over, then get together with a couple of old friends for lunch. Tom Benson and Lyle Foster are here."

"How about tomorrow?"

"Good. I'm in the wing headquarters building. I'm the Twentieth Wing's Training and Tactics Officer. The security guard can give you directions. I'll see you in the morning."

Russ called the embassy motor pool and arranged to pick up a staff car at the end of the day. He told Miss Rutherford that he would be out of the office tomorrow, spending the day at Upper Heyford Royal Air Force Base. She had a map.

Russ entered the city of steeples and towers, turned north on A34, and drove slowly through Oxford's narrow, crowded streets. Soon the ancient city was behind him and a sign told him Weston-on-the-Green was twenty-three miles ahead. The drive into the Cotswolds was unhurried and pleasant.

Josh's call had puzzled him. It had to involve controversy, for the Twentieth Wing flew F-111s, and controversy had followed that fighter since day one. He had, just as all aviators had, followed the new tactical fighter's development closely. *McNamara's folly.*

Robert McNamara, while Secretary of Defense in the Kennedy administration, had been eager to prove his renowned management style and had seized his first opportunity with the high-profile Tactical Fighter Experimental program, called the TFX. It had been the most important fighter development in twenty years. The secretary had overridden Air Force procurement procedures and had prematurely awarded the contract for the advanced fighter to the General Dynamics Corporation.

Production had been a series of delays and problems. There were several crashes during test flights. Political criticism raged. Senator John McClellan called the TFX a "billion-dollar blunder," and Senator William Proxmire described it as "defective and dangerous." McNamara designated the TFX the F-111, called it the "can-do-all" aircraft, and directed the Air Force to put it in operation at Nellis Air Force Base. Design flaws and technical failures resulted in numerous more crashes, specific causes usually unknown. To ward off increasing criticism and controversy, McNamara deployed the plane into combat in 1968, and of the first thirty scheduled sorties, four of the aircraft crashed en route to North Vietnam. The F-111 was brought back. McNamara resigned from office. During the F-111's first eighteen months of operation, seventeen of the fighters crashed, and there were numerous groundings. Problems were identified and corrected, and the F-111 had been sent to war again in 1972. Now the first F-111 wing augmenting NATO had been positioned in England.

Militarily, there was nothing more important to the defense of Western Europe than the F-111. It was NATO's single most important weapons system, critical to its force structure. In addition to the 20th Fighter Wing, two or three more F-111 wings were planned for Europe.

Russ put Josh's call out of his mind, willing to wait for an explanation. He would know soon enough. He accelerated to the speed limit and settled in for the remainder of the drive.

He had not been able to put Friday night out of his mind. That had been four days ago, and he had hardly thought of anything else since.

Beyond the stone fences, swollen meadows rose and fell in smooth contours. The rural Midlands were exactly as described in books he had read as a boy. He slowed to enter the village of Weston-on-the-Green and followed the well-marked route through the town. Next was Middleton Stoney.

It was a beautiful morning for a drive. The road curved through the farmlands. The autumn sun burned through the haze. Enveloped by the scent of mown hay, he passed an ancient pub on the left, a wooden sign proclaiming it THE BLACK BOAR. The charm of the Cotswolds lay everywhere. He drove through Middleton Stoney, and a few minutes later he was at the gate of Upper Heyford Royal Air Force Base.

The old brick of Upper Heyford was visible through the gold and yellow leaves. He pulled up to a wide gate manned by security guards, showed his credentials, and asked for directions to the wing headquarters. Moments later he parked in a visitor space in front of the two-story brick building.

"Russ!" called out Josh Sims, striding toward the car, grinning and extending his hand with enthusiasm. "The sky cops called, said you were on your way." They shook hands and with his free hand Josh pounded on Russ's shoulder. "Thanks for coming."

They entered the building and went to Sims's office. Sims gestured toward a chair and went straight to the coffeemaker. Without asking he began pouring coffee into two heavy mugs. "Do you still take it black?" Before Russ answered, he followed with "How was the drive?"

"Enjoyed it. And yes." He looked around the office. A teakwood nameplate on the desk had carved elephants flanking Sims's name. It was one of those things everyone brought home from Thailand. Pictures of the famous "swing-wing" fighter from various views lined the wall. "How do you like flying the F-111?" Russ asked.

"I don't, but the early problems experienced at Nellis have been corrected. It performed extremely well during the Christmas bombing of

Hanoi. Flew sorties throughout the eleven days. It did a hell of a job."
Sims handed him the mug.

"Yeah, that's what I heard." Russ looked at a photograph of the aircraft
with wings swept back. "The night after Christmas one flew over the
Hanoi Hilton at rooftop level."

"But it's not the all-purpose, multimission wonder that McNamara
boasted it was. I don't like the mission. Long-range, low-altitude penetration. Nuclear-weapons delivery." Sims looked directly into Russ's eyes.
"It's just about perfect for the European mission—war lines into the
USSR."

"Flying low level at night in bad weather," Russ mused, still looking at
the photos. "Too close to terra firma for me."

"It's one hell of a terrain-following system. Flies you down at two
hundred feet automatically. Computer-controlled."

"I don't care how good it is, that's not my idea of fun."

"Nor mine," said Sims. "Takes a lot of training."

"How's the Twentieth Wing doing?"

"We've got problems. Very serious problems."

"What kind?"

"We've busted—failed—our first two operational-readiness inspections. Our first *two*. Heads have rolled. The first wing commander was
fired. The second is hanging by a hair." Sims stuck a cigarette in his mouth
and lit it with a Zippo. "We're on the verge of failing our third ORI, and
when that happens it won't be just careers being ended, it'll possibly be
the end of the F-111 in Europe."

"Hell, Josh, it's the backbone of NATO's planned air capability."

"We're reminded of that every day. You can imagine the pressure being put on us as the first F-111 wing in Europe."

Russ shook his head in disbelief. "The Twentieth Wing failing its
ORIs. Incredible."

"Yep. And if it continues, NATO could be forced to review its future."
Josh took a long drag from the cigarette.

"What's causing you to fail ORIs? What kind of problems are you having?"

"The worst kind. Substandard aircrew performance."

"What? Are you serious?"

"You heard me. The pilots aren't hacking the mission." The F-111 pilot paused to emphasize his words. "Believe me, I'm not kidding at all."

"Why? What's wrong?"

"Inadequate training. How does that grab you?"

"You said that I might help because I'm at the embassy. What can I do?"

"Russ, we've got good pilots in this wing, but they can't get proficient. Our mission is low-level. Night. Bad weather. Two hundred feet above the ground. And we simply don't have enough low-level training routes or practice target ranges."

"Why not?"

"That's what we'd like to know. We keep proposing new ones for the embassy to negotiate with the British government. We work damned hard to design proposals that present relatively few problems to our British friends. You know, avoiding chicken farms, populated areas, historic sites."

"And?"

"We submitted the proposals to the proper directorate; the Office of Military Affairs. I talked to your predecessor just before he left the embassy and he told me he never saw them. Someone at a higher level handled them. And disapproved them." Sims said disgustedly, "As a result, we fly the same mission routes over and over. We can fly them in our sleep. Training value is absolutely nil."

Russ sipped his coffee and listened.

"More than with any other fighter, proficiency in the F-111 requires productive, daily training flights. Demanding, low-level flights. Every day counts. What was adequate for the F-100 and F-105 isn't for us. We've got to have new routes, more difficult routes, for effective training."

"Can't your wing commanders get something done?"

"The first one tried and got fired. The present wing commander is under so damn much pressure he just keeps putting pressure on the aircrews."

"I understand."

"It's been frustrating as hell. Every proposal we've submitted to the embassy has been turned down. We've proposed every kind of route and bombing range this island will allow, with as few potential problems as possible." Sims slumped in his chair. "Quite frankly, we don't know what to do. But I'll tell you this: we are sick and tired of taking it in the ass just because we can't train properly."

"What do you want me to do, Josh?"

"Just find out what it is with those guys at the embassy. Find out what they want."

"And?"

"And we'll do everything we possibly can to give it to them—anything to get realistic training."

"Tell me, do you think you can improve on the proposed routes and targets you've already submitted? Can you come up with anything better?"

Sims's answer was deliberate and flat. "In all honesty, no." He took a slow, deep breath. "But we can try."

"Give me the six best proposals you've got, Josh. I'll hand carry them through the system and find out where the problem is."

Relief swept over Sims's face. "You've got it, Russ."

"One other thing. The proposals that have been rejected, they were returned from the embassy with a cover letter, right?"

"Yeah, that's right."

"Whose signature was on the letters?"

"Eads," Josh Sims answered. "Brigadier General William E. Eads."

Russ left Upper Heyford immediately after lunch with Sims, Benson, and Foster, planning to be back at the office before the close of business.

Sealed cardboard cylinders lay in the backseat, labeled "confidential" and containing maps and proposals for flight training routes and targets.

He thought about his conversation with Josh. ORIs were extremely demanding. Usually, a fighter wing failed them because of technical problems. Failure of aircraft systems. Avionics. Munitions issues. Seldom was it because pilots were unable to meet the mission requirements. His mind was filled with questions. Why couldn't the wing obtain more training? Why were requests for more training routes and targets denied? Why was there no explanation for denying their requests? Only letters of rejection by General Eads.

He hadn't hit it off with Eads, but he vowed to meet with the general as soon as possible to find out what had happened to the fighter wing's requests. Surely, the problem could be resolved quickly.

Back in London, he nodded to Vivian Rutherford's mock surprise as he entered his office. "I didn't expect you back today," she said, following him to his office door. "Your messages are on your desk. Nothing urgent. May I get you a cup of coffee?"

He accepted her offer as he placed the cylinders on his desk and sat down. He glanced at his messages, tossed the small stack aside, then picked up the telephone and dialed. "Ted? This is Russ Jefferson."

"Hello, Major. How's it going?"

Ted Sanders was a captain in the embassy Air Attaché's office. It was a lowly post, but he had flown combat over North Vietnam and he was the only man in the embassy that Russ trusted with the question he was about to ask. "Oh, I'm slowly getting the feel of things, I guess," Russ said, managing a disparaging laugh. "I suppose someday I'll figure out what I'm doing here."

Sanders chuckled. "Let me know when you do, Major. I've been here a year and I'm still trying."

Miss Rutherford placed the coffee mug on his desk, and Russ nodded his appreciation.

He asked, "Ted, has the Air Attaché's staff reviewed any proposals for low-level training routes and bombing ranges submitted by the wing at Upper Heyford?"

"No, we haven't."

"Are you sure?"

"Absolutely sure. I'm the only navigator on the staff. I evaluate proposed routes."

"Is it possible any proposals were reviewed by the Air Attaché's office before you came on board?"

"Nope. There would be a file on it." Now a suspicious tone crept into Sanders's voice. "What's this all about, Major?"

"I was visiting with some old friends in the fighter wing. Some questions were asked, and I didn't know the answers. That's all." His answer sounded lame, but Sanders didn't press it. "Ted, keep my questions under your hat, will you?"

"Sure thing, Major. No problem."

He replaced the phone and leaned back. So, the proposals had never reached the Air Attaché's staff. That left only two officials who could have rejected them: Admiral Frank Fleming and General William E. Eads. And Eads had signed the letters.

His telephone rang. He glanced at his watch—almost five. He picked up. "Major Jefferson speaking."

"Major Russell *T.* Jefferson? Hello. This is Ava."

"Well, Miss Gardner, this is a pleasant surprise."

"Ava," she said again. Then, sounding curious, "It is?"

"An incredible surprise."

"Why? Was I so rude Friday night?"

"No, of course not."

"I was a terrible hostess, wasn't I?"

"Not at all. Just very busy. Telephone calls. You seem to have a busy schedule."

"I suppose it appeared that way, but it's just that I never have a schedule of any kind. I'm really an uncomplicated kind of person."

He had to laugh. "Of course you are."

"Oh, I am," she insisted.

"I enjoyed the evening."

"So did I, Major. Honestly, I did. Being with someone from North Carolina. Gives me a chance to talk naturally and know I'm understood."

"I'm sure you would find me easy . . . to talk to," he said mischievously.

"Oh, it's more than that, honey. You'd be amazed how rare it is that I meet someone who has the slightest idea of what it's like to be from the South." She was talking now as if they were friends. "And does this little southern girl, who's been away from Dixie so long, miss having a young southern boy to talk to occasionally? Honey, do you even have to ask?"

"I'll start dropping my R's, and find my recipe for hominy grits."

"And I must apologize to this southern boy for my bad manners Friday. I was just in one of those menopause moods, I guess."

Her words surprised him. He made no reply.

"And I must make amends. I'm having a few friends over this Thursday night. Please come and give me a chance to redeem myself."

"It'll be my pleasure."

"Good. Thursday at eight. And, Major . . ."

"Yes?"

"You don't need to bring any more wine."

"If you say so."

"Or flowers."

He laughed as they hung up, and then he swiveled around to look out the window. Invited to her home, again. He was going to see her again. Unbelievable.

Six

Russ Jefferson stood to one side of the room observing the assembly of guests at Ennismore Gardens.

Muted voices mixed with music, laughter, the sounds of ice clinking in glasses, and expensive dresses rustling. There were perhaps thirty people of varying attire, accents, and manner in the large room, seemingly with one common trait: talking endlessly about the most trite and trivial topics possible.

The crowd represented a wide range of ages. There were married couples, escorted dates. A few—like Russ—were there alone. Several of the women were quite pretty, two or three even beautiful. But none compared to the hostess.

Ava's black dress was strapless and cut low at the back. A diamond necklace and matching earrings glittered almost as brightly as her eyes, reflecting a seemingly infinite array of brilliant colors. The perfect hostess, she moved from guest to guest, conversation to conversation. Her charm warmed the room, and even in the atmosphere of exaggerated gaiety and teasing flirtations, her laughter could be heard above the others.

When he arrived, she had greeted him with a brief hug and a kiss that missed his cheek, and there was a faint fragrance of vanilla. "I want to be with you later," she had said, smiling affectionately, before moving on to other late arrivals.

During the first several minutes Adolfo Gonzalez, a Spanish politician, Falah Zabari, an Iraqi general, and a British poet named Stephen Spender had introduced themselves to him, and the briefness of their interest in him was exceeded only by his in them. From across the room, the actress gave him a lingering look and that smile again.

He checked his watch. Still early. Drink in hand, he shifted his weight to the other foot. A very distinguished-looking man came to join him at the side of the room. "Major Jefferson?"

"Yes."

"I understand you're Ava's new American friend." The man smiled and extended his hand. His grip was firm and dry. "My name is Hooker. Sydney Hooker." He released Russ's hand and looked over the crowd. "Have you ever seen such a pocket of untapped natural gas in your entire life?"

"Oh, I'm sure they're discussing very important things." Russ examined the slender man more closely. Late sixties. Dark hair, gray at the temples, thick and combed slickly so that it shone in the light. His mustache fitted his face perfectly; a natural part of the man. He wore a tailored three-piece suit.

"Rubbish, my boy." Hooker laughed. "They are actors, politicians, writers, and professional partiers. You could lump them all into one large ball—if that were feasible—and *still* not find one informed view on any serious subject." He sipped his drink, then added, "And that includes me, of course."

Russ smiled, saying nothing.

"Ava also told me you're a fighter pilot. Were you in Vietnam?"

"Yes."

"Terrible dilemma. Terrible." Again Russ chose to remain silent. "I was in World War II, in the RAF. Flew Spitfires." Hooker paused thoughtfully, seeming moved by the memory, then continued. "I like to think I still have a feel for flying fighters—even flying combat—but I haven't a clue about the wonderful technology you chaps have in your modern fighters."

"I'm not sure how wonderful it is."

"What are you flying now?"

"I'm not. I'm in a staff assignment."

"Ah, yes. Ava said you're assigned to the embassy. I have a few friends there."

"That's a few more than I have." Russ had no idea why he said that.

"Things a bit nippy at Grosvenor Square?"

"No. To be quite honest, it's me. I'm not quite suited for the embassy."

Hooker laughed. "Spoken like a true fighter pilot," he said. "We've never belonged behind desks, have we?"

Hooker continued. "I do hope you're enjoying London, Major."

"I haven't really seen much of London yet."

"We must do something about that." The older man paused a thoughtful moment, then asked, "Do you play golf?"

"Yes, I play."

"I enjoy the game also. Shall we play a round? We have some marvelous courses in London, and I can introduce you to some chaps."

"Thank you. I would enjoy that." Still he watched Ava, admiring her hourglass figure, seeing how irresistible she was to every man in the room. He hoped she would look at him again. He wondered when he would have an opportunity to talk to her. "Have you known Miss Gardner long?" he asked.

"Oh, yes. More than twenty years."

"Then you're old friends."

"Longtime friends. At my age you avoid the word *old*."

"Quite a woman," Russ said, his eyes remaining on her. She was standing with two men, listening attentively to the taller one as the other handed her a fresh drink. She looked up at the tall man as though he was the most charming man she had ever known and as if whatever he was saying was the most interesting thing she had ever heard.

"She is, without doubt, the most exciting and beautiful woman on this planet," said the Englishman, his voice deliberate. "And you, my boy, seem to have caught her fancy. I've seen those looks she's been giving you."

"She seems very interested in the man talking to her right now."

Hooker shook his head. "She's just being the proper hostess to that bloke. She can turn that on whenever she wishes. The looks I noticed her giving you were different, my young friend."

Russ wasn't at all sure that Hooker was serious, and he was paying little attention to the Englishman as he watched her. She was simply conversing—listening, talking, laughing—and he was completely fascinated by her.

Hooker smiled at the American's expression. He had seen it on other men when they looked at the actress. He waited another moment, then asked, "Do they release you from the embassy on weekends?"

"Yes." Russ took his eyes from Ava and glanced around the room restlessly.

"I'll call you one day for that round of golf. Our good weather won't last much longer. We should make it soon." Hooker sensed the American's impatience. "I'll be off, now, my boy. I need to say hello to some of the other guests. Let's chat again soon," he said as he turned to leave.

Russ made his way to the bar and ordered his second drink. He had never been to a party like this. Not likely to ever go to another. He thought about squadron parties that were also filled with laughter, but honest and natural laughter among friends. Like this one, those parties were filled with flirtations, but his kind of people and the people at this affair could hardly be more different. He wondered what Noonan would say and do at this little shindig. His friend would, without a doubt, have insulted and offended at least half of the guests in some hilariously delightful way by now. His mind flashed a warning: *don't think about Noonan.*

With a fresh drink in hand, he retraced his steps to his solitary spot against the wall, overhearing conversations with accents he couldn't recognize.

He saw that Ava had moved to another small group. Someone was handing her a new drink even as she finished one. Again she smiled at him and nodded. He nodded an answer.

When he arrived, she had said she wanted to be with him later. Now he was beginning to wonder if they would be together at all. He knew he was being impatient and unreasonable. Of course he was.

Suddenly a blonde, only a few pounds from plumpness, stepped beside him and said, "Hello, lonely stranger."

"Hello," he answered, still looking across the room.

"I'm Regina, Reggie if you prefer." She waited for him to complete the exchange of names. When he didn't, she asked, "Who are you?"

He turned to look at her. She had big blue eyes, smooth skin, a wide mouth. Her lips were full. Her hair was a thick mane of yellow-gold, and her low-cut dress emphasized the size of her breasts. By the time he told her his name, her smile had disappeared. Her eyes widened, her lips parted slightly. "You're an American?" Her blue eyes were fixed on his scars.

"That's right."

"What are you doing in London?"

"Not much," he said seriously.

"Are you a good friend of Miss Gardner's?"

"No."

"Neither am I. I was brought by Count Lardass over there." She nodded toward a heavy man wearing a dark gray, double-breasted suit, a style preferred by the more conservative class of English men. She turned back to Russ, again examining his face. "Who are you with, luv?"

"No one."

"Tall, dark, and handsome, and all alone. That makes you a terribly intriguing character." Her voice lowered. "And mysterious."

"You have an overactive imagination."

Her smile widened. "You've no idea how active my imagination is."

"Isn't it time you returned to your count or duke or whatever?"

"No, he doesn't miss me. Besides, I'd rather be with you." His look was disapproving. "Well, I *am* attracted to you." She took a deep breath, her breasts swelling, her dress drawing dangerously near inadequacy. "It's . . . well, in part it's the scars."

He said nothing. No one had been so direct about them before.

Her voice became huskier. "You excite me."

Wearily, he said, "I don't mean to be rude, Miss . . ."

"Reggie."

"I honestly don't mean to be rude, *miss,* but I really have no interest in games just now."

"Nor do I. Are you a race-car driver? A Hollywood stuntman?"

"No, on both counts."

"It doesn't matter." She smiled with those full, soft lips. "I don't wish to annoy you. I only wanted you to know that I find you terribly attractive. The scars. I *do* hope you aren't self-conscious about them." She picked up a matchbook from a nearby desk and opened her small purse. "I'm sorry if I've embarrassed you." She pulled a silver pen from her purse and scribbled inside the matchbook as she talked. "But I do hope you call me sometime." She handed the matchbook to him. "This is my number," she said, smiling, and she walked away.

Without looking at it, he dropped the matchbook into his pocket, then checked his watch. Surely it was just a matter of time before he had an opportunity to join Ava, to spend a few minutes with her. He would continue to nurse his drink until then.

Suddenly from across the room came the sound of breaking glass. He looked in the direction the noise had come from, and though her back was toward him, he instantly recognized the black strapless dress and her dark hair. It was Ava. A broken vase lay on the floor beside the stereo, apparently knocked off when she raised the top of the cabinet to play a record. Now, as she fumbled with the sound system's controls, there was the loud, unnerving sound of the needle scratching across a record. A second attempt, and then Spanish music filled the room.

She turned, kicked off her shoes, and strode toward the center of the room, bare arms raised, fingers working as if playing castanets. She began dancing in small, precise steps to the flamenco guitar, her hips moving rhythmically, an arrogant set to her head and shoulders, the overall effect a brazen, natural sexiness. Her eyes held Russ's.

The crowd clapped in time to the music, and she extended her arms toward an older man with a gray goatee, inviting him to dance with her. He politely refused, blushing. She turned to the Iraqi general, demanding that he dance with her, and when he, too, declined she took a defiant stance, feet set wide apart, hands on her hips. "What's wrong with everyone?" She tossed her head and her eyes flashed dangerously. "Am I not cultured enough for you bastards?"

A swarthy man stepped forward, preparing to join her.

"No, no, no!" she cried scornfully, moving away from him. "I'll choose who I dance with, goddamn it!" Once again her eyes gazed steadily into Russ's.

She was obviously drunk, yet her steps and words were precise, unimpaired.

Russ watched and waited. "There she goes," said the man standing next to him. "She's wonderful until it gets dark and there've been too many martinis. And then it's Ava from hell."

She danced forward, her hips swaying to the music. "Such a *wonderful* group of men," she mocked. "All of this power and money, and all so goddamned *civilized*. Not one of you could hold your own against the poorest Gypsy in all of goddamned Spain!" She took a glass from a man, drank its murky contents, then threw it against the wall and resumed dancing.

Several guests prepared to leave, whispering as they made their way to the door. She watched them, an arched eyebrow and a sarcastic laugh her only reaction.

"Let's go to the bars, Ava!" shouted a man in the group surrounding her.

She stopped dancing. "Yes, let's do. We'll race our cars to Soho. Dance all night."

She turned to a young man with tanned skin and long hair, his open silk shirt revealing strands of gold chains. She grabbed his arm and said, "I'll take you." Then she turned to another older man. "And you."

She strode on, scanning the men at the bar. "It's going to be a *wonderful* night of bar crawling and dancing, but *not* with you . . . or you . . . or you," she said, pointing to one man after another. Then her eyes returned to Russ and she stopped in front of him.

"And I had thought the climax . . . the end of this evening would be just us," she said in a low, provocative voice. "I thought . . . a fun romp . . . just the two of us. So handsome and irresistible, but I saw you with that woman." She tossed her head and laughed contemptuously. Then, her voice back to normal, she said, "Stay here, Major, with your fat blonde."

"Come, Ava," implored the tanned man with the gold chains.

"Yes, let's go," she said, laughing, and joined the others. Noisily they were out the door and into the night.

Everyone stood motionless, only exchanging glances. It was as if no one knew what to do in the aftermath of the storm. There was an empty, breathless depression, a vacuum in the sudden absence of noise and movement and energy. Russ looked at the door through which she had disappeared. Why had she said those things to him?

"Don't take it personally, my boy." It was Sydney Hooker. "She didn't mean what she said. She's having one of her nights. She can seem cruel when she's like that." Most of the guests were gathering their coats and leaving. Two or three still stood at the bar, ordering more drinks. "Sometimes things just become too much for her. Then she drinks too much and strikes out at anyone unfortunate enough to be in the same room with her."

Russ examined his own feelings. He had watched her drinking martinis throughout the evening; the moment one glass was empty, there was another. The charming hostess had become a different woman. She was insecure and desperate. Volatile. The Barefoot Contessa. He thought something deep inside her brought out this different person, a beautiful woman trying to escape from very ugly demons.

"Those wicked moods don't occur so often now," said Hooker, "but her sudden up swings and down swings still happen. When she's drinking, she can become violently unpredictable. That terrible temper can lead her to cruelty. To thrown glasses. It has cost her many friends."

Still staring at the door, Russ hardly moved.

Hooker looked at the young American with a knowing expression and said, "Let's meet for lunch tomorrow. At my club. We can talk." He removed a business card from his inner coat pocket, quickly wrote an address on the back, and handed it to Jefferson. "Tomorrow, at one."

Seven

Russ stepped into the large room, carrying the cylinders he had brought from Upper Heyford.

The American Air Attaché's office was among the more prominent in the embassy, but the attaché's junior staff officers were relegated to a room in the far corner of the basement. Only with specific directions could anyone possibly find it. It was a "bullring" arrangement: five desks in an open bay area, separated by partitions.

He saw Ted Sanders at his desk and walked toward him. Air Force Photographic Services' standard airplane pictures covered the windowless walls. "Nice view you have here, Captain."

Sanders grinned as he extended his hand. "It's somehow fitting with our lowly station. You know, slave quarters." He shook Russ's hand vigorously and offered him a chair.

Sanders wore navigator wings and four rows of ribbons that described one hundred missions over North Vietnam. Russ saw the Air Force Cross, the Distinguished Flying Cross, and the Air Medal with clusters. Sanders had been there, all right.

"What's this?" asked the captain, nodding at the cylinders.

"Proposals for low-level training routes and bombing ranges." Russ glanced around. He saw no one. "From the fighter wing at Upper Heyford."

"I see."

"I have a favor to ask."

"Let me guess. You want my help to get them approved."

"I want you to help me find out what the problem has been," corrected Russ. It was time to be honest. He looked around the room again to make sure there was no one to overhear him. "Can this be confidential—between us?"

"You've got it, Major."

"These six proposals have been previously submitted to the embassy." He removed the rolled maps from the cylinders. "The favor I need is for you to confirm if they've been previously reviewed by the Air Attaché staff. Then I need you to evaluate them to see if they're acceptable. See if they generally satisfy the criteria required by the British government."

"And?"

"And tell me what you think," Russ said. "I'll keep your name out of any follow-up discussions."

"Leave them with me, Major. I'll call you by noon."

"Thanks." He thought of Sydney Hooker. "I've got a lunch appointment, but I'll be here until after twelve."

The rest of the morning was filled with routine staff work. Shortly before noon, Vivian Rutherford called him on the intercom. "Captain Sanders is on line two."

He checked his watch and punched the blinking light. "Not quite noon, Ted."

"It wasn't a tough job, Major," Sanders replied. "Number one: none of these proposals have ever been submitted to the Air Attaché's office. Number two: these are well-planned proposals. I think they avoid all of the problems that would cause objections by the British government."

"Did you see *any* reason for rejection?"

"No, and I gave them a close check. The guys at Upper Heyford did a good job on them."

"Anything else, Ted?"

"I'll do anything I can to help these guys get what they need, but . . . I have one suggestion."

"What's that?"

"You told me the letters rejecting the wing's prior proposals are signed by General Eads. I assume, and I suspect that you do as well, that he made the decisions."

"A reasonable assumption."

"But we don't *know*. If you're determined to hand carry the proposals through the embassy, plus USAFE, plus *Whitehall,* I suggest you don't do it behind his back. Be right up front. Tell Eads. He may boil you in oil, but there's also the chance that he's *not* been the one who's killed those proposals. He may have just handled the administrative part of it. In any event, I think you should tell him. After all, he *is* your boss."

"Yeah. I'll tell him."

"And I'll have these back to your office today, Major."

"Good. Talk to you then."

He pushed the button for the intercom. "Miss Rutherford, call General Eads's secretary. Ask her if he's there; if he's alone. If so tell her I'm on my way for a visit. Only need five minutes."

He didn't wait to hear about the deputy director's rules regarding appointments. He stood, straightened his uniform coat, and walked past Rutherford, who was already on the phone with Eads's secretary.

Rutherford's brown hair was pushed back for the receiver, and she listened to the protest from Eads's office. She smiled as she watched Jefferson walk purposefully to the doorway and disappear.

Russ took long strides down the hall to the door marked DEPUTY DIRECTOR OF MILITARY AFFAIRS and entered. A woman with a streak of gray extending from her widow's peak protected the general's door.

"May I see the general?" he asked.

"Yes, go right in, Major."

He stepped in and went to the front of the desk. Eads gave him a cool glance, then returned to his review of a letter. Russ stood comfortably, waiting.

The senior officer lowered the letter to the desk and leaned back, looking at Jefferson. "I've agreed to this interruption, Major, but make it quick. What's this all about?"

"Thanks for seeing me, General. Won't take a minute. Just wanted to brief you on a project I'm going to be working on."

"A project?"

"Yes sir."

"*I* assign your projects, Major Jefferson."

"I understand, sir, but this is an exception." He tried to make his question sound innocent. "Are you aware of the fighter wing's performance at Upper Heyford?"

"I know they've had some problems."

"I was invited to Upper Heyford Tuesday. They wanted to talk about very serious problems—problems that have a direct bearing on their combat-readiness training and their mission capability." He paused to let the words settle in. He had used two phrases that established absolute importance: *combat readiness, mission capability.* A discussion following *that* precursor would not be treated lightly.

The general said nothing.

Russ continued, "The crews of the new F-111 wing can't train properly because they don't have enough training routes and bombing ranges. They fly routes that are so few and so canned that the training value is zero. They say they can fly them in their sleep. It's the major reason for busting their first two operational readiness inspections. It can't go on."

"And your project?" the general asked carefully.

"Just to help them get more routes and ranges. They have submitted formal proposals through proper channels, but for some strange reason the submissions keep getting bounced back." The general's eyes clouded. Russ said evenly, "Their proposals are well prepared but rejected every time, right here at the embassy." Eads blinked. "And my project is to find out why."

The general said in a low voice, "There may be complexities involved that are beyond their scope of understanding—and yours." Russ's face hardened into a cynical expression. "There are usually more to these decisions than one might think," Eads said as he got to his feet, stepped to a small table, and picked up a file. "There may be political sensitivities. Important bargaining chips."

"Some Harvard graduate in the State Department can negotiate those lofty issues, but right now I've got to help the fighter wing get what they need."

"I told you a moment ago, *I* assign your work, Major Jefferson."

"This has to be done, General."

"No, Major," the small man said evenly. "You are *not* going to take on this so-called project."

"Am I to understand—"

"I think you understand me completely."

"That is your final word on the matter, General?" Russ asked, incredulously.

"You will consider this matter closed and you will not address it again. *That* is the final word from your commanding officer."

Without thinking, Russ blurted, "That's bullshit from a professional penguin!" *Good Lord, I'm doing it again.*

"What did you say?" The voice quivered in controlled rage.

"A penguin. It eats and squawks and never flies."

"You can't show me that kind of disrespect!"

"I just did." *God, Russ, why don't you just jump off the career cliff?*

The general slammed the file down and his face turned red as he started to speak.

Russ didn't wait. His words came fast and sharp. "You know how critical the F-111 is to NATO, General. The most crucial component in its entire force structure. There are eighty F-111s at Upper Heyford at a cost of about a billion dollars. There are a couple of hundred pilots and weapons systems officers and each cost the taxpayers over a million dollars for just their basic flight training." He paused, then continued, knowing he had gotten in too deep to be able to ever get out. "There is a support organization of maybe two thousand trained maintenance specialists, weapons specialists, and all sorts of other technicians, and God knows how much in equipment and weapons. The United States government has maybe a couple of billion dollars tied up in that wing, and they can't train properly because some stupid jerk won't let them fly over a mink farm or something."

Eads's eyes were slits.

"They're here to fly *war lines,* General, but some dumbass in the embassy won't let them fly their missions!"

"You can't talk to me like that!"

"I can when I have to."

"I'll have you *court-martialed!*" The older man was almost screaming.

Russ turned and left the office, slamming the door behind him. He would send the proposals to USAFE headquarters right away. That very day. Screw Eads.

The taxi turned onto St. James's Street and approached Sydney Hooker's club. Russ looked forward to lunch with Hooker. His encounter with the actress still seemed unreal; maybe a conversation with one of her best friends would help him know her better. The taxi pulled up to the curb and stopped. He saw Hooker striding toward the club in a bowler hat, holding an umbrella and a folded *Times.* Russ paid the driver and stepped from the taxi into the light rain.

"Hello," Hooker called, and he started collapsing his umbrella. "Let's go in for whiskey, get the chill out of our bones."

Russ followed the well-dressed man through the high door with the polished engraved brass plate that read HAILEY. They walked through an alcove and past a wide staircase to the dining room, which was spacious and expensive in every detail. The walls, pale cream with gilt-edged panels, were illuminated by a large crystal chandelier. Across the room a log burned in a massive fireplace.

"Most of London's clubs are located in this area," explained Hooker. "On St. James's and Pall Mall. Since the eighteenth century." He gave Russ a brief smile. "Pall Mall isn't a well-known street, and of course Americans think it's named after one of your popular cigarettes."

They sat at a table near a window. The glow of the fire contrasted with the grayness of the day.

"The great London clubs are very old, and membership is handed down from generation to generation." A distant look came into Hooker's eyes. "I will never forget my father bringing me for the first time. I had no idea what to expect. I was terrified in case I spoke when absolute silence was required or sat in the wrong chair. Would I be acceptable? How was I to know?" He laughed and his eyes twinkled.

"We have nothing like this in America," Russ acknowledged.

"The great clubs are no longer so aristocratic—if ever they were—but they are still the places where one can find the best food and drink in London." Hooker beckoned a steward. "Are you ready for a drink?" he asked Russ.

When their drinks arrived, Hooker said, "Cheers" and sipped his whiskey, looking at Russ over the rim of the glass. He was eager to get to know the younger man. He enjoyed fraternizing with fighter pilots. Plus, he was always interested in Ava's bullfighters.

"Many things have changed about the gentlemen's clubs over the years, but according to tradition, they are still to some extent intended for a certain sort of gentleman. For example, the Savage is still the primary club for writers and others associated with literature." He thought for a moment, a perplexed look crossing his handsome features. "I don't know exactly, but I suspect the Hailey was for every sort of scalawag."

Russ laughed. He enjoyed the company of Sydney Hooker.

The steward returned. Hooker asked, "Russ, do you mind if I order for us? A meal that has been a principal in London for generations."

"Not at all."

Hooker instructed the steward to bring braised beef in Guinness with fresh vegetables prepared in broth. Dessert, he added with a smile, would be bread-and-butter pudding. The steward left and Hooker suddenly became serious as he addressed Russ. "I know you were shocked by Ava's behavior last evening."

"It was certainly a surprise."

"Being singled out for special attention by her, as you were last night, can be an overwhelming experience."

"Why me?"

"Green-eyed jealousy," answered Hooker. "She had been looking at you all evening as though she had found another bullfighter."

"As you said, it was a shock."

"You know, you shouldn't judge her. Really, you shouldn't. Sometimes a young man, out of youthful pride, can be very resentful when a woman shuns him publicly. I hope you won't judge her harshly. She is volatile, volcanic. She drinks too much. But, my young friend, when she is your friend, she will kill for you. And if she wrongs you, she will do anything for your forgiveness."

Russ took a sip of his drink as he waited for the Englishman to continue.

"She is quite vulnerable. Not at all the hard, self-centered, demanding person the press made her out to be. She could never protect herself against the cruelties of the movie industry and its tycoons. They fed on her, used her, but she got little back. So at the peak of her career, when she was perhaps the most recognized woman in the world, she ran away. She couldn't fight them, and she had to survive, so she simply ran away."

"Has she regretted it? Running away?"

"No. I think being a movie star, proclaimed the most glamorous woman in the world, was everything she never wanted. None of that was as important to her as living the way she wanted. Having some control over her life."

"She was out of control last night."

"She's known abuse. Her life has been tempestuous, but she never deserved to be the world's symbol of scandal and immorality."

"Why are you telling me this?" Russ asked quietly.

"Because she likes you."

"After last night, I would say that's debatable," he said, laughing cynically.

"No, it isn't. I saw how she looked at you. And, my young friend, would it be fair to say that you look at her with, well, *admiration*?" He smiled. "There's no mistaking that look, my boy."

"Of course, I admire her. She's incredible, but she belongs to an entirely different world."

"As I said, she's run away from the movie world. And I suspect you are running from a past world, also, my boy. Something you are trying to forget?"

Russ looked at him in surprise.

The gentle rain scratched at the window, and the log in the grate toppled over with a swirl of sparks.

Trying to forget.

The heat, humidity, and smells of Southeast Asia permeated the briefing room even before dawn. The captain pulled the large map into view, sliding

*it silently along its rails from concealment behind a curtain. He used the tip
of his telescopic stainless steel pointer to tap the largest symbol on the map.
"Gentlemen," he said, "today you're going downtown." The room became
quieter. "Two big-time targets: the Paul Doumer Bridge and the Yen Vien
railroad yards."*

*Jefferson and Noonan exchanged glances. Downtown meant Hanoi. Jef-
ferson studied the map. Yellow lines represented routes to the targets, leading to overlapping symbols of Hanoi air defenses. No surprise. The Paris
peace talks had fallen through again, and hundreds of fighters were going
north today. Navy and Air Force. Operation Linebacker. It would be the
biggest operation since the first two years of the war, but it came too late.
Much too late. The war, as everyone in this room knew, was lost.*

*As the officer continued, Jefferson glanced around. Thirty pilots sat in
the large briefing room. Some studied every minute detail of mission information. Some wore expressions of resigned dread. Some were sipping from
cans of V8. All were resolved. This was what they had trained for, and they
would fly the mission as best they could, but not for flag or country. LBJ and
the Washington crowd had taken care of that long ago. They would do it for
one another and for others who had gone before them and hadn't come
back. The pilots were well aware that this was the largest strike in five years.
They also knew it was too little, too late. Five years too late. The war was a
tragic waste. The only thing left was to get the POWs out.*

*Jefferson looked at his hands, then he folded his arms and hid them.
They had been shaking. It just wouldn't do for the others to see that they had
a nervous leader.*

Eight

A dumbass penguin? He really called the general that?" Irene Harrington gave her friend a look of disbelief.

"That's what he said," repeated Joanna Thompson. "A dumbass penguin that never flies! That only eats and squawks! I couldn't believe it, but I heard it with my own ears. *To the general!*"

The three women were having lunch at their table near the corner, as they did two or three times each week, but today's conversation was more exciting than usual, and it centered on Russ Jefferson. Vivian Rutherford listened with a bemused smile. Her new Air Force guy in Military Affairs was becoming the talk of the embassy.

"What else did he say?" asked Irene as she took a cigarette from her purse. She held her lighter poised.

"Well, remember, this is in strictest confidence," Joanna said solemnly as she frowned at the cigarette. "The general threatened the major with a court-martial, telling him that he could not show him that kind of disrespect." She seemed to enjoy the role of eyewitness. "The major said that it was really quite easy to show him that kind of disrespect—and *other* kinds as well."

"He *didn't!*" Irene lit her cigarette, exhaled toward the ceiling, and turned back to her friends.

Joanna looked around to see that no one could overhear her, then continued. "General Eads's blood pressure went through the roof. He was raving the rest of the day. Stuttering and stammering."

"I can't *believe* it!" Irene said. "A major—saying those things to a general!"

"Eads yelled at me three times to get an appointment with Admiral Fleming, who's been in Washington a week," Joanna said in a hushed tone. She glanced around, then continued with an even graver tone of confidentiality. "He stormed off to the restroom. When he came back he was trailing toilet paper all the way down the hall!"

"Oh God, how wonderful!" Irene squealed. "What was Major Jefferson like when he came back to the office?" she asked Vivian. "He must have been really uptight."

"No, not really."

"Far out," Irene said, and sighed. She tapped an ash from her cigarette. "Major Jefferson is stirring things up around this old place."

"Yes, he is," agreed Joanna, whose patience and control were now exhausted. "And can you blow your smoke in some other direction?"

"Oh, Joanna, you're just like all the other ex-smokers," said Irene.

Vivian was no longer listening. Joanna would, of course, repeat often the exchange she overheard between the new major and the general. She would first tell her close friends in "total confidence" and then her casual friends with equal confidentiality. Within hours the story would spread throughout the embassy, and people would be talking about Russell Jefferson for a very long time. The new major was an instant embassy celebrity.

Vivian wished Jefferson would allow her to become his ally. His confidante. She had always been there to take care of her guys, but not this one.

He was a loner. One thing about him, though, he was a far cry from the typical embassy bureaucrat, compromising always and never standing up to a superior. And he was a far cry, too, from most of the career-hustling, cover-your-ass type military officers usually assigned to this place. And, she told herself, she liked him.

Russ stepped off the elevator and nearly bumped into Ted Sanders.

"Hello, Major," Sanders said. "I hear you touched base with the general. That you informed him of your plan to get the Upper Heyford proposals through channels."

"Just as you suggested."

"Yeah, but jeez, I didn't suggest that you call him a *penguin.*" A narrow smile worked at the corners of his mouth.

"I've never been very subtle—or smart."

Sanders chuckled, then became serious. "I've been notified that your proposals arrived in Germany. They've been received at USAFE headquarters. The whole package. An old buddy of mine has been assigned to review and recommend. He telephoned this afternoon with a couple of questions. It went well. I told him to call if any other questions come up. And he will. We'll take care of it."

"I really appreciate your help."

"No sweat. Oh, one more thing."

"Yes?"

"I hear that the junior officers can hardly wait until the next formal occasion when tuxedos are required. They want to use their penguin-suit jokes." He laughed again. "See you around, Major."

Russ regretted that his exchange with Eads had become so widely known. He didn't want to have a reputation for being a hot dog or a cheap-shot guy. He entered his office and Miss Rutherford told him "that lady" was on the line again. He hurried to pick up the phone.

"Major, this is Ava." Her voice was flat. Emotionless.

"Hello," he said somewhat guardedly.

"May I see you?" There was no hint of the laughter that always seemed just below the surface. "I would consider it a real favor. I promise not to keep you more than a minute or two." She paused. "Please?"

"Of course. When?"

"Would today at five-thirty be all right? My flat?"

"I'll be there."

"Thank you," she said, and hung up without saying good-bye.

He turned to look out the window. This was the first time he had spoken to her since the night of her party. He had thought of her often, wondering if he would ever see her again. Wondering if she would ever want to see him. He checked the time. In spite of the tiredness he had heard in her voice, his excitement began building. Only a couple of hours and he would be on his way.

Time passed quickly. Two reports written and several telephone calls later, and it was almost five. This time would be different. He would show her that he was an experienced man, just as experienced as any of those at her party. He would go directly from work and arrive in uniform. Sans flowers, sans wine. He would tell her that he had only a few minutes, that he was taking valuable time from his busy schedule. The uniform would make him appear more mature, he thought. Surely, with its insignias, its rows of colorful ribbons, and its silver wings, it would add a certain . . . well, manliness.

As he started to leave he thought of something. He went directly to Gerald Graves's office and knocked, not waiting for an invitation to enter. A few seconds later he reappeared with one of the lieutenant commander's cigars in his hand. That will do it, he thought. A cigar would make him seem older, give him character.

She looked through the partially opened door. "Hello," she said. Unhurriedly she opened it fully. "Please come in."

She wore a long-sleeved white shirt, a plain khaki skirt, and light tan sandals. She seemed small. He followed her into the room, which seemed empty and quiet in contrast to the last time he had been there. She extended a hand toward a chair and said, "Please, sit down."

"Thank you," he said, aware of a great difference in her. Something was wrong. Her walk was not her usual, unselfconscious stride. He took the chair she offered. "It's good to see you."

"I had to see you." She sat down in the other wing chair and took a deep breath. "Major, I'm sorry for the way I acted Thursday night. I was a real bitch I'm sure. I'm told I particularly owe you an apology." She dropped her eyes momentarily, then raised them again. "I'm told I was especially mean-spirited to you."

"Don't give it another thought. Really." Earlier in the afternoon he had thought he would tell her that, even if she was famous and wealthy, *no one* treated Russell Jefferson like she had, and . . . the thought had trailed off into a deep, dark mental abyss filled with other worthless thoughts.

"I asked you to come so I could apologize." Her voice, normally husky, sounded thin. "To ask you to forgive me."

"You're forgiven," he said in a soft, serious voice, hoping it made his words more convincing.

"It was just inexcusable for me to treat you badly, after you've been so helpful and kind to me. Being drunk is no excuse. I really am sorry."

He looked at her more closely. She was pale. "Are you okay?"

"A little tired, maybe." She looked him over. "May I tell you how handsome you are in that impressive uniform?"

"You may."

"Very handsome," she repeated with a wan smile, her words sounding indifferent.

"Thanks, but you don't sound at all convincing."

She didn't react to his expressed doubts. "When I lived in Spain I was once invited to the nearby Air Force base to see an aerobatic demonstration." Her voice was still flat. "Aren't they called the Thunderbirds?"

"That's right." He nodded. "The United States Air Force Thunderbirds."

"I watched their entire performance, and I was impressed by the beauty of it. Such precise maneuvers, so close to each other. Just above the ground and so fast."

"They put on quite a show," he agreed.

She rose and walked slowly to the fireplace. "I had a chance to meet the pilots. They invited me to a party after their show, and they gave me an orange flight suit with my name and the insignia of a one-star general sewn on it." He leaned back, watching her and listening. "They told me the maneuvers they fly are the same maneuvers that all fighter pilots fly on a daily, routine basis." She looked at him. "And you are one of them, aren't you?"

"I've never flown with the Thunderbirds."

"But you flew those planes in combat. Incredible." She blinked, as if to clear her vision.

"Are you all right?"

She lifted a hand to her temple and closed her eyes. "I'm fine. Just . . . a little dizzy." She rested her hand on the mantel for balance.

"Sit down." He moved to her quickly, taking her arm and leading her to the chair. "Sit here while I get a glass of water."

He released her hand and had started toward the kitchen for water and a damp cloth when he heard her say, "I'm so . . ." He looked back just in time to see her fall to the chair. There was a soft moan, and then she slid unconscious from the chair and collapsed onto the floor.

With two strides he was there and knelt at her side. Her breathing seemed regular; he placed a finger on her pulse. It was racing. He hurried to the bar and dampened a cloth with cold water, then rushed back to place it across her forehead. There was no response, no sign that she was regaining consciousness.

He had no idea what had happened, no idea what to do.

He scooped her up effortlessly and carried her to the door of her flat. He had no trouble opening it, and he kicked it closed behind them. From the top of the stairway he shouted at the doorman, "Roberts! Get a taxi, and hurry, Miss Gardner is ill!"

The damned lift will take forever. She was light in his arms, and he swept down the stairs to the building's entrance. Roberts seemed uncertain at first, unsure if he should do what the American said, but then he flagged a taxi and hurried back to hold the wrought-iron gate for them.

"The nearest hospital, where is it?" demanded Russ as he carried the limp body across the wide sidewalk.

"On Praed Street, guv'ner," the driver answered. "St. Mary's. It's right at Paddington Station."

"Just across Hyde Park," said the doorman, no longer hesitant. He held the taxi door open. "Less than five minutes, sir."

"Call the hospital, Roberts!" he commanded as he carried her into the taxi. "Tell them we're coming, right now! Go!"

She had been unconscious for more than two hours. He had sat in her hospital room, paced the hall outside her door. Now he sat beside the bed. Her face was pale, her breathing even.

He checked his watch. Two hours since the doctor had first examined her in the ER. A nurse came into the room, watched her for a moment, then left. The nurse had looked in on her frequently with the doctor's instructions to notify him when she awakened. He rose from the chair. It was time to pace again.

"Hello," she said weakly.

"Hello, yourself." He took a step toward the bed.

"How'd I get here?"

"I brought you."

She looked at him vaguely. "Well, Sir Lancelot . . . seems as though . . . I'm becoming your . . . personal damsel in distress."

"That's right." He started toward the door. "I'm searching for fire-breathing dragons every minute of the day to slay on your behalf." He stepped out the door, looking left and right. He got the attention of the nurse and motioned to her.

"So, you're awake, are you?" clucked the nurse at the bed. "How're you, luv?" She took an arm, feeling Ava's pulse. She stared at nothing for a moment, concentrating on her count, then she lowered the arm to the bed. "I'll go get the doctor now. Have him here in just a minute."

Five minutes later the doctor—tangled gray hair, wrinkled face, wearing a green surgical coat that looked as if it had been slept in—entered the room. He placed his hand at her temple. "How are you feeling?" His voice matched the deeply lined face.

"A little wobbly." She waited until he removed his hand, then asked, "What happened?"

"You had a transient cerebral ischemic attack, what we call a little stroke."

"What caused it?"

"Shhh." He clamped the stethoscope into his ears and placed the round sterling-silver piece on her chest. He listened, repositioned, listened and repositioned. Finally he straightened and hooked the stethoscope around his neck again.

"What caused it?" she repeated.

"A temporary interruption of blood flow to the brain."

"Some might say the only thing that flowed to my brain this weekend was alcohol." She attempted a weak smile, answered only by Russ's scolding frown. "But it's over now, isn't it, Doctor?"

"Yes, but it is very important that you understand this was a warning." The doctor lowered his voice and leaned toward her. "This attack told you that you must take precautions against a cerebral vascular accident—a stroke."

"You don't mean another little stroke, do you? You mean something more serious."

"Yes. A *very* serious stroke is exactly what I mean."

"What will cause a *very* serious stroke?"

"Well, my dear, there are three major causes of strokes. One is blood vessels becoming occluded." He leaned forward and thoughtfully rubbed his chin as he ran his eyes over her. "That condition is referred to as cerebral thrombosis. I don't think that's what we're concerned with here. Cerebral thrombosis is associated primarily with people older than you."

"Thank you." Again the attempt at humor.

"The second is the cerebral hemorrhage, which results from the rupture of a blood vessel in the brain. This condition is more common for people fifty years of age or so."

"Ugh," she grunted dejectedly.

"And third, there is a cerebral embolus—a condition associated with rheumatic heart disease. Tests will determine what the cause for your symptoms may be."

"I can go home, can't I? Return for the tests?"

"No, my dear. We're going to keep you here where we can keep an eye on you."

Russ wondered if the doctor knew who his patient was. The old boy was turning on the charm, no doubt about it.

"How long will I be here, doctor?"

"Two or three days. But make no mistake about it, you have been given a very serious warning and we are going to learn as much as we can."

"What if it's one of those blocked-artery things?"

"There are corrective measures. Surgical procedures. Anticoagulant therapy." He smiled and patted her leg. "Don't worry about those things now. Let's wait and see. Try to get some rest." He shot a warning glance at Russ.

The doctor left the room with a promise that he would see her the next morning.

Russ sat in the chair beside the bed. "Sounds like you're going to have to stay put for a while." His throat tightened and his voice wavered. "But I'd say you're in very good hands."

"Then why are you so nervous?"

"Me? I'm not nervous."

She looked down at the cigar that he was holding tightly. "I didn't know you smoke cigars," she said.

"I don't."

"You just enjoy *twisting* them, I gather." She gave him an understanding look.

He dropped the tortured cigar into the wastebasket near the bedside table. "Since you're remaining overnight, I'll get things that you need."

"You don't have to do that."

"Nonsense. Help me with a list. Toothbrush. Hairbrush. Makeup. Is that about it?"

"Really, I can't ask you to—"

"Look, you're going to have to allow me to help you. Your maids, doormen, and servants aren't here now." He shrugged. "Like it or not, you only have me."

She smiled. "You will do quite nicely, I think." She looked around. "If you can find my purse, the key to my flat is in it."

"Sorry, lady. I didn't bring your purse. We left in kind of a hurry."

She nodded. "Roberts will let you in. At the telephone there's an address book with the telephone number for Paul Mills and his wife, Spoli. Tell her what happened and ask her to go over and pick out some things for me. You don't need to rummage through my clothes."

"Okay."

"Tell her that I'm only going to be here for a couple of days. Tell her *not* to pack traveling trunks for a goddamn safari."

"I'll tell her."

"And ask her not to tell anyone. I don't want a crowd in here." Her eyes pleaded with him.

"Don't worry. I'll be back in an hour."

"I hope so." Her voice was small.

He could see she meant it. The moment seemed awkward. Someone else should be there with her, to comfort her. He stepped closer to her and took her hand in his. "You'll be just fine. And I promise, I'll be right back." He held her hands for a long moment, smiling.

"It's just that . . . I'm scared. I'm so scared."

When he returned with a small suitcase and a makeup bag, she was asleep. As he unpacked her things, a nurse came in. "She'll sleep like a baby tonight," she said. "We gave her something to make certain she has a good night's rest. Come back tomorrow. She'll be awake then."

He looked at Ava, sleeping comfortably. He admired her beautiful, tranquil face, then slipped out of the room and left.

Nine

Russ pressed the hospital elevator button. A few seconds passed and he punched it a second time. And again.

It was late the next morning, and he had wanted to be with her at the very start of visiting hours, but he had been held up at the office. There were four telephone calls to return, two letters to draft, and then, after handing the letters to Miss Rutherford and asking her to cover for him, he had finally escaped. He had stopped to get flowers, then hurried to the hospital thinking about how frightened she had been the night before.

"Frightfully slow, these lifts," commented the man standing by him.

You got that right, he thought as he impatiently pushed the button again. The elevator arrived. Soon he was nearing her room, straightening his tie, and checking the bouquet in his arm. He put on a big smile to greet her, stepped through the doorway, and found the room empty. The bed was made, the bedside table cleared. His smile disappeared. Every other surface in the room was covered with floral arrangements and bouquets in vases.

The nurse who had been on duty the night before was nowhere to be seen. There was a nurse behind the counter, concentrating on paperwork. He cleared his throat and she looked at him. "Miss Gardner . . . room 359 . . . is something wrong?"

"Sir?"

"The patient in room 359. Where is she?"

"She's having tests just now." The nurse glanced at her watch. "She should be returning soon."

He went back to the hallway, walked up and down thirty feet of it for several minutes, then returned to her room. He sat down, wondering what the tests were showing when a sudden noise at the door interrupted his thoughts. Three orderlies maneuvered a gurney, its stainless-steel sides raised, through the doorway. She lay on the gurney, covered by a sheet.

Russ rose, moving to the side of the room and pulling the chair clear of their path as they drew the gurney alongside the bed. He tried to greet her with his smile, but she was hidden behind the railings and behind the men, who laid her in the bed with a practiced proficiency. There had apparently been an ongoing teasing, and as they straightened things up and readied to leave she said in a tired but game voice, "Get out of here you bastards, and don't ever ask me to go out with you again."

They laughed, said good-bye, and left.

She was very still. Her face turned toward Jefferson. Stepping to her side, he said, "Hello."

"Hello, yourself." She looked at his bouquet.

"Just thought it would brighten up a dreary room." He looked around at the massive array of flowers, then at his small bouquet. "I guess I needn't have worried."

"That damned Spoli," Ava said wearily. "She was told not to send trunks of clothes, so she sends banks of flowers. I'll give all of these to the nurses—except yours."

"There's no need to do that."

"There are other people in this joint who need flowers." She attempted a smile. "Besides, what else could a rescued damsel do for her hero?"

"Well, for openers, she can get some rest." He moved a half-step closer. "You've had a tough morning. You're tired. Why don't you take a nap?"

"And you?"

"I'll have lunch."

"I would love to see you again."

"Then I will return after lunch."

"Isn't today Tuesday? Aren't you working today?"

"No. I told everyone I was taking a holiday."

"Holiday?"

"Yes. It's an anniversary. A very historic anniversary. On this date sixty-five years ago the Chicago Cubs won their only world championship."

She gave him a fond, disapproving look as she shook her head slowly. "Will you really come back?"

"If you like."

"I wish you would."

"Then I'll see you later." He patted her arm and left the room.

"Hi," she said drowsily. "What time is it?"

"Four-thirty." His chair was next to her bed.

"Oh. I *did* sleep, didn't I?"

"You needed it. You've been through a rocky couple of days."

"You could add Thursday night to those days. It was pretty rocky in its own right." Her eyes softened. "I'm truly sorry."

"We've been through all of that," he said. "What really matters is how you're feeling."

"I don't know. A little tired."

"Is there anything I can do?"

"You've done everything."

God, she is so beautiful, he thought. *A stroke. In the hospital all night and day. No one's done her hair. No makeup. And she is absolutely gorgeous.* He couldn't help himself. "Ava, you are so beautiful," he said.

"That's kind of you, but I don't like to hear that."

"But it's so true."

She laughed softly. "No, honey. There was a time when I could stay out all night drinking and dancing, then pin up my hair with toothpicks from the night's supply of martini olives, wash my face with soap, and show up on the back lot at dawn looking pretty for the cameras. But that was when I was young. They say I was beautiful then, and maybe I was. Not now."

"But you are."

"Honey, stop saying that."

He felt he had gotten out of line. "Maybe I should leave and let you get more rest."

"Please, don't," she said quickly. "I wish you would stay. Can you?"

"Of course I can. Do you feel like talking?"

"Not really. But I would love to listen to you."

"I'm not much of a talker."

"Oh, the strong and silent type." A weak smile reappeared. "I've costarred with your kind."

"No, no. I'm certainly no leading man."

Her eyes rested on his face. "Russell *T.* Jefferson." She was reflective for a moment. "What is the *T* for?"

"Thomas," he answered.

"Russell *Thomas* Jefferson."

"My mother was from Virginia."

"But you grew up in North Carolina."

"Charlotte. I was born there and grew up there. My father worked for the newspaper; my mother was a teacher. Active in the community. A terrific mixed-couples tennis team." He took a breath. "They made sure my childhood was rooted in God, family, country. They gave me a good start.

I had a typical boyhood for Charlotte, North Carolina. At least, for white boys."

"You went to college."

"Uh-huh. University of North Carolina, at Chapel Hill."

"What did you study?"

"Political science."

For the first time in days he saw her smile. "Well, of *course.*" She laughed softly. "What in the hell else would Russell *Thomas* Jefferson major in?" He gave her a chagrined look. "Did you intend to go into politics?"

"No. Just wanted to understand it." He wanted her to rest, so he went on. "My family was in politics for several generations. North Carolina, South Carolina, and Georgia. My dad was the editorial writer for his newspaper, and that kept him in the middle of the political scene."

"You're very proud of your father, aren't you?"

"And my mother. They had fun, but they didn't duck any of the tough issues. They were among the first to oppose segregation in Charlotte and that part of the state."

"Are they retired, or still working?"

"They're dead." His voice was flat. "They were killed in a car accident. 1961. They were driving to Chapel Hill to see me."

"I'm so sorry."

"It was tough for a while."

He was silent. Returning to memories he stored in a deep, safe place. She waited. Self-consciously—for he had exposed more of himself than he normally allowed—he adjusted his posture in the chair. "For a silent type, I'm talking quite a lot."

She wouldn't allow his discomfort. "What do your friends call you?"

"At home it was Russell, and that carried into college. In the Air Force it's been shortened to Russ. Fighter pilots like short words."

She was thoughtful for a moment. "I think I will call you R.J." She seemed to be thinking it over, then asked, "Do you mind?"

"No, if that's what you prefer."

"Thank you, R.J." She decided she liked the sound of it. "Are you married?"

The question caught him off guard, and he looked at her blankly for a half-second. "No, I'm not married."

"Were you ever?"

"Yes. Once."

"When?"

"We got married five years ago. She left in 1970. She got the divorce this year."

"I would like to know about it. Please tell me." She paused before adding, "Unless you'd rather not."

To his own amazement he heard himself say, "No, I don't mind telling you." A small nervous smile pulled at the corner of his mouth. "We had a short engagement. 1968. It was a great year to be in love. Terrific love songs and romantic movies. *Romeo and Juliet* and *Doctor Zhivago*. Great year for a sound track to a love affair, all right."

"Who was she?"

"A girl from an old California family with old California money. And she was the quintessential California girl. We met at a party near Venice Beach. A very popular bar where the groovy people hung out. Lots of booze, lots of grass. There were plenty of those parties in '68. Wouldn't be surprised if some of them aren't still going on." She waited for him to continue. "It was just all too much. A trendy Marina del Rey–type bar. The Beach Boys filling the room. A balmy breeze." He smiled. "And there she was. Hard not to fall in love under those conditions."

"I know," she said. "I've walked into my share of those romances, R.J., on starry, perfumed nights."

"Maybe we should change the subject before we get totally depressed," he said. "On a more serious note, during your tests, did you see the doctor this morning?"

"Yes."

"What did he say?"

"Not much, really. He wants to wait for the test results."

"But he said *something*."

"Standard lecture—or sermon. You know, proper diet, proper exercise, avoid stress. I'm sure he's part-time physician, full-time southern Baptist preacher."

"Because he did say something, didn't he?"

An almost imperceptible movement of her head gave her chin a defiant set. "The ass said I would, regardless of test results, be on potent blood-pressure medications."

"And?"

"And I will have to stay off the booze." She glared at him. "There. Are you satisfied?"

"You *are* going to do as he says," he said. "You do know that, don't you?"

"Telling me I have to do something is not a good way to get me to do something," she said with a soft belligerence.

"But you will?" He looked sternly at her, making it more an order than a question. He straightened in the chair. "I should leave," he said, looking at his watch. "They'll want you to eat soon."

"R.J., what happened to your marriage?"

He leaned back. "Crashed and burned." His forehead creased. "Two years after we were married, I was assigned to the Fighter Weapons School. That's the Air Force's Top Gun program at Nellis Air Force Base, just outside Las Vegas. Several weeks of air-combat training—old-fashioned dogfight stuff with edge-of-the-envelope technology. It was a real honor. Only the top three or four percent of fighter pilots got selected, and I was walking on air."

She reached toward the tableside drawer for her cigarettes. He could reach them more easily. He removed one from the pack, lit it, and handed it to her.

"Jenny wanted to do Vegas, so we gave up our apartment in Victorville and moved. Found a neat place on Tropicana. It couldn't have been better. God, I loved Nellis, and the program." He thought of the crusty alkaline desert surrounding the world's most sophisticated fighters and most advanced operations. "It was great."

"And Jenny?"

His voice flattened. "She was doing what she loved, going to the posh gambling rooms along the Strip. Enjoying the glitz. High-heeled glamour. Drawn to all that money—and the men who had it."

He stopped and tried a crooked smile. She waited.

He shrugged and continued. "I came home one night to find her gone. And she stayed gone. She was working as a hostess in the high-stakes rooms at Caesars Palace. The muscles in his jaws tightened. His eyes clouded, pain returning to them. "I remember her toga, her costume, had silver glitter sprinkled all over it. Glued on somehow. She looked like she was covered with stardust. Anyway, she was working the pricey rooms and meeting wealthy men. Three months after leaving Victorville, she left me for the Strip."

"What did you do?"

Through a tight, narrow smile, he said, "Finished my training. Went back to Southeast Asia for another year of my war."

The movie star's eyes were drawn to the scars on his face.

"It was a bad year," he said.

The first F-4 Phantom taxied slowly into position on the runway and braked to a stop. Jefferson's thumb pressed the UHF transmission switch. "Udorn Tower, Buick Flight's number one for takeoff." Buick 2 pulled up to the right and slightly behind Jefferson and Noonan. Buick 3 and 4 were farther behind them. The four F-4 Phantom jets created a sinister, dangerous appearance in the dawn, their aggressive shapes accented with bulky clusters of bombs under their wings.

From the backseat Noonan advised Jefferson that the others were in place, and then he began the "before takeoff" challenge-and-response checklist. The same procedure was being followed in the identical manner in each of the aircraft. No item was too small, no item unimportant, as they checked aircraft systems and controls. When they completed the checklist, Noonan said, "Russ, my man, we're ready to go."

Jefferson looked over at his wingman, raised his gloved hand, pointed up, and rotated it in a circular movement, the signal to run up their engines. He pushed the throttles forward while holding the brakes, rechecked engine instruments, then he gave his wingman an exaggerated nod. He released the brakes, moved both throttles to the outboard detent, and with the explosion of afterburners the F-4 accelerated down the runway with a great roar.

"Buick One's on the roll," he transmitted to the tower. The aircraft shook as it rolled faster across expansion cracks on hard tires, and raw power pushed them faster until objects left and right became a blur. Quickly he glanced at his instruments, catching the go-no-go speed of 141 knots, accepting the fact that no matter what happened now, he was committed to attempt takeoff. Moments later, at 172 knots, the fighter lifted off the runway. Positive rate of climb. He raised the landing gear, then the flaps, and at 350 knots he came out of afterburner. Squared away, he now made the next required call. "Udorn departure, Buick One airborne, squawking code three-four."

"Roger, Buick One. You're cleared as filed to twenty-six thousand. Squawk ident."

Without looking, Jefferson reached for the transponder and pressed the spring-loaded switch. "Buick One, ident."

"Radar contact," called the controller.

Jefferson began his departure turn to the right. Buick 2 was moving in close. Buick 3 and 4 closed in the turn, sliding into position. Buick Flight was joined, and they climbed into the clear, bright skies of a beautiful morning.

They were on their way to war.

Ten

Joanna Thompson looked up, startled to see General Eads standing at the door. With a practiced smile, he said, "Miss Thompson . . . er, ah . . . Joanna, will you come in here, please?"

She attempted to regain her composure, picked up her stenographer's notebook, and stood, smoothing out her skirt. Tension had been high in this office the past several days, ever since the stormy encounter with Major Jefferson. She patted her gray-streaked hair as she neared his door.

"Have a chair, Joanna." The general's eyes never left her as she sat down. She carefully swept her skirt under her with one hand. She held the notebook in her lap, pencil poised.

"Joanna, I need these notes typed for the Jefferson report." He picked up several pages of notes from the green blotter on his desk and looked at them solemnly. "These are the charges."

"I see," she said gravely, as though true justice was surely to be served.

"I think you will find them to be in the proper order. Prepare them in the same format we've been using." He took on an expression of regret. "Jefferson has gone too far this time. Too bad, but perhaps I'm doing him a favor in the long run. If he continued to be so irresponsible, he could face even more severe circumstances in the future."

"Will there be anything more, sir?" she asked flatly. She didn't believe his feigned regret for a moment.

"No." His mouth tightened as if trying to repress a smile. "That will be all for now. I believe I have all I need."

The taxi driver stopped at the hospital's front entrance to let his passenger out. Excitement and anticipation surged through Russ as he hurried through the lobby. Since talking to Ava yesterday, he felt more alive than he had in two years. It seemed strange that she was treating him like a friend, depending on him. Now the sights of the world seemed more colorful, its aromas sweeter, its sounds more musical. He expected that she would be released today, and she would be eager to get back to her flat. He would take her home.

The doorway was jammed three-deep with newspaper reporters and photographers. Loud, relentless voices asked endless questions about her illness, her next picture, and her current love affair. Were the rumors true that she and Sinatra would reconcile soon? He couldn't hear her voice through the din. Photographers checked their watches, tiptoed, and held their cameras high over the heads of those in front of them, taking photographs blindly, for the evening-edition deadline was only minutes away. Splashes of brightness filled the room. He got glimpses of jeweled women and well-dressed men, friends and show-business people. He wondered if Sydney Hooker was there.

He felt left out, distant from her, and he retraced the steps he had taken so eagerly just minutes earlier. He left the hospital and walked along the street unaware of the golden sunlight filling the afternoon, the sights and sounds of autumn in London. Now it was just another day. Now there was no excitement. Now there was only the matter of his runaway daydream and the need to return to reality.

He should have known that she wouldn't need him to take her home. She had friends, colleagues, hangers-on, and former lovers to do those kinds of things for her. He should have known better. He wasn't a part of her world.

He looked for a taxi.

The next morning blustered in raw and cold. The front had been forecast, bringing with it a two-day cold snap, but the weekend was predicted to be sunny and warmer.

Russ and Ted Sanders left the conference room together and walked side by side down the wide hallway. "Boring staff meeting," Ted said out of the corner of his mouth.

"Consistent with everything else around here," Russ replied. "Not exactly exciting."

"Just before the meeting, I called my buddy at USAFE to check on his review of the Upper Heyford proposals. He told me it's a done deal. He forwarded them to his boss with a recommendation for approval. They've been approved by both the Operations and Training directorates. I told him I would be in Ramstein this week, that I'd pick them up and hand carry them back. I'll have them here Monday for you."

"I never expected them to sign off so quickly."

"Helps to have friends in high places," said the captain with a wry smile.

"Why are you going to Ramstein?"

"USAFE is holding a hurry-up conference on the fuel crisis. Two days to study its effect on flight operations. Lots of possible implications."

"Scary subject."

"If it gets any worse, it's going to be a hell of a lot scarier."

"I appreciate your help, Ted. Hope you have a good conference."

"See you Monday," said the captain as he started down the stairs to the basement.

Back in his office, Russ slumped behind his desk. He had to find some way to fight off this letdown, this sense of disappointment that had been with him since he left the hospital yesterday.

He straightened, pressed the intercom button, and said, "Miss Rutherford, please bring me today's message traffic." She had the thick file on his desk in minutes. Distribution was indicated by stamped squares in the upper corner of each document, and General Eads's scrawled initials in the "Deputy Director" square recorded his earlier review of the file. Jefferson scanned each intelligence report and each ops order relating to U.K.-based wings. There was nothing noteworthy.

He struggled with two letters that had to get out this morning. After an hour, second drafts were still dismal and he took them to Rutherford. "Can you fix these up?" he asked as he handed her the letters. Each was covered with penned changes, personal editing in his hieroglyphic style.

She shook her head slowly as she looked at them, like a mechanic gazing at a dead motor, and then she smiled and assured him she could rescue his failed efforts. He turned to go back to his office, but she stopped him with a question. "Is something wrong? I mean other than these letters?"

"No," he answered. "Everything's fine." He returned to his office and slumped in his chair. Miss Rutherford had seen right through him. She could obviously tell that things weren't going well for him just now. Nothing was fine.

His meeting with General Eads had been a bad scene. He leaned back, tapping his pen on the desktop. That wasn't his way of doing things, talking to a general that way. And the warning of a court-martial wasn't an empty threat. Majors don't push generals around and mouth off as he had. Bad beyond belief.

He had been off base not only with the general but with Ava as well. It really was quite stupid to think she needed him to take her home from the hospital. Or for anything else. He had been there when she had no one else. That was all. It had been simply a matter of necessity that he took her to the hospital, that he stayed with her because she was scared. There had been no one else, but now, as always before, she had her rich and famous friends.

He lit a cigarette and swiveled to face the window.

How had his life become such a mess? How does a man screw up his world so completely? What had once meant so much to him was now lost. And days had become meaningless steps leading nowhere . . . until his accidental encounter with Ava.

The illusion of his boyhood fantasy materialized before his eyes; that irresistible image making him feel alive and vital. But he had made too much of it. It was just that he happened to be there when she needed someone and no one else was.

He turned to the desk, stubbed out his cigarette, and pushed the file away. He'd somehow get through the day.

"God, I know the doctors are glad I'm gone. I turned their hospital into a madhouse."

Sydney Hooker followed the actress into her flat, carrying the suitcase and makeup bag. "It's always good to return to home and hearth," he said.

"Thank you for bringing me, Sydney."

"I had to do my part," he said, laughing softly. "I can't have that young American taking over altogether." He took the luggage to her bedroom and laid both pieces on the bed.

"Even though your motives aren't honorable, I appreciate you."

"I could do much more for you, you know," he said, following her into the kitchen. "No appreciation required."

"We've been through this a million times, Sydney."

"Then let's go through it again. It isn't good for you to be alone, not even having Carmen with you. Not with these problems you're having."

"The doctor is treating my problems." She put the kettle on to heat.

"Not all of them."

"What do you mean?"

"Your financial needs."

"I don't need to be treated financially. I can still get roles that pay well."

"Then why don't you?"

"I will, when they offer me a decent one." She put cups on the counter.

"They don't care if they get you good parts. They only care about box office."

"This last script they sent—God, it's terrible."

"They've used you. Just as the men in your life have."

"My husbands haven't used me."

"Perhaps not, but other men have during the time I've known you."

"They didn't—"

"The hell they didn't! I saw what George C. Scott did to you. Your face was bruised. Your eyes were swollen shut."

"It was the booze, baby."

"My God, stop being that woman raised in the American South. It *isn't* all right for your 'menfolk' to beat you up. You don't have to take that!"

"What do you Brits know?" She smiled at her old friend. "Ever since Vivien Leigh played Scarlett, you think you're experts about the South."

"I'll tell you what *this* Brit knows. I know you need stability. You need to marry me and spend the rest of your life with me. You need to be protected. Loved."

"Dear Sydney, I once told you—"

"I don't care what you told me. I would provide you with security."

"You are the sweetest thing in the world, but you know I could never marry for those reasons. I could never even accept alimony from my husbands."

"Stop being so stubborn, Ava. You've earned little money the last few years. There are no prospects that you will. Inflation is soaring. Costs in London are outrageous."

"I'll get a part soon. I always have."

"Even so, you don't know if you'll physically be able to do it. Your doctor told you that you must take it easy."

"Let's change the subject, shall we?"

"Very well. But I'm not giving up. And I'm not leaving."

"Good. Your tea is almost ready."

He was silent a moment. "How is the American? Your new bullfighter?"

"I don't know. I'll call him later today."

The telephone in his flat was ringing as he came in from work. No one called him at home. It had to be Ava. Hurriedly he picked up the phone. She was home. "It's great that they released you," he said. "You've gotta take it easy, though."

"I will. My agent sent over a script. I'll read it."

"You're thinking about making a picture?"

"It's too early to know. It's been two years since I've done a film. It was with Paul Newman and John Huston. It grossed well last year. Did you see it?"

"No. I, uh, didn't see any movies last year."

She paused. This wasn't the first time he had referred to "last year" in that tone of voice. "R.J., where *were* you last year?"

"Vietnam."

"Honey, I don't mean to be insensitive, and if it's none of my business, just say so, but when were you burned?"

"Last year," he said.

In a very soft voice she asked, "R. J., will you take me for a walk in the park tomorrow?"

"Viv, you must warn Major Jefferson," Joanna Thompson said urgently.

Vivian Rutherford knew that Joanna was worried. The general's secretary seldom called her at home, after work. "But the report can't be substantive, Joanna. He's missed a meeting or two, and he's said some things he shouldn't have, but that's hardly reason to bring charges against him."

"Eads has more than missed meetings."

"Eads needs an important incident to make his case."

"He has one. He ordered Jefferson to never send policy matters to USAFE headquarters without his approval. It's documented. A memo of record."

"And?"

"He has discovered that Jefferson forwarded several proposed F-111 training routes and bombing ranges without getting approval. He's going to court-martial him. Insubordination."

"Is there any chance he'll change his mind?"

"No. He's a real bastard, Viv."

"I love it here," said Ava. Cara heeled perfectly at her mistress's left.

The hazy mist of the autumn afternoon hung over the rich foliage. They walked near the eastern edge of Serpentine Lake, through the Dell, and watched as a red-jacketed girl rode a large gray horse along the bridle path.

"The bridle path was originally named the Route de Roi," she said. "No one calls it that anymore." The sounds of the galloping horse faded away. "I love it this time of year, this time of day." She looked about at the soft veil of the fog fading the edges of distant trees. "On warm summer days, everyone comes here. But on days like this, wet and cool, you see those who *truly* love their park." She smiled up at him. "You can forget that you're in the middle of a huge city when you're here."

"And you like that?"

"I love that." She laughed softly. "I'm just a country girl."

He laughed too. "Yes, of course you are."

"Oh, it's true. The North Carolina I grew up in was very different from yours, R.J." She stepped around a small break in the stone walk. "The North Carolina I grew up in was small towns, dirt roads, tobacco fields. I ran around barefoot half the year. Shoes were expensive. Besides, I loved the feel of soft mud and dirt under my feet, stream water between my toes. I was free. I still try to recapture that feeling every chance I get."

"I find that hard to imagine."

"Don't scoff. I was a real tomboy. I swam in the creeks, climbed trees just as high as the boys. And I took as many risks."

Unhurriedly they followed the path along beds of dark yellow flowers. A small flock of birds swooped from the line of trees nearby, bringing a single bark from Cara. They met a solitary older man who smiled and nodded to them.

"This was once wild countryside, until Henry VIII enclosed it as a hunting preserve."

He looked at her in surprise.

"Somewhere near here"—and her hand made a sweeping gesture—"the crown jewels of France are hidden. In the late 1700s, King Louis's mistress brought them here and buried them, supposedly between here and Trafalgar Square. Some historians believe she buried them in the Royal Mews, which were demolished when Trafalgar Square was built." She looked at him with a mysterious smile. "But I don't think so."

"What do you think?"

"I think she chose a natural, beautiful site—like this—to hide them."

"Why do you think that?"

"Because it's what I would have done," she said quite seriously. "She died on the guillotine, never revealing to anyone where she hid the jewels."

Across the lake a small boat skimmed across the misty water.

"You were young when you went to Hollywood, weren't you?"

"Just a baby. I was terrified. A quick screen test got me a contract, one of those standard minimum-wage type things that give you no privileges at all but hold you in their complete power." She turned up her collar and put her arm through his. "We were told what to do, when to do it and how, and we were paid very little. I used to joke that we were the only kind of merchandise allowed to leave the store at night."

He looked down at her arm. In complete amazement he realized she was holding his arm. She wanted to hold his arm as they walked!

"I spent most of my first six months in Hollywood doing publicity photos. I remember how excited the studio was to discover that I knew how to milk a cow. They were overjoyed! What a marvelous publicity shot, a starlet who could milk a cow." She gave him a slight smile. "No one ever said it was an intellectual profession, R.J."

The feel of her arm thrilled him. He had never felt so proud.

"MGM never wanted to use me in anything. The studio sold and traded me as often as they could. Like a prize hog. Believe me, honey, that does not do much for the ego."

"Was there anything you liked about Hollywood?"

"Well, I did love the late nights and clubs, anywhere you could dance all night."

It was like the first night. He wanted to think of something clever to say, but the immensity of walking arm in arm with her overwhelmed him. He felt like the awkward schoolboy again. "You've never told me what the doctor concluded from your tests."

"He thinks I should have the surgery," she said.

He was silent for several moments as they walked. "In the hospital, I said that you would have to depend on me because I was the only one there." He turned to her. "I fully realize that's not the case anymore, but you can still depend on me, you know."

"And, in the hospital, I said you would do." She looked up into his eyes. "You will do quite nicely, I think."

The four jet fighters moved as one in a delicately choreographed formation, slashing past small puffy clouds with supersonic savagery. They were part of a strike force that would, in exactly thirteen minutes, attack the well-defended Yen Vien railroad yards.

Captain Russell Jefferson looked toward the point on the hazy horizon where the gray forms of Hanoi and the flat, meandering Red River would soon appear. Beads of sweat lined his forehead. He and the other members of Buick Flight would soon be diving down at the railroad yards through a hailstorm of anti-aircraft fire and then, at low altitude, release their bombs before pulling out of their steep dive, hoping to escape the firebox. He felt the cramped confines of the cockpit become tighter. Sweat now ran into his eyes, his nerves anticipating the imminent battle.

He would be okay. Race-car drivers spoke of a state of mind when they are unaware of their speed and the dangers of the race; aware only of the racing line they view through a red mist. Jefferson knew that, once in the battle, he, too, would view the enemy through his own red mist.

The fighters—camouflaged in irregular patterns of subdued tans, browns, and greens—were eight minutes out. Precisely on time.

It was time to get ready. He depressed the UHF button. "Buick Flight, arm 'em up."

The response was simple but deadly. "Buick Two, armed hot."

"Buick Three."

"Buick Four."

Jefferson tried to shake a disturbing premonition. He'd had it since the briefing. Hanoi defenses. One thousand guns in the area of the bridge and railroad yards in addition to nearly four thousand guns in the Hanoi defense ring. More than two hundred surface-to-air missile sites, and each site could fire tens of missiles. When the defenses had been briefed this morning he found himself being unusually aware of detail. Not like him. Again he tried to shake off the disturbing feeling, but it wouldn't go away.

Five minutes out now. Time to push back all fear and uncertainty.

Eleven

ouse of Commons. May I assist you?" It was a perfect telephone voice. Professional.

"I beg your pardon," Russ blurted. He was sure he had heard correctly. "Did you say *House of Commons*?"

"Yes, I did, sir. May I be of assistance?"

"Er, ah, Sydney Hooker, please."

What in the hell? Hooker's business card, their lunch at the club. Nothing had indicated his business number was at Whitehall. Well, well.

"Mr. Hooker's office," another polished voice said.

"Mr. Hooker, please. Major Jefferson calling."

The secretary thanked him, told him it would be just a moment, then put him on hold. Sydney Hooker. A Member of Parliament. The last few days had held lots of surprises. A moment later the connection clicked to life again.

"Russell, my boy, how are you?"

"Fine, Sydney, or is it proper to call you Sydney? I had no idea I was telephoning a right honorable gentleman."

"Of course. All of my friends call me by my first name."

"I hope this isn't a bad time."

"There are nothing *but* bad times here," the man said with a chuckle. "I *do* have some people waiting for me, so I will need to rush a bit. What can I do for you?"

"You told me you have several friends in the RAF?"

"Yes." Hooker drew out the one word. "I do have some friends with our air forces."

"Do you know anyone who would be involved in the approval of training areas for the United States Air Force units? Especially the F-111 units?"

"I think so. In fact, I may know just the chap. Squadron Leader Ian Palmer, with the Air Ministry."

"I need a favor, Sydney. Would you introduce me to him? I need him to consider proposals for new low-level routes and bombing ranges for the F-111s at Upper Heyford. It's urgent."

"I could introduce you."

"And perhaps you might get him to . . . well, to favorably consider the proposals?"

"Let me see if I understand this correctly. You not only want approval of your proposals but, as you Americans always do, you want it quickly?"

"Well, yes." Russ was embarrassed.

"That isn't something I should do, apply political leverage to influence his judgment in such a matter."

"Of course, I understand—"

"Good. Now, it so happens that Palmer is trying to sell a car just now. A sports car." Hooker paused, a signal that this was important. "You could ask to make an appointment with him to see the car. You could consider purchasing it."

"Yes, I could."

"Very well. I'll give you his home number. Call him after work about the car." Hooker read the number to Russ.

"I'll call him tonight," he said. "Thank you, Sydney."

"I hope I've been of some assistance." He sounded pleased.

Russ hung up, rose from his desk, crossed the floor to the coffeemaker, and poured the steaming liquid into a cup. He returned to three letters awaiting his signature. He could proofread them, of course, but that was a total waste of time whenever correspondence came from Rutherford's typewriter. He signed them and tossed them into his out basket.

Sydney. A Member of Parliament.

There was one other call to make.

Ava answered on the first ring. She sounded good. Rested. He began with an exaggerated forcefulness. "You have," he said, "invited me to dinner and to a party at your home."

"God, do you have to remind me?" Her laughter was soft. "Let's *do* try to forget, shall we?"

"Now it's my turn. It's only fair that I take you to dinner."

"Oh?"

"To your favorite restaurant."

"I don't have one. I don't go to restaurants often. Do you have a favorite, R.J.?"

"You're talking to the original peanut-butter-sandwich kid."

"It doesn't sound good for us, does it?"

"Okay, I'll make this an exception. I'll choose the restaurant. This Saturday evening."

"R.J., I really don't know—"

"And the theater. I have tickets to *The King and I*. Want to eat before or after the show?"

"R.J., I'm not—"

He cut her off. "This is Wednesday. You have three days to get ready. That's enough time to prepare for Attila the Hun."

"Very well," she said with a laugh.

"Great. Saturday at seven."

The Ramstein conference had progressed to midafternoon Friday, a gray, cool day in Germany. Thursday had been a full day of meetings, and now as they neared the end of the agenda, a fifteen-minute break had been called.

The subject was critical to the United States Air Forces in Europe, and the conference was attended by representatives of each operational wing and staff from headquarters and from the U.S. Embassy in each country that hosted Air Force units. For two long days they had examined the implications of the predicted fuel shortages on flight operations. The outlook was unnerving, as the impact was expected to be enormous.

The coffee bar was crowded as several men lined up to be served. Lieutenant Colonel Scott Mitchell needed one more cup of coffee to make it to the end of this marathon. He glanced at his watch as he stepped up to the Formica-topped counter, and then he noticed that the man standing next to him had been introduced the previous day as the representative of the American embassy in London. "I'm Scott Mitchell," he said to the younger man, and he reached to shake hands. "I'm from the Sixty-third Squadron at Torrejón."

The captain accepted the hand. "Ted Sanders."

"So, you're with the embassy in London."

"Yes sir, that's right."

"I have a good friend there." Mitchell paid for his coffee and turned to face Sanders. "An old buddy. He's only been there a couple of months. Russ Jefferson. Know him?"

"Yes, I know him."

"He's a good man."

"The best," agreed Sanders.

"How's he doing?"

"Fine. He's doing fine."

"I visited him about a month ago. He sure as hell wasn't doing fine then." Mitchell looked levelly at Sanders. "Now, how's he really doing?"

Sanders returned the colonel's look without blinking. He sipped his coffee slowly, eyeing the other man thoughtfully. "You say you're a *very* good friend?" he asked cautiously.

"Yes, I am, Ted. Russ and I go way back. You can be frank with me. I'm the guy who'll crank up his support network if and when he needs it, and right now I want to know how he's doing."

"Well, if you want to know the truth, he isn't good . . ."

"Why are you wasting my time with this?" she said with scorn as she threw the script on the table. She stepped to the window and lit a cigarette.

"It's a wonderful role, Ava," said her agent. The stout man rubbed his puffy eyes as though to ease a headache. "And to costar with—"

"I don't give a damn about costarring with Charlton Heston. For Christ's sake, I've starred with Gable, Peck, and Mitchum." The mention of film giants pushed her agent into a silent reluctance, but she knew it was only momentary. She waved the cigarette toward the table. "That script! It's a bigger disaster than the earthquake this picture's about."

"Picture making is flat just now, Ava," said the other man in the room. The producer was well dressed, standing patiently near the fireplace, smoothing out an imaginary wrinkle in his sleeve. "There aren't many good roles available."

"So I should accept bad roles in bad movies?"

"This will be a fine film."

"It's trash."

"No, it's not, Ava," said the producer. He examined the sleeve closely to make sure the wrinkle was gone. "This role is you, darling."

"This? Me?" She arched an eyebrow. "I'm Pandora. The Barefoot Contessa. Lady Ashley! And you say that—"

"This role will let you express yourself," the stout man insisted. "You can get inside the skin of this part, Ava."

"All of these years, directors have been perfectly happy for me to just stand there and look beautiful. That's all they wanted. And now you're saying I'm going to be stretching my skills as an actress?"

"That's right," the agent said quickly.

"You have no shame, do you? You'd say anything to get me into this embarrassing film, just to get your ten percent, wouldn't you?"

The agent began to protest, "Now, Ava, baby—"

"Don't 'baby' me. I may be at the end of my career. I may not be young and beautiful anymore, but I will not be a curiosity piece in such drivel as this! Go back to your Hollywood offices, and don't call me until you've found something worthwhile."

"You're making a mistake, Ava," said the producer.

"No. And you can tell the others that I will not be put in front of the cameras like Errol Flynn was, like a drunken has-been curiosity."

"But Flynn *was* a drunken has-been."

"You just don't get it, do you?" A soft expression replaced the stern one. "He had style, honey. Real style."

Saturday morning was clear and cool, a perfect day for getting out of London, and as Russ drove, he knew tonight would be perfect for the theater.

"I'll be at my cottage this weekend," Ian Palmer had said. "You can see the Alfa there." And he had given precise directions, making it easy to follow the series of country lanes.

Russ had taken A23 from London to a secondary road outside of East Grinstead. The road followed tree rows and stone fences, and beyond the Rowden Bridge he turned south onto an even narrower road crossing hedgerows and country meadows. The squadron leader had referred to the lanes as backdoubles, and had assured Jefferson they would save many miles and minutes. Russ was beginning to wonder if he was lost when, after a particularly sharp right turn past a row of hedges, the cottage appeared in front of him.

The "cottage" was more than he had expected: a two-story, stucco-and-timber Tudor-style house. A gleaming red Alfa Romeo Spider two-seater, top down, was parked in the driveway. A large man was polishing it, and he stopped and started toward the VW as Russ braked to a stop. He got out and they introduced themselves.

"A nice day," observed the RAF officer.

"Yes. We're lucky the cold snap ended before the weekend."

"You mentioned on the phone that you're with the U.S. Embassy."

"Yes. On assignment."

"I'm on assignment too. To the Ministry of Defense from the RAF. But now let me show you the car. I was just out here dusting her off a bit. Want her to look her best, you know."

The gravel driveway crunched under their feet as they walked around the car. "Uhhmmm." Russ expressed a knowledgeable appreciation. "A beauty."

Palmer, enjoying the reaction, waited quietly.

Russ circled the sports car slowly, walking around its rear, admiring the little red rump. He didn't have to pretend. It was very well kept. "Too bad you have to sell it."

"I'm being posted out of country. It's better for her not to sit."

He knew how to approach Palmer. He had done his research on the car. "Ah, the lineage of the Alfa Spider. Not the most powerful, but exciting to drive, don't you agree?"

"She is." The Englishman looked wistfully at the red car. "I've always loved her looks, as well."

"Pininfarina styling, perhaps at its best," Russ agreed. He would lay it on a bit thicker. "Rear drive. Five-speed gearbox. Disc brakes. Twin-cam engine; revs up to a six-thousand-rpm red line."

"You should drive her. Try her out."

"I'd like to. Thank you." Russ gave the man a confident look. "Any idiosyncrasies?" It was a question about an intimacy, the equivalent of asking the man about the sexual preferences of his wife.

"Oh, no," Palmer quickly answered. "She starts, even when cold, with two or three prods of the throttle," he said proudly. "Wonderful road manners. No unwanted twitches with this one. If you drive her right, she'll corner as if she's on rails."

"I may consider buying it . . . since you have to sell it." Russ opened the door and slipped into the driver's seat. "You told me on the telephone that you would sell it for three thousand pounds, I believe."

The big man laughed. "No, I told you I'd sell her for three thousand *five hundred* pounds." He paused, still smiling. "Nor did I say I *had* to sell her." He got into the car.

In his best bargaining manner, Russ pretended disbelief of the stated price. "A bit steep for me, I'm afraid. I don't suppose you'd consider selling it for less." He keyed the ignition and the motor caught instantly.

"Oh, I don't know. As you can see, she's in fine condition."

"Yes, that's true." He frowned while making a difficult judgment. "I'm shopping for a good car, but I hadn't considered more than three thousand." He relaxed the frown. "Maybe three thousand two."

Palmer stroked his chin. "I'll have to think about that."

"While you think about it, we'll take a short drive." He drove slowly out of the driveway, onto the road. "You say you're assigned to the Ministry of Defense. I may have a task soon that will require the coordination of the Air Ministry."

"Indeed. What might that be?"

"Obtaining approval for new training routes for the F-111," Russ said absently, carefully changing gears. "Routes and bombing ranges. But I don't suppose you have anything to do with that sort of thing."

"I would have *everything* to do with that," Palmer said. "My shop is responsible for dedicating special operating areas for military aviation, and that includes the United States Air Force."

"You don't say," Russ said, pretending to be surprised. He looked about the car's cockpit and checked the gauges. "Is it difficult to get new areas approved?"

"That depends. We don't look favorably upon Yank training areas that create problems for British citizens." The smile returned.

"Of course. We've emphasized nuisance abatement as the highest criteria, avoiding populated regions, sensitive areas such as stockbreeding and animal training. And we'd avoid all historically significant locations, of course. We planned sites for bombing ranges that allow approaches from over water—the Isle of Man, the Wash."

"Sounds as if you have the right idea."

"Maybe we can talk about our proposals in detail, say, one day next week." It was time to cast the lure. "I'll give you a few days to consider my offer on the Alfa and then join you again. I'll take it for a real test drive, and we can discuss the training needs of the F-111."

"Sounds jolly good. But I daresay I'm not likely to accept that paltry sum for such a fine car."

"It has quite a few miles on its clock." The expected game of bargaining honorably continued. "Perhaps if you think about it . . ."

She leaned toward the mirror for a closer inspection and approved. Her makeup was just fine. Her hair was as she liked it. Her dress carefully chosen. A very special night. A night with R.J.

She rose from the dressing table and glanced about the bedroom. Candles in place. Wine in the fridge. She crossed to the bed and turned back the silken cover. She was looking forward to the evening she had planned with R.J. After the play and dinner, when they returned to her flat.

So handsome and virile. So eager. And, she told herself, it had been so long since she had enjoyed the physical pleasures of an unencumbered passionate affair.

She patted the cover in place. Yes, it was going to be a wonderful night with R.J.

Their taxi was washed in reflections from the garish neon of Piccadilly Circus as it crept through the snarled traffic around the statue of Eros. London's West End was vibrant with its theaters and cinemas, and Russ took in the dazzling scene.

"Enjoy it while you can," Ava said. "The Prime Minister's going to darken all England this month."

"What do you mean?"

"The fuel emergency. You know, depleted coal reserves. It'll be like the blackouts of the blitz all over again. London in the dark."

"When?"

"Very soon. Any day now."

"All of London?"

"All of England."

"How do you know that?"

She smiled mysteriously. "Sydney tells me everything. He's an MP, you know."

"No. You don't say."

The taxi stopped in front of the Criterion, and they hurried inside. Ushers were immediately at their side, escorting them to their seats, for Russ had called ahead and told the theater management that Ava Gardner would attend that evening's performance.

She wore a dark coat with a black velvet collar; her necklace and earrings glittered. The audience recognized her before they were halfway to their seats, and they rose to their feet and began applauding. She smiled beautifully and nodded, acknowledging them. The applause continued until after they were seated. He helped her remove her coat but left it draped over her shoulders.

"Nice reception," he whispered.

"Very kind of them," she said softly.

The lights dimmed and *The King and I* began. He stole an occasional glance at her, finding it impossible to keep his eyes away. Her perfume intoxicated him. It was still astonishing that they had become friends, and that she now sat beside him. Turning to him, she smiled, then returned her attention to the stage.

She had only looked at him . . . and he felt light-headed and giddy.

At that moment across London, the third floor of the U.S. Embassy was dark except for the office of General William Eads. He sat at his desk reading the report again, reviewing every word to ensure that nothing had been omitted. It made a compelling case that Major Russell Jefferson was, indeed, guilty of the charges made: disregarding directives, missing mandatory meetings, conduct unbecoming an officer. Insubordination. He had disobeyed clearly defined orders from his superior officers.

Eads put the report down and examined the cover letter. Satisfied, he leaned back and stared into space. It was critical to create circumstances with the F-111 that would reshape future NATO decisions. Major Jefferson had become an obstacle.

Now timing was crucial. Eads had to make his move before Admiral Fleming returned from the Pentagon, for the Navy admiral would be reluctant to act on the charges as presented. Fleming would dig into the background of the facts, evaluate the circumstances behind the charges as completely as he would their merit. No, Eads had to take care of Jefferson before Fleming returned.

The Air Attaché was precisely the officer Eads needed to be in charge of court-martial hearings. General Sam Elliott was motivated by one goal: to make certain his record with the embassy was spotless, that no problems by embassy Air Force personnel detracted from his record. He was determined that there would be no paperwork describing a troubled climate during his watch. He would hear the Jefferson case and make a quick decision, based purely on political considerations. In General Sam Elliott's way of doing things, the sooner it was over, the better.

Eads leaned forward and scrawled his signature across the bottom of the letter.

He glanced at the calendar on his desk and saw that Miss Thompson had made an appointment for Jefferson. Monday, nine-thirty. Her note explained that Jefferson had requested the meeting but had not stated why he needed to see the general. He would cancel that appointment first thing Monday morning.

Jefferson had blown it. No more meetings.

Russ led Ava across the marble-floored lobby of the Dorchester Hotel and they entered the elegant Terrace Restaurant. The maître d' showed them to a secluded table and took Ava's coat. The VIP treatment was evident as the maître d' seated her. Russ sat directly across the table.

"Are you trying to get us into the gossip columns, R.J., dining at the favorite restaurant of movie stars?"

"It is?"

"Oh, yes. Elizabeth and Richard dine here frequently. David Niven. Albert Finney."

"I didn't know," he lied. He had read that the beautiful restaurant with its cream-colored walls and gold-leaf moldings *was* the favorite of film stars, and he had selected it on that basis alone.

The headwaiter addressed them. "May I suggest that you begin with mousseline of game and goose liver," he said carefully, "accompanied by aspic and pear. Perhaps a braised-lettuce soup and glazed scallops with sliced crayfish?"

A few moments later, the appetizers arrived. Russ wanted everything to be perfect for her, but the other diners were looking at them. He was afraid they would irritate her, and she saw the concerned look on his face.

"At least in London people are polite," she said quietly. "They may recognize you, but they respect your privacy. In America they wouldn't allow us to eat. They would knock your soup in your lap."

"A pain in the neck after a while, I suppose."

"No. A pain in the ass. I'm not complaining, but you'd think people would understand that we need to eat like everyone else, for God's sake."

Waiters appeared again bearing filet of lamb, wild mushrooms, and miniature potatoes. Russ played the part, tasting and then nodding in approval of the wine.

"You have to understand," he resumed after the waiters disappeared, "that people like them—like me—don't dine in the same room with someone like you. Hollywood stars. We aren't accustomed to breathing the same air." He sipped his wine. "We aren't quite sure how to act."

"You seem to know, R.J."

"I'm just fakin' it," he admitted with a smile. "My knees are knocking." Then, more seriously, he said, "You know what I mean."

"Sure I do. I remember the first time I was in the presence of Clark Gable."

"That's heady company, all right," he muttered.

"He was a long-established star when I first saw him. The epitome of manhood, and make no mistake about it, he was the real thing." She sipped from her wineglass.

What am I doing with someone like her? Russ wondered.

Nearly an hour later they finished their meal with a chestnut parfait with raspberries. Russ had not once felt awkward or embarrassed with her, and now he was thinking how terrific they were together.

"R.J., we need to discuss something," she said seriously.

"Oh?" *Something is wrong. Something embarrassing.* "What do we need to discuss?" *Good grief, is she going to tell me I don't measure up to Clark Gable?*

She leaned forward slightly. "This place is terribly expensive," she said in a low voice. "Please let me help with the bill."

He smiled, relieved. Nothing was wrong. Nothing at all. "It's okay. I don't need help with this. Really."

"They pay you flyboys better than I thought." She settled back in her chair, looking at him fondly.

"No, we still do it for the glory," he told her. "Fame and glory."

He expected her to smile at his silliness, but instead she closed her eyes and slowly shook her head. She bowed slightly, eyes still closed. She pinched the bridge of her nose. When she looked back at him, her eyes seemed unfocused.

"Are you all right?" he asked.

"Yes. But let's go now."

Moments later they were in a taxi, and Ava sat near him as they made their way to her flat. "R.J., I can't remember enjoying an evening more," she said.

"I'm glad you accepted my invitation."

The taxi stopped at her gate.

"Please, don't bother to get out." Soft light from the streetlamp illuminated her face, emphasizing the soft shadows of her cheekbones and the cleft in her chin. "Thank you, so much. It was an evening I'll never forget." She kissed him briefly, lightly, on the lips. "Good night, R.J.," she said. She slipped from the taxi and disappeared through the gate.

He could only sit, staring after her. Roberts was at the door.

The faint scent of vanilla still hung in the darkness. The taste of her lipstick remained on his lips. She said she had enjoyed the evening—that it was an evening she would never forget! Impossible! But it had happened. It was *happening*. She said she liked being with him. He *heard* her.

And she had kissed him!

Surely this wasn't a dream.

Surely to God he wasn't on that filthy, damp concrete floor, dreaming in order to survive the fear and the hopelessness. Surely this wasn't a dream from which he would awaken only to discover that he was still in his small, rat-infested cell, hearing screams from a distant room. Or worse, from his own.

It wasn't. He knew it wasn't He could *feel* her. He could *taste* her!

"You 'aven't planned to sit 'ere all night, 'ave you, guv'ner?" The driver looked at him curiously.

He gave his address and looked vacantly out the window as the taxi made its way down the quiet street.

His heart soared with happiness and he couldn't get "I Have Dreamed" from *The King and I* out of his mind. A song about the joy of a new romance, whose words repeated over and over in his head.

She closed the door behind her and leaned against it. Eyes closed, she waited for the dizziness to stop. Oh God, it was still happening. The dizziness. The blackouts.

Twelve

The actress sat at the breakfast table with her second cup of coffee, struggling with her anxieties. The dizziness last night had ended her evening with R.J. prematurely. She had wanted so to spend an intimate night with him. She just knew that she would enjoy him.

He was a decent guy, removed from the phoniness of show business and café society. Genuine and honest, but such a sad young man. In spite of the humor he used when flirting at times, there was a deep, private sadness in him. Terrible secrets were hidden behind his wall, but she believed she could help.

She picked up the phone and dialed. "Good morning, R. J.," she said. "How are you this morning?"

"Fine. Having my second cup of coffee." She didn't know if he was asking about her dizziness, but she didn't want to discuss it. "Mornings aren't really too bad without a hangover."

"I'm just glad you're following doctor's orders."

She didn't respond to that. "I know you're terribly busy today—you people with ambition usually are, even on Sunday—but I wanted to talk to you."

"I had supposed that you have always been ambitious."

"You couldn't be more wrong, honey. The truth is I've always been happiest doing nothing at all. I have never understood people who think work is the most important thing in the world, and spend their lives at it."

"I've *had* to treat my work as the most important thing in the world," he said with a grunt. "Not ego. Survival."

"But you aren't flying fighters now. So what are you doing?"

"It's so boring here, I don't even want to tell you."

"C'mon, R.J. You sound so secretive." She became playfully inquisitive. "Do you have a woman over there?"

"How did you know?"

"I've always heard that fighter pilots are like Italian men—if they aren't chasing a woman, their lives just aren't worth living." Her voice took on a thoughtful tone. "Hmmm. Being with an *Italian* fighter pilot. Now, there's a thought."

"No girls here. Tomorrow's a big day for me at work, and I'm just loafing around."

"I want you to know how much I enjoyed last night. Thank you, again."

"It was my pleasure."

"Oh, my, R.J. You're such a charmin' southern boy."

"You like charming southern boys?"

"Of course I do, honey."

"Does that mean you'll go out with me Tuesday afternoon?"

"Well, I don't know." Her laugh was soft. "Just where are you going Tuesday?"

"To the country."

"Any country in particular, R.J.?"

"Just any old country road. It's a test drive."

"What are you testing?"

"A red Alfa Romeo Spider. The weather's supposed to be good."

"I'd love to go with you, R.J."

"Great. I'll call you not so early Tuesday morning."

"I'll be waiting."

Monday did not turn out to be the big day Russ expected. Just before nine-thirty Joanna Thompson had called to tell him that General Eads had canceled his appointment. No reason was given. Russ had called back several times throughout the day, only to be told that the general was busy; he had ended up wasting the day. The secretary made excuses, but they were obviously contrived.

That was yesterday. Today would be different. Today he would find a way to accomplish that one important task: he would see the general. He was determined not to show that cocky contempt toward Eads. His arrogance was out of line—and dangerous. He had to cool it.

Carrying a file under his arm and three cardboard tubes, Jefferson walked down the hall to Eads's office and went in. Miss Thompson looked up from her typewriter with surprise. "Major Jefferson," she said as he approached her desk. "Good morning."

"Good morning. Is the general alone?"

"What is this?" she asked with a sly smile. "Another of your famous, no-notice visits?"

"Seems that's the only way I can get in to see him. Is he in?"

"He is, Major, but he has an appointment in five minutes. I can ask him if—"

"I won't need five minutes," he said, and he started toward the closed door.

She picked up the telephone and tapped the general's intercom button; her call was answered just as she saw Jefferson open the door. "General,

Major Jefferson is . . ." It was useless. She really wasn't surprised that the major was doing this. He had, after all, called her five times yesterday asking to see the general, asking for only ten minutes. Each time the general had refused even though there had been time, and there was no question that her attempted explanations sounded entirely phony. No, she wasn't at all surprised to see the young officer storm in today.

She hoped she would be able to overhear what he said this time.

Russ shut the door behind him as Eads put the telephone down. He walked over to the chair, pulled it closer to the desk, and sat down. "I'll only take a few minutes, General," he said. "I know you have an appointment." He leaned forward and placed the file on the desk, then placed the tubes beside it.

Eads's anger was obvious. "What is this? What is the meaning of this intrusion, Major?"

"The meaning of this, sir—and I do apologize for barging in—is that I have six proposals for new low-level training routes and bombing ranges for the F-111, two in each tube. They are ready for your approval."

"Damn it, Major, I've told you—"

"The Twentieth Fighter Wing has put a lot of time and effort into developing these proposals, each one approved by the wing commander."

Eads's face flushed.

"The Director of Operations and the Director of Training at USAFE headquarters in Ramstein have approved all six of these proposals." He stared into the hard eyes. "They endorsed the routes completely and urged their immediate implementation."

The general exploded. "Major, I ordered you not to forward anything to USAFE without my written approval. I gave you a direct order—a legal and clear order!"

"It seemed necessary, sir." Eads's jaws tightened. "I have also coordinated with the Ministry of Defense's Royal Air Force staff officer responsible for reviewing and recommending special operating areas for military aviation in England." A slight stretch of the truth didn't bother Jefferson at all just now. "The Ministry of Defense has been *most* complimentary about the proposals' criteria for nuisance abatement."

Eads could barely control his rage.

"General, everyone else in the loop has given these proposals very high grades—people *above* you in the pecking order."

"Major, for reasons that exceed your scope of understanding, I won't approve these proposals. Now, get out of here and take those with you."

"No, General. It's just not going to work that way." He had sworn not to lose control today, but . . . "Not this time."

"You had . . . better . . . I'll call . . . security police!"

"No, *you* had better, General," Russ said obstinately. "You haven't the most remote idea, do you? It has just never occurred to you that these men at Upper Heyford are assigned one of the most difficult missions in the world, has it? They are under *real* stress, General, not like the paperwork world you live and prosper in."

"Don't tell me—" Eads began.

"I *will* tell you, General, for there appears to be a lot that you just don't understand." He took a deep breath. "A lot of these guys at Upper Heyford flew the F-111 over North Vietnam, December '72. The Christmas bombing. Remember?"

"I promise you, Major, you're not going to get away with this."

Anger flashed in Russ's eyes. For the first time in his life he hated a man who wore this uniform. "Those guys flew the F-111 into Hanoi every night. It was the most violent eleven nights of the air war, and it brought the North Vietnamese back to the peace table. It ended the war and it got guys like me out of the Hanoi Hilton."

"This is a different scenario, Major." The voice and eyes were cold.

"This is the same scenario, damn it! They survived McNamara and they survived the generals of the Seventh Air Force in Saigon, and now they're going to survive you."

"You're way out of your depth, Major."

"Perhaps we both are. The importance of the F-111 to NATO is greater than either of us can comprehend."

"I'll have you court-martialed!"

"Maybe so, General, but these guys may have to fly their war lines to the USSR, two hundred feet above the ground at Mach two, and *you* aren't going to be the reason for their lack of preparedness!"

"You have no idea the command issues I must consider—"

"You've been watching *Twelve O'Clock High* again. Just sign the goddamn things, General, and get 'em out of here."

"I haven't studied them yet." Although brusque and formal, it was a surrender.

Russ's look was one of total disgust, "Okay, look them over before you sign off on them. I'll pick them up tomorrow morning." He leaned over the desk, into the general's face. "Accept it: you're boxed in. Every office higher in the chain has approved these. You can't do anything by not signing off, except look stupid." He stared into the man's eyes for a long moment. "Do you read me?" He turned and left.

As he walked through the outer office he saw the admiring look of Miss Thompson. The general's ten o'clock appointment was waiting. It occurred to Russ that Joanna Thompson was responsible for the penguin story circulating through the embassy. He stopped at her desk, knelt beside her, took her hand, and, ignoring the surprised look on her face, said, "Joanna, Joanna, Joanna. Please say you'll come away with me. Tell me you'll be mine forever!" Then he was up, and no sooner had he kissed her cheek than he was out of the room.

The man waiting for his appointment looked at Joanna Thompson in disbelief, then gave her an uncomfortable smile.

Outside the office Russ shook off the lingering discomfort of his meeting with Eads and checked his watch. It was not so early Tuesday—he'd call Ava and confirm the time for their afternoon drive.

Being with her was the most important thing in the world. He thought of Saturday night: the scent of her perfume; that extraordinary face faintly illuminated by the Criterion's stage lights; her softness and warmth as she sat next to him; the taste of her lipstick. And it wasn't only because she was glamorous and famous—it was more than that. She understood what it meant to live on the edge. The excitement of risk. She understood matadors. Maybe she would understand fighter pilots.

Ava and Russ stood at the top step in front of her flat, looking down over the iron-rail fence at the small Italian sports car. "That's it," he gestured grandly with a hand, "waiting for today's great test drive."

"It's gorgeous, R.J. It's exactly right for you."

"Maybe. We'll see how we like it." He glanced at his watch. His F-111 conversation with Ian Palmer had taken longer than expected.

He took her arm and led her down the steps. "A beautiful day, but too cool for the top to be down. It was pretty nippy coming over here from Westminster." They were through the gate and at the car. "It'll just take a minute to put the top up." He glanced at her as he unsnapped the leather cover of the stowed top and began raising the framed fabric into place.

"Where are we going, R.J.?" she called across the car.

"To the southeast."

"Oh."

He came back to the curbside and opened the door for her. "Get in, and watch your skirt." She wore a long, dark skirt over boots. Her black turtleneck and leather coat weren't enough for top-down driving today. "Just a couple of clamps inside to lock and we'll be on our way."

The Alfa started immediately, and the soft flutter of exhaust made him smile at her. He slowly pulled away toward Knightsbridge Road, where he turned right onto Sloane Street, lined with expensive shops. The one-way lanes took them around Sloane Square, and then they picked up the Chelsea Bridge Road in front of the Royal Hospital. "We'll take the A22 out of London," he told her as he checked his mirrors.

"And you only know that you're going *southeast*?"

They drove past Ranelagh Gardens and its thick rows of trees. "Once out of London, we'll just follow the car's nose."

"Tell me, R.J., just how *long* do you intend to follow its nose?"

"I don't know. Told Palmer I'd have it back tonight."

"He's a trusting soul."

"Well, not altogether. After all, he does have my VW."

They crossed the Thames and soon were clear of city traffic. The Alfa's throaty exhaust note provided a pleasant accompaniment as they accelerated on the open highway. She spoke loudly to be heard. "I've had sports cars. My favorite was a white Jaguar XK-120."

"Would you like to drive this?"

"No, I don't think I should, R.J." There was a brief pause. "I can't."

"Why not?"

"I don't have a license. They've taken it." She continued, "There is this problem, you see. I'm a terrible driver. I don't have the Jaguar because I wrecked it like all the other cars I've owned." He looked across at her and she gave him a helpless, "what can I say" shrug. He shook his head, laughing.

Soon the A22 brought them to Godstone and the junction with A25, and he turned west. "I want to be off the main roads. To drive through the villages."

"The lovely English countryside."

"When I was a boy I read about foreign lands and imagined what they were like. I've been to some of them, and usually they failed to live up to my imagination." He pointed at the surrounding countryside without removing his hand from the wheel. "England's different. A few days ago, I drove through the Cotswolds along old Roman roads. It was just like I always imagined."

He shifted down as they approached Bletchingley, slowing to join the parade of two or three other cars on the main street of the small village. An ancient building of stone and timber gave the street the appearance of

Tudor England. A sign identified it as the Hooker Inn. Russ nodded toward the building. "Another Hooker. One of Sydney's relatives, do you suppose?"

"I don't know. Could be the other kind of hookers."

They reached open road again, and he drove quickly, checking the tach. The Alfa was impressive. He concentrated on his driving, and she allowed him to enjoy the car and the road without distraction. Suddenly, the shrill scream of twin horns sounded and an old but beautiful MG-TC, with its top down, overtook them. Its driver wore a wool cap and an RAF sheepskin flying jacket. As he pulled ahead he raised a heavily gloved hand in greeting.

"That's the true spirit of British sports car drivers," Russ said, laughing. "I have to admit I'm not so hardy."

They crossed a narrow bridge, drove between old timbered cottages, and then they were in Brockham Green, with its graceful spires. Cottages of tile, brick, and board crowded the street, some half-plastered and half-timbered. Quickly they were out of the village, following winding, narrow roads. "This is terrific," he said. "I can see why you live in England." After a pause he asked, "Why *did* you move to England?"

"I had a misunderstanding with the Spanish government. They thought I owed them lots of taxes. I didn't think I did."

"You chose England rather than the United States. Don't you miss Hollywood and living the life of a movie star?"

"I never considered myself one," she said seriously. Then she laughed, "I was only a sex goddess, R.J."

"You were one of the biggest stars in Hollywood."

"I suppose, but when that was happening I was in that scandalous, explosive marriage with Frank. Then I went to Spain."

"To escape?"

"Yes, and I was fascinated by Spain from the first. Felt a real kinship with the place. The flamenco made me feel alive. Bullfights. Pageants. Fiestas. I loved it and I stayed."

"And never regretted it?"

"No. I was enjoying life and those romantic, star-filled Spanish nights."

"And wrecking XK-120s."

"Afraid so."

"And enjoying bullfighters?" He gave her a jealous smile.

"Well, yes . . . but that was before I knew a fighter pilot, R.J.," she teased.

"You were at the peak of your popularity, weren't you?"

"Yes. The publicity department was sending out thousands of black-and-white photos of me every week."

Before he realized what he was saying, he blurted, "One of those was to me."

"What?" She raised an eyebrow and a smile slowly appeared.

Now he was really embarrassed, but it was too late. "I was one of those who wrote for an autographed picture. 1952. You were wearing a brief, black thing and black mesh stockings."

"How old were you, R.J.?"

"Twelve," he admitted.

A moment of realization shocked her. She turned away so he couldn't see the expression on her face. God, he was young enough to be her son!

Russ had driven as far as the day would permit if he was to get back to London by a reasonable hour. A sign told them that Chiddingfold was two miles ahead. "Would you like to stop for something to eat?" he asked.

"Let's do. There'll be a pub here."

Moments later they drove through the village and past its spacious green square.

"There." She pointed toward a half-timbered structure beside a pond. A large wooden sign said CROWN INN. He pulled into the near-empty parking lot at the side and parked under a large tree. Ducks swam idly among the water lilies. They got out and followed a narrow walk past rose vines to the front door and entered.

The Crown Inn was obviously the favorite alehouse of locals, for although the parking lot was almost empty, the pub was noisy and crowded. A carved wooden plaque hung on the wall inside the entrance. It read:

CROWN INN

THE OLDEST PUB IN ENGLAND
EDWARD VI WAS OFTEN HERE, QUAFFING ALE
AND STAYED HERE IN 1552.

They took the table at the wall, and soon a waiter greeted them with a broad smile. He took their orders for sandwiches, a shandy for Ava, a dark beer for Russ, and disappeared into the kitchen behind the bar. They settled into their seats and looked about the old tavern.

Everything about the place was dark and aged. Solid wooden walls were decorated with wrought ironwork and horse brasses. Windows were filled with wisteria vines. Across the room a sturdy round table held a wheel of cheese, big jars of green pickles, and pickled onions. At the far wall a small fireplace crackled.

A crowd of older men lined the bar. Some wore overalls, some the tweed of gentlemen farmers. Their conversations were filled with lively, loud laughter. A dartboard served as a well-worn field of battle for gray-haired men contending for drinks.

Their sandwiches came. Ava enjoyed the food and her shandy and watched with an amused smile as Russ ravenously attacked his sandwich. Cheers and groans from the bar told of changing fortunes in the contests. The crowd noise began to change, quieting to a low buzz, and the old men were now stealing glances at the two Americans. Now differences of opinion were being argued in loud whispers. Russ could hear some of what was said.

"Y'er daft, y'are."

"It bloody well *is*."

"Could be, the looks of them east and west."

"Tomkins, y'er a blinkin' fool, you are." A hearty laugh. "But you always 'ave been."

"The bloody cheek! I'll prove it."

"Have a go, mate. Can't kill you, can it, now?"

One of the men started toward them, and Russ said to Ava, "You're about to have company."

The man shuffled to their table and tipped his old, formless cap. "G'day, miss. Sir. My name's Tomkins. Nice day, ain't it?"

"Yes, it is." She looked up at the gray-haired man with the deeply lined face.

" 'Tis nice now, but you'll see, we'll have to pay for it," warned the gentle voice.

"We'll just have to enjoy it while we can." She smiled at him.

The older man looked down at his shoes, hesitated before raising his eyes again, then managed a nervous laugh. "S'cuse me, miss, but, well, you see, my friends 'n' me, we've had a slight difference of opinion . . . upon which we've wagered drinks, you see."

"Yes?"

He screwed up his face with a questioning look, the chiseled lines becoming even deeper. "Could it be . . . miss . . . as some of my mates are sayin' . . . could it be you're the famous American cinema star?" He waited, unabashedly admiring her.

"Tell me honey, how did you bet? Do you believe I am?"

"I said you were, miss," he said proudly.

"Do you *really* believe I am?"

"Me knickers are in a bit of a twist if you're not, miss."

Smiling, she took a deep breath, rose, and walked purposely toward the group of men. She stopped, placed her hands on her hips, and said, "Gentlemen, I'm Ava Gardner. It's a great pleasure to meet you."

Tumultuous cheers erupted. The men slapped one another on the back with loud congratulations and demands for their drinks—the first one would be for the lady of course—and their noisy laughter filled the room.

"Order up, you losers. I knew it was her all the time, I did."

"Yeh, pay up, lads." Tomkins was back in the group.

"Pay for the drinks and don't worry," a man with silver hair said to his friends. "You'd only spend it on fripperies like food and bills."

Mugs of ale were placed on the bar, and several men tried to hand Ava the first one. She laughed, accepted one of the drinks, and lifting it toward Russ, toasted him. He raised his dark beer to her in return.

Then from behind the crowd came the plaintive sound of a harmonica. The pub became hushed as a little man wearing work clothes and a tweed cap, one foot upon the rung of a stool, began to play louder.

Russ recognized the song immediately, as did Ava. It was "Can't Help Lovin' Dat Man," a song she had performed in *Show Boat*.

The little man hunched his shoulders, covering the harmonica with both hands, his nose and chin nearly meeting at the instrument, and he closed his eyes for a moment, as if to somehow find the sweetest sound possible. He found it. The only sound in the pub was the harmonica.

The man opened his eyes and, looking at her as he played, arched his brows as if to ask her if she recognized the song. She stepped closer to the bar. Two men lifted her effortlessly, lightly seating her on the bar. She crossed her legs, and the split of the long skirt fell open at the knees.

When the harmonica player had played back to the verse, she joined him. It was as if the key light were on her, her face aglow, her eyes alive. All of the men looked at her in complete adoration, their faces reflecting a near reverence. Softly she sang Julie's lament of having no choice but to love one man, just as fish have to swim and birds have to fly.

Shadows lengthened across the road as the autumn afternoon waned. "You weren't completely surprised," Russ said, glancing over at her. "I know you had some idea they were talking about you. How did you know?"

"I heard one of them say something about 'east and west.' "

He steered through a sharp, well-cambered curve. "East and west? What does that mean?"

"It's an old cockney expression meaning 'breasts.' I'm not being vain, R.J., it's just that I *was* the only one in the place with tits."

He laughed. "I think you're wonderful, do you know that? And you sounded just like you did in the movie."

"Thank you, honey, but that wasn't my voice you heard in the movie. I just moved my mouth."

"I think you're wonderful anyway."

"It isn't important what you think of *me* today, R.J. The important thing today is what you think of the car." She glanced about the interior approvingly. "You *are* going to buy it, aren't you?"

"I don't know. I like it. The Alfa Romeo has been a great Italian sports car since the thirties." He glanced at her. "But, typically, I didn't develop much of an interest in Alfas until I saw one in an American movie."

"Which movie?"

"Dustin Hoffman drove one in *The Graduate*."

"The studio tried to get me for the Mrs. Robinson role, but they hired Anne Bancroft and she was wonderful."

"Why didn't you do it?"

"Honey, I had just moved to London and I didn't want to be running back and forth like a demented pigeon. So I turned it down." She shrugged, "R.J., you've got to believe me, I'm not good at being a Hollywood star."

"I think you're a magnificent Hollywood star." Then he added, "I think you're a magnificent woman."

"You're prejudiced because I once took the time to personally sign a photograph, seal it in an envelope, address it, and mail it to you." She patted his cheek fondly.

Above the jungle and rice paddies the four fighters screamed on at 540 knots, the calm sky and green earth incongruous with the violence waiting ahead.

Thirty miles from Hanoi, Jefferson made his inbound turn to the north, feinting an attack on Gia Lam. As deception went, it wasn't much, but it was all he had just now. He signaled for his flight to cross over into an echelon formation. They'd skirt the eastward edge of the heavily defended Paul Doumer Bridge in their approach to the railroad yards.

"I'm getting Fan Song signals, Russ," said Noonan. "They're tracking." The surface-to-air guidance radars were activating the F-4's warning systems. Appropriately, the aural warning signals sounded like a diamondback rattler.

The Fan Song radar guided Russian-made SA-2 surface-to-air missiles. The SA-2 looked like a white telephone pole, 32 feet long. It carried a 350-pound warhead to altitudes of 85,000 feet at speeds of Mach three. It was deadly.

The sight of surface-to-air missiles rising out of the splash of fire and smoke was dramatic. The SAMs would climb high before coming down at them, squeezing the strike force from above while the anti-aircraft artillery saturated lower altitudes. That's the way it worked, and it worked well. Too damn well.

The F-4 strike force thundered on. Ahead, surface-to-air missiles climbed majestically, brilliant white contrails rising into the sky from every direction. From the apex of their arc, they nosed over and accelerated to twice the speed of sound as they dove toward selected targets.

Orange and red explosions created clouds of black and brown and gray smoke below and ahead of the strike force. Anti-aircraft artillery. "The natives seem slightly pissed today," said Noonan. "We've got one guiding on us, Russ!"

A white contrail to their right bent toward them. "Buick Flight, SAM at two o'clock," called Buick 3. Just ahead of the contrail, the long and lethal SA-2 was visible and coming fast. Coming straight at them.

"Buick Flight, let's take it down a bit," transmitted Jefferson, and as if pushed by a single puppeteer the four fighters nosed over in a rapid descent, bobbing and weaving as they watched the missile. They sliced through the haze with afterburners shooting fire behind them. Immediately they saw that the missile wasn't tracking them as it continued along its path, making no attempt to correct to their lower altitude. It passed over them, guiding on its target, but it wasn't aimed at Buick Flight. Not this time.

The enemy had given its greeting. "Ah, there you are," they seemed to say. "We've been waiting for you."

Thirteen

Joanna, did General Eads sign the Upper Heyford proposals?"

It was the day after Russ had left the proposals with General Eads, and now Vivian Rutherford stood before Joanna Thompson's desk. Russ had doubted, in fact, that the general would approve them. He took nothing for granted. Rutherford told him she would find out for sure.

"Eads signed the proposals before leaving the embassy yesterday," said Joanna.

"Did you see his signature on them? Is there any possible way he could 'lose' them?"

"Viv, I stood there and watched him sign them. I took them to the Director of Military Operations for final approval by Admiral Fleming. The admiral is due back Monday."

"Okay, Joanna. Thank you."

"Well, I knew it was very important to Major Jefferson," she said, and then in a conspiratorial whisper she asked, "What's this all about, Vivian?"

"I'm not sure about the specifics. But Major Jefferson said it was critical."

"It's also very important to Eads. That ass is going to court-martial Major Jefferson for this."

"We can't let that happen."

"I don't know how we can stop him. But I did make Mildred promise that she'd put those proposals ahead of everything else on the admiral's desk."

Rutherford walked directly to Admiral Fleming's office. Fleming's secretary greeted her with a smile.

"Mildred, I'm tracking the progress of some important staff work. Priority stuff."

"Yes?"

"Six proposals by the wing at Upper Heyford, under a cover letter signed by Major Jefferson. General Eads has signed off on them, and Joanna said she forwarded them to Admiral Fleming."

"Yes, I know what you're talking about. In fact, Joanna brought them to me herself."

"Would you do me a favor, Mildred? Would you put them on the top of the stack for the admiral? Arrange for him to review the proposals as soon as he gets back? It's very important."

"Of course. I owe you a favor or two, Viv."

Miss Rutherford returned to her office and reported to Jefferson the status of his proposals. "Eads definitely signed them," she said. "The proposals are on Admiral Fleming's desk. They're the first thing the admiral will see when he returns Monday."

"Miss Rutherford, what would I ever do without you?"

She gave him a smile and went to her desk.

Satisfied that the obstacles were hurdled, Russ dialed Squadron Leader Ian Palmer and told him the proposals would be delivered to the Defense Ministry next week, "probably Tuesday or Wednesday." Palmer promised to act promptly, then with exaggerated sadness lamented having let the

Alfa go for so little. Russ offered to sell it back, at a 25 percent profit. They hung up, laughing.

One last call to make. Upper Heyford. He could hear the appreciation in Josh Sims's voice. "If there's ever anything we can do for you, let us know; I owe you one."

Miss Rutherford entered with an outgoing piece of correspondence. She placed it before him, and he was preparing to sign it when the telephone rang.

"Hello, R.J." Ava's voice sounded so alive. "I just wanted to thank you for the drive and ask how the negotiations worked out. Did he accept your offer? Did he come down on the price?"

"Well, no. Not quite."

Her disappointment was clear. "Oh. So you didn't buy it, then?"

"Uh-huh, I did. But, you see, he offered some other concessions that . . ."

Rutherford looked at him curiously. Major Jefferson's voice always took on a different, lighter tone whenever the mysterious lady called, and it had that tone now. She left the office and closed the door behind her.

"I think that's wonderful, R.J.," Ava said, laughing lightly. "You may not drive the hardest bargain in the world, but you just had to have that car."

"Well, I have it." It was more of an apology than a boast.

"Let's celebrate. I have an old copy of *The Barefoot Contessa,* and we can watch it tomorrow night. No booze. Popcorn and Coca-Cola. What do you say, R.J.? Do you know how to run a projector?"

"I do, but I can't. Not tomorrow night."

"Well, well. Sounds suspicious. Got a date, R.J.?"

"No. An obligation. Can't we watch it Sunday night?"

Now there was a soft chuckle. "R.J., I do believe you're trying to hide something. It's a woman, isn't it?"

"It's Cindy and Greg Powers. Greg was my roomie during pilot training. I was best man at their wedding." He swiveled to face the window.

"They're coming into London tomorrow. A one-week visit. They'll stay with me tomorrow night and the next day they'll find a hotel."

It would be good for him to be with old friends, she thought. He was holding in a lot of painful emotions, and perhaps he could talk about those feelings with close chums. "That's great, R.J. I hope you have a good visit. Do you plan to introduce me to them?"

"Are you kidding?" he blurted. "Greg's from the Arkansas Ozarks. Meeting a movie star would totally blow his mind." Then after a moment's thought he asked, "You were kidding, weren't you?"

"I suppose so."

Russ sped past the Parkway Cranford exit on the M4 motorway. The next exit would be Heathrow. He checked his watch. Good. Right on time.

He had calculated a time to arrive at the passenger-pickup zone, considered all factors: their arrival time, processing through customs, collecting their baggage. He had even allowed for time walking to the exit. It would be a minor inconvenience if Cindy and Greg had to wait for him, but nothing compared with his problems if he arrived early and wasn't allowed to park and wait. He had absolutely no idea how one negotiated a once-around-the-block at giant Heathrow. He could imagine five or six hours. Fortunately, he still had the VW. He would sell it soon, but it was a lifesaver for this run.

He saw the Heathrow exit, turned off the highway, and had surprisingly little trouble following the signs to the arrivals gates. Now if only his calculations were correct. A space was open at the curb in front of the TWA doors. His two friends waited under the overhead shelter. He parked and leapt from the car, throwing an arm around Cindy and pounding Greg's shoulder. They loaded the luggage and moments later were making their way back to the M4.

Conversation began their first moment together and continued as he entered the motorway, but he concentrated on his driving, for traffic was heavy. Soon the massive motorway became the Great West Road, and his passengers were silent now as they viewed London. He turned onto Warwick Road, and minutes later they were at the door of his flat.

He led them to the guest room and gave them a quick tour of the flat, then he showed them where the booze was kept and drinks were poured.

"A toast to my favorite couple in the world," Russ said sincerely, lifting his glass.

Cindy was neither beautiful nor cute in the usual sense, but Russ had never known any woman as likeable as she. Her personality and manner made one immediately desire her as a friend, and when she became a friend you wanted her as a best friend. She lowered her glass and smiled widely at him. "Gosh, Russ, I've missed you *so* much. It's been so *long!*"

"About four years," said Greg. "It was when you were at Nellis. Vegas. You were in the Fighter Weapons School."

"Yeah, that's right," Russ agreed. "A long time."

Cindy gestured with the glass. "But I see you haven't changed at all— strongest drinks in town." She knew Vegas was a sensitive time in Russ's life, when Jenny was spending so much time at the Strip and things were getting rocky in their marriage. Cindy wouldn't let the conversation hedge near that. "Russ, I need to shower and clean up."

"Of course. Let me show you where to find towels."

Later they relaxed in the small den, the reunion still an exciting pleasure. Russ had gotten fish and chips at the corner, and they had more than half emptied a bottle of Gordon's. The two travelers were tired, but they weren't going to end this evening at an early hour.

"Russ, we do appreciate your invitation." Greg sipped his drink. He had the perfect face for a politician. Innocent. Trustworthy. He was taller than Russ, perhaps an inch or two over six feet. "We tried to line up a hotel for a week, but God, everything was so expensive."

"London isn't easy on the pocketbook."

"We'll find something to fit our budget tomorrow."

"You can stay here as long as you want. Stay the entire week."

"We're not going to intrude on your privacy for a week, old buddy. Swinging London has the biggest reputation in the world for willing and able women, and I suspect some of them find their way to this pad."

"No, I don't get around much. I get lost in London."

"This is a great place to be lost in," said Greg. "Terrific pad and neighborhood."

"Speaking of getting lost, are you still flying C-135s?"

"Yep. It's the only way to go."

Russ shook his head. "I still can't imagine you guys getting in those big, ugly mothers with so many engines and so many people."

"I can enjoy hot coffee on a mission, can you? Plus, it takes a real man to fly the biggies."

Cindy stood and gathered glasses. "Here we go, just like always. The big boys talking airplanes. I'll pour drinks."

The two old friends continued their conversation until Cindy returned and handed them their drinks. "Okay, you guys, enough about airplanes," she said. "I want to talk to Russ." He took a sip and grimaced, a shudder running through him. He gave her a dubious, accusing look. She winked at him. "Well, if it's too strong, don't blame me. You taught me everything I know."

He lifted the glass toward her in a salute and smiled.

"Now," she said in her softly demanding way, "tell us about your social life."

"Josh Sims is at Upper Heyford. I had a good visit with him the other day."

"That's not what I mean," said Cindy. "I mean your *social* life."

"I don't have one."

"Russ, I *know* you." Her frown was that of a mother who suspects her little boy of mischief. "Honestly now, have you found romance?"

"Nope. I only work. You know, shoulder to the wheel, nose to the grindstone. You can't imagine how hard it is to join the social swirl with your shoulder and nose in that position."

"Damn it, Russell, stop that."

"It's the truth. Embassy work is tough duty. Really tough. Leaves no time for frivolous things like girls."

Greg laughed, took a big sip, then screwed his face tightly into a look of pain. "Jeez, Cindy! What are you trying to do, get us drunk and then take advantage of us?" He looked at Russ. "Tell her what she wants to know, before she pickles our brains in this stuff."

He smiled and insisted, "Really, I don't do anything. I don't go anywhere. Don't know anyone."

Suddenly the doorbell rang. "Who in the world?" Russ said. With a half-dozen strides he reached the door and opened it. He couldn't believe what he saw.

She stood before him. She could have been dressed for a New Year's Eve in Monaco with the Rainiers.

Ava swept through the doorway and entered the room; splendid in a low-cut, bright red dress with a mink stole across her bare shoulders. Her hourglass figure was breathtaking, her luminous skin and green eyes a fascinating vision. He had never seen her more beautiful.

She stopped in the center of the room. "Darling, I have only a moment and I *do* hate to interrupt your evening." Her sparkling eyes fell on his guests, who sat unmoving, amazed. She looked back to Russ and held a gloved hand toward him. "But I simply *had* to return this." She held something small in her outstretched hand.

He approached her, raising his hand cautiously.

"It's your cuff link, darling. I found it on the floor this morning." Her laugh was soft and suggestive. She placed it in his hand. "It must have fallen from the table next to the bed."

Cindy and Greg stared at her, eyes wide with disbelief. No. No, it couldn't be. It was impossible—but it was right there before them, more glamour and excitement in one person than they had ever imagined. No. But it was. Russ Jefferson was introducing them to *Ava Gardner!*

"It's so nice to meet you. I do hope you enjoy your visit in London and your time with R.J."

Russ watched in admiration. She was absolutely incredible.

Cindy and Greg simply sat in silent awe, mechanically clasping her hand as she offered it.

"I really must go now. Again, so nice to meet you both." She turned and they watched her glide unselfconsciously across the room. Russ went to open the door. She stopped and said good night to Cindy and Greg, then she looked up at Russ affectionately and kissed him. Then, with a wink and a quick, mischievous smile, she was gone.

Cindy looked at Russ in astonishment and in a flat, hollow monotone, said, *"You don't do anything . . . you don't go anywhere . . . you don't know anyone. Is that what you said?"* She and Greg looked at each other with quizzical expressions and lifted their strong drinks, not lowering their glasses until they were empty.

Russ smiled at them. Ava had been magnificent. God, how he loved her!

Jefferson turned in on the target, and the strike force swung in behind him. Sixteen fighters.

"Russ, my man, SAM launches. Multiple launches!" Noonan's warning was brief, but his tone was urgent.

"Got one dead ahead." Jefferson called to his flight, "Buick, SAM at twelve."

"Roger, Lead. Tally-ho. Got another one at nine." Jake Robinson sounded disgusted.

The SAMs were everywhere, rising out of the billowing smoke of their launchers, climbing to a high arc, their white contrails streaking behind them.

"Got a visual on the railroad yard?" Noonan's voice was tight.

"Not yet. Watch for SAMs."

"Any particular dozen?"

Surrounded by the contrails, each pilot searched desperately for the surface-to-air missiles tracking his airplane, but it was simply impossible. There were too many.

"Tally-ho on the railroad yards," transmitted Jefferson.

Countless flashes lit the railroad yards. Each was an anti-aircraft battery firing at them. Orange and red explosions crept closer, leaving clouds of black and brown. Dark smoke filled the sky.

"Railroad yards at eleven o'clock, Buick Flight. Thirty seconds." Jefferson paused. "Let's step down, Buick." The four F-4s pushed over and started down to fifteen thousand feet, maneuvering more erratically now, dancing individually within their own formation. The twelve others followed. In moments they would roll in on their target. "Ten seconds," called Jefferson.

Noonan silently began measuring time. "Mississippi one, Mississippi two, Mississippi . . ." Jefferson rolled sharply to his left, pulling over into a nearly inverted entry to his steep dive.

"Buick Lead's in," Jefferson called as he rolled into the dive-bombing pass.

"Two's in," echoed his wingman.

The others followed into the rain of anti-aircraft fire, a high-speed train of fighters now obscured in smoke. They were in a steep dive. Lines of tracers streamed past the F-4s, crossing at all angles. Jefferson and Noonan felt the shudder of explosive concussions.

"Thirteen thousand . . . twelve . . ." Noonan called out their descent, his eyes fixed on the spinning altimeter and airspeed indicator as the F-4 screamed toward the ground. Releasing precisely at the correct parameters was all that mattered, and he continuously read off altitude and airspeed.

They were immersed in violence. Orange and red explosions. Dirty clouds of smoke. Deadly tracers. Anti-aircraft artillery. An F-4 to their right vaporized in massive blasts. Jefferson shut it out. He had to. He had somehow *learned to shut out the danger, the violence, concentrating solely on his goal: the target.*

Jefferson made corrections to put the sight on his target. The AAA gunners were also correcting their aiming points, and the fireworks came even closer. And closer still.

"Eleven . . . unhh!" Noonan grunted as their F-4 took a hit. No time for distractions now, and somehow the two men maintained their concentration on the task that had become the purpose of their lives. Noonan tried to keep a steady, even voice as he continued to advise Jefferson. "Ten thousand . . . nine thousand, Russ . . . ready . . . ready . . . pickle now!"

Jefferson released the bombs and pulled the control stick back into his lap to recover from the fast, steep dive. Good pass. Good bombs. Eight G's jammed them hard into their ejection seats as the nose of the fighter pulled through the horizon and Jefferson shoved the throttles full forward and into the detent. They pulled away from the target, afterburners blazing, the airplane shuddering violently. Tracers streamed past the canopy, then an antiaircraft shell exploded just behind their left wing. The explosion flung the fighter wildly as jagged pieces of metal raked the Phantom.

Jefferson wrestled the aircraft back under control.

"Egress heading's two-seven," blurted Noonan, his voice rattled by the intense turbulence. "We're hit bad! Can you fly her?"

Buick 2 was just behind them. "Jesus, Lead, the natives are really after your ass."

"I think they just got a piece of it." It was bad. Fire warning lights glowed. The control stick vibrated in his hand.

"Lotsa fire back here, Russ!" Noonan knew they couldn't last long.

"Buick Lead, Two's at your five. You've got major damage, Lead. Fuel or hydraulics fire. Left nozzle's closed."

Jefferson checked his instruments and warning lights. There were no questions to ask. His plane was engulfed in a massive blast of flame, a long column of smoke trailing them. At most, only seconds remained before they had to leave the doomed fighter. "We've gotta get out, Noonan . . ."

His wingman transmitted the same warning. "Get out now, Buick Lead!"

"Eject, Noonan!" ordered Jefferson. "Eject!"

"See you on the ground, my man." Noonan sounded almost bored, and then there was the deafening roar of the rear canopy jettisoning and the ejection seat firing.

Before Jefferson could blink, a dazzling white flash filled the cockpit, drawn by the suction of an incredible draft. The flash blinded him, but he remained conscious of the aircraft lurching drunkenly out of control.

In spite of the pain and windblast, he again shut out the danger and focused on what he had to do—he pushed his head back against the headrest, tucked his chin, and sat as erectly as possible. Then he grasped the ejection handles and pulled.

Fourteen

"How much are these?" Russ completed his examination of the jewelry. The necklace and earrings reflected an infinite number of dazzling colors.

The pinched-faced man behind the glass counter handed the American a small white card from the case. The card had numbers written on it. Very high numbers. His slick black hair gleaming in the light, the thin man looked over his thick glasses at Jefferson. There was no mistaking being looked down upon.

Russ replaced the card, handed back the jewelry, and looked about in a bored manner as if nothing interested him. "I don't think these are quite right," he said, and the clerk lifted his nose another degree or two. Russ nodded and walked out past the brilliantly lit displays of shimmering diamonds, dark red rubies, and gleaming gold.

He stepped onto the mist-shrouded street.

The necklace and earrings were just right for her, but the price was more than a half-year's salary. Shouldn't have bought the Alfa. His gift had to be special, something meant just for her. He didn't know exactly what he was looking for, but he knew these were the kind of shops where he would find it.

Ahead was the Burlington Arcade. Carriage lights hung from vaulted roofs reflected in glass fronts. He entered the elegant corridor.

Russ smiled to himself as he remembered Ava's unforgettable visit when Cindy and Greg were there. There was no longer any question about it—his heart simply soared with love for her. He could think of nothing else, wanted to be nowhere but with her. She filled his thoughts and his dreams.

He reached the end of the arcade, turned onto Burlington Gardens, and crossed over to Bond Street. The mist was heavier now as he surveyed each shop window he passed. These weren't just any shops; they bore the most famous names in commerce: Gucci, Maglie, Cartier. Jewelers, fashion boutiques, and art dealers selling goods and products few could afford. He knew he wasn't viewed as a promising customer, someone worthy of preferential treatment. He didn't look like a big spender.

He walked through the crowded street of shoppers and tourists, and then he saw it. It was centered in the small spotless glass window of Warrington's, surrounded by draped blue velvet. He hurried in. The store was serenely quiet, its thick carpet absorbing sounds. Two fur-bundled women examined clocks at a far counter.

"May I assist you, sir?" A woman in a dark dress approached him.

"In your window, the small doll."

"The *Detherage*?"

"I suppose. May I see it?"

"I'll get it for you." She went to the window and returned with the doll.

He examined the intricate detail, turning the doll carefully in his hands.

"It's a very old doll," the clerk explained. "Made of the finest china in the 1850s. A rare example of early Detherage." She waited for an expression of recognition and appreciation; when she didn't get it, she continued. "It's simply priceless."

"Really?" He smiled at her. "Literally priceless?"

"Of course not," she said, smiling, and told him the price of the doll.

"Very well, I'll take it," he said. "Please wrap it carefully. It's for someone very special."

A few minutes later he left the shop, carefully holding the precious package. The mist was light and he felt like walking. He followed Bruton Place to Berkeley Square. Finding this gift reinforced his belief that destiny had brought him to something—no, to *someone*—incredibly rare. He walked past Claridge's Hotel, turned onto Grosvenor Street, and headed toward the embassy. It was a wonderful walk. Atop the embassy building the massive eagle and American flag loomed against the gray sky. The converging sidewalks on Grosvenor Square took him past the statue of Franklin Roosevelt.

The elevator doors sighed quietly and let him out on the third floor. Then he was at the outer office. "Hello, Miss Rutherford," he said cheerfully.

"Well, hello, Major." A puzzled smile appeared on her face as she watched him walk past.

"Keeping the wolves at bay for me, Miss Rutherford?"

"I'm trying, Major. I'm trying."

After removing his coat and throwing it onto a nearby chair, he cautiously picked up the package and unwrapped it. Holding the fragile object carefully, he examined it even more closely than he had in the store.

In every detail it was a perfect image of Ava as she had appeared in *Show Boat;* more incredible, it was the exact costume she had worn in her biggest musical scene of the film: "Can't Help Lovin' Dat Man." The precise, impeccable facial features were hers. He recalled the scene in the Crown Inn last week, when old men had basked in her every move as she sang that song. God, how she could create magic!

Russ leaned back in his chair, gazing at the small wonder on his desk. He couldn't wait to see her.

He knew it seemed foolish. He was trained to make reasoned, calculated decisions. He had led men into a hailstorm of enemy fire, his split-second decisions affecting their lives. He was experienced beyond his age. Yet, since meeting her he had acted like a kid. Clumsy. Embarrassingly immature. It seemed crazy, but there was an explanation: his dream was there, there with him. It was understandable that her beauty, her style and glamour overwhelmed him. He had somehow entered her world, and she had made him feel alive. He wanted to feel this way forever.

And now he knew. He would follow his heart, even if it meant giving up forever everything that had once been so important to him—flying fighters, his career in the Air Force. Those things had once made him feel so alive, but they didn't matter anymore. The only thing that mattered was being with her. All he wanted was to feel the way only she could make him feel. And he would do anything to make that happen, including resigning from the Air Force.

There was a knock on his door and he rewrapped the doll, placing it in his desk drawer.

Gerald Graves entered and lowered himself into a chair. "How's everything going, Russ?" he asked.

"Not bad." Russ reached into his desk, withdrew a cellophane-wrapped cigar, and tossed it to the Navy officer. "Here. And thanks."

Graves caught the cigar and examined it. "Better than the one I gave you," he said. He looked up, his eyes boring into Russ's. "There's scuttlebutt going around about you."

"Oh?"

"Rumor has it that General Eads has submitted a report to the Air Attaché charging you with serious stuff." He paused. "The word is Eads and Elliott have agreed to take legal action against you."

"What do you know about General Elliott?"

Graves raised an eyebrow. "He's a very smart man, politically. He's not shy about doing whatever's necessary to protect the establishment. He will *not* allow an internal squabble to harm the Air Force's image in this embassy."

"We certainly don't want anything to hurt our *image*."

"It's being said that Eads is out for your blood." Graves's eyes held as steadily as his voice. "You've got to take this very seriously, Russ."

"I always take generals seriously."

"This is no game. Eads is really out to get you."

"He's been screwing over the F-111 wing at Upper Heyford. My God, Gerald, the F-111! Someone had to do something about it."

"You could have found a better way. You've pushed too far. He's documented all sorts of insubordination on your part."

"Eads is a gutless staff nerd."

"The Air Attaché isn't. General Elliott's your problem now, and he's as solid as they make 'em. Believe me, he's not going to hesitate to fire some young major, some loose cannon."

"You know something, Gerald? I don't care anymore."

"That's your resentment talking. We've all felt the same way at times."

Russ lit a cigarette. "The guys who flew up north didn't compromise their principles. How can I?"

"This isn't a matter of compromise. It's a matter of a senior officer's authority over a lower-grade officer." He shifted his weight in the chair. "You've got a great career ahead of you. You could be a squadron commander in a couple of years, a full-bird colonel wing commander before you're forty. You've got a realistic shot at two, three . . . hell, even four stars."

Russ inhaled deeply and released the blue smoke. "It just isn't important to me anymore."

"This career was so important to you at one time that you were willing to risk life and limb for it, to measure up."

"I know, but it's a little like flying combat. A lot of things seemed important until you entered the firestorm, then nothing mattered except the one purpose you lived for—putting the bombs on the target. Now, nothing else matters except the one thing I want to live for, and that has nothing to do with the United States Air Force."

"So be it." Graves looked levelly at him and rose to his feet. "I'll be going. Just wanted to warn you that the generals are ready to make their case against you."

"Thanks, Gerald." Russ stood. "Thanks a lot."

The Navy officer paused and said, "Oh, by the way, Brenda wants you to come over for dinner soon. Next week?"

"We'll see. Thank her for me."

Graves left the office, closing the door behind him. Russ remained standing there, staring at the door and smoking his cigarette.

Everything Gerald said was true. He had devoted everything to this career. His war record singled him out as one of a few who were considered for future stars in the Air Force. Fast burners on the career ladder. Nothing had ever mattered as much as flying fighters and his career in this uniform.

But now she had come into his life.

Russ hurried up the steps in the deepening darkness of the evening. In spite of a light rain, the night was unusually warm for this time of year, almost balmy. He nodded to Roberts as he entered the building, then he crossed the foyer and stepped into the lift.

Ava answered the first ring of the doorbell. "Come in, R.J.," she said.

He put three LPs and a package on a table and struggled free of his coat. "It does rain a lot in London, doesn't it?"

"So it rains sometimes." She looked up, her eyes engaging his. "It rains everywhere, sometimes. And I happen to like the rain."

"Me too."

"How was your day, R.J.?" she asked over her shoulder as she took his coat to the closet. "Things okay at the embassy?"

Unusual that she would ask, he thought. She had never asked about his work before. "My day was all right." He held the package out to her.

"What's this?"

"Just something you should have," he said. "Open it."

She removed the ribbon, opened the small box, and lifted out the doll. Her eyes widened. "Oh . . . oh, R.J.!" She held the doll in both hands, studying it with childlike fascination.

"It's over a hundred twenty years old," he said. "And," he boasted proudly, "it's an early Detherage."

"It's *beautiful*! That's the same dress I . . ." She looked at it in wonder. "How did you get this made?"

"No, you gotta believe me. It's old. It's you in *Show Boat*, and the unbelievable thing is, it was made in 1850."

Like a little girl, she held the doll to her chest. "Oh, R.J., this is such a special gift. So very special. Thank you so much."

"You're very welcome."

She looked at it again. "I just can't believe it."

"I know. How could it be identical? Costume. Everything. There's some kind of major karma here."

"How could you remember my costume in that scene?"

"Easy. I saw *Show Boat* four times. Plus, your picture on the soundtrack album. You were wearing that dress."

"Honey, this was so sweet of you. I'll keep it with me all the time."

He turned and picked up the LPs. "I've brought some easy listening. You don't care for my rock-and-roll records, so I thought we'd try these." He casually looked at each and said, "We have Henry Mancini . . . Mantovani . . . Sinatra . . ." He glanced at her, waiting to see her reaction.

Her expression didn't change; she was still studying the doll, and then put it down. "How about a gin and tonic, R.J.?" she asked, then went to the bar and began putting ice into glasses.

He put the first record on. When she returned with the drinks, he lit her cigarette and they sat quietly facing the fireplace, listening.

They sipped their drinks and said little as the first record played. The record ended, the second dropped into position on the turntable, and the needle lowered into its groove. It was Sinatra. Closely he watched her face, her eyes. "This is a live recording of his show at the Sands. 1967, wasn't it?"

"1966, and the son of a bitch can sing," she said, smiling.

"He's been doing it a long time."

"And he does it well." She sipped her drink, never taking her eyes off him.

"It's always good being with you," he said softly.

"I like to be with you, R.J. I value our friendship."

He moved to the floor and sat beside her chair. He looked up at her and took her hand. "I wasn't exactly honest a few minutes ago when you asked about my work at the embassy. The truth is, things aren't going very well."

"What is it? What's wrong?"

"I've gotten into a hassle with a senior officer. A general, my boss."

"Are you in trouble? I mean, are you in official trouble because of this hassle, R.J.?"

"Probably, but it doesn't matter. You see, I've made a decision. I'm resigning my commission."

"But your career. Your flying."

"My career is going down in flames. Within days it'll be just a smokin' hole." His eyes searched hers. "But that isn't important. What *is* important is that I will be able to stay here in London. I'll be free to live the life I choose."

"No, honey. You're wrong."

"But don't you understand?"

She released his hand and stood up. "Let's go out onto the balcony. Get some fresh air."

She draped a sweater over her shoulders. He followed her through the French doors. They stood at the wrought-iron railing and looked down on the small park. The rain had stopped. A fine mist created silver halos around the distant streetlights.

She turned to him; faint light filtering softly through the curtains let him see her face. "Honey, I want to tell you something."

"Sure."

"Not long after I went to Spain, I visited a ranch where they bred fighting bulls. I joined the crowd around the ring to watch the spectacle of the bulls being trained. I loved the excitement and I wasn't shy about drinking my concoctions, my *solasombras*. Then I had this great idea to sit on a horse as it worked with the bulls in the ring. Someone in authority, and sober, should have stopped me, but no one did."

She took a drink, then continued. "So, I was off, galloping around the ring when they let a young bull in. The bull charged, and as I leaned down to stick in my banderilla, the horse reared and I fell. My face smashed hard against the ground. All I can remember is hooves pounding all around me."

He listened quietly.

"The accident left a large lump at my cheekbone. A very large, scary lump. I thought my career was over. I went to see Dr. McIndoe at his East Grinstead hospital for the Royal Air Force. Archie has performed miracles with RAF pilots. I saw many who were so terribly burned. Some had hardly any face left; some didn't have limbs." She looked into the darkness and her voice became softer. "Their treatment was long and agonizing. I met a lot of them and we danced and laughed together. They were so brave I could have cried."

She took a cigarette from its case, and he raised his lighter for her. The brief flame illuminated her face. She inhaled deeply and resumed. "The thing that struck me most about those men was they never complained. They never quit." She spoke carefully. "Tell me about last year, R.J."

He shifted his weight. "Ah, really." He shrugged. "There's not much to tell."

"Please," she said. He stood still, staring into the night. "It's very important to me, honey."

His throat was tight and he coughed softly to clear it. "It was the tenth of May and we took off at dawn. One of our biggest strikes at the most important targets in North Vietnam. My target was the Yen Vien rail yards. We knew it was going to be tough because the North Vietnamese had rebuilt their air defenses during the Paris peace talks. We knew there would be heavy losses."

He leaned forward against the iron railing, still looking into the night. "I led a flight of F-4s. It's a two-seat fighter, and my backseater was my best friend. His name was Noonan." A note of pride crept into his voice. "We weren't only buddies, we were very, *very* good in our F-4. I swear he knew what I was going to do before I did. And we were ready that day. It was our fifty-third mission north, and everything was normal until we got to the target."

He rubbed the side of his nose and continued in a flat voice.

"Sixteen F-4s were making runs on the rail yard. We led them in. Anti-aircraft fire was thick; the sky was full of smoke and crud. Tracers were like a laser show. Noonan and I rolled in and flew a good pass, putting our bombs on the target. We took lots of hits. We pulled off the target, then realized we were on fire. Our F-4 was an inferno and we had to bail out. Noonan ejected first. Without the canopy for protection, I was covered with fire. That's when I got this." He raised a hand and touched his face near the eye. "I ejected," he said simply.

"I landed in a rice paddy. Hit hard. I was nearly blind, and by the time I got my act together I was surrounded by a dozen North Vietnamese regular army troops. They threw some ropes on me and dragged me to a village." He paused. "Just a small, godforsaken village in a godforsaken jungle." His voice became harder. "And I don't even know the name of it."

She could hear the pain in his voice. "Does it really matter, R.J.?" she asked quietly. "Why does the name of the village matter?"

He didn't seem to hear her. "They dragged me into the village. The soldiers and the villagers were standing around something. Something lying in the dirt. I couldn't see what it was. They pulled me over to where they were, and then I could see . . . it was Noonan. They'd torn his flight suit and G suit off. He had lots of blood on him. Black-and-blue bruises and blood. Stones lay on the ground around him." A sob caught in his throat. He struggled with the words. "They had stoned him, Ava. He was alive, but they had *bludgeoned* him."

He took a few breaths and continued. "They treated us like some evil creatures from some distant planet. We were captured very near the target, so they hated us the way you might expect, I guess."

He shook his head slowly. "I don't know why they didn't stone me. They forced me into a bamboo cage. Then they dragged Noonan to the cage and pushed him in. There was barely enough room for both of us. I held him. He was unconscious, barely breathing. Bleeding everywhere.

"The sun was hot. Bugs crawling all over us. I didn't have any way to protect him from the heat and stink, but I tried to keep the bugs off. He recovered consciousness once. Although he could barely speak, he said I'd done a lousy job selecting accommodations on this trip. He was delirious all afternoon. A woman brought us a bowl of yellow water. I forced some down Noonan, but it only made him vomit. Before night, he started shaking. Blood poured from his mouth. He died in my arms. No treatment. No help. Died in that cage."

He lowered his head. "Noonan was the best friend I ever had. We took on everybody in billiards, racquetball, bridge. In anything. We were a team and maybe the best damned crew to ever strap into the F-4. And I got him killed."

She reached toward him, to show him it was all right if he didn't want to talk anymore, but he stopped her hand with his and went on.

"They kept us in the cage all night and the next day. I held him and tried to keep the flies off. Before night they took him out of the cage. I don't know what they did with the body. I don't even know the name of the village. Later, I was paraded through several villages and put in the Hanoi Hilton."

"That's the prisoner-of-war barracks?"

"Yeah. I was singled out because I led the bombing mission. One of the guards—I called him 'Chipmunk'—had lost two brothers at the Yen

Vien rail yards. He wanted revenge, and that eye-for-an-eye stuff was very serious business with him. He tied my arms and legs behind my back and left me lying on the cell floor for I don't know how long. They put some kind of rice broth on the dirty concrete floor for me to lick up, but the rats got it first. Both my shoulders were broken. The only way I could bear it was to mentally remove myself. Shut out the pain. Shut out the fear. When they tortured me, I willed my mind to solve a puzzle, a puzzle I visualized. A thousand-piece puzzle. I shut everything else out somehow.

"Later, some guy tried to fix up my burns. The first several weeks were really bad. The last few weeks the guys who enjoyed their torture games eased up, but in spite of what Jane Fonda says, things were really mean and nasty in there."

"Oh, R.J."

"I didn't do well, compared to others. Most of the guys who got there before me resisted their tormentors much better than I did. Maybe it was because they believed we would win the war." He shook his head. "I had no such belief. I didn't expect the president, the Congress, or the people to do a damn thing to get us out. So I had no faith or hope. Plus, the Chipmunk never gave up on his goal of killing me a little each day.

"Our politicians got us into a war that they had no plan to win, not even a plan to get out of it. Inconveniently for them, however, there were a lot of guys dying and the American public got tired of it or bored with it or both, so they pulled out.

"One day buses suddenly drove up and started taking us to the airport. General Giap and Uncle Ho had won the war, and we were on our way home."

His soft laugh was sarcastic. "On my first night home I was at a restaurant and at the next table three men were complaining about how tough it was to make sales. Insurance, shoes, or something. Worried about sales quotas." He shook his head and took a deep breath. "And of course, college kids had become very trendy. Burning their draft cards and their campus buildings. Abbie Hoffman and Timothy Leary were the heroes. We were the bad guys. It really wasn't what we had in mind when we signed on to fly beautiful, fast fighters."

He stood straight, his voice still emotionless. "I spent the next five months in the hospital at San Antonio. Major body-repair job."

She put her hand on his arm.

"Oh, well. It's like Noonan would say: 'Things don't always turn out the way you expect, otherwise poker would be a real bore.' " He turned his face up toward the wet night. He said quietly, "I really miss Noonan."

Ava was overcome by his anguish. "Oh, R.J.," she said as she put her arms around him and held him tightly.

She felt warm and soft. He hid his face in her hair and tried not to cry. He desperately needed her to comfort him, to console him. He needed to be free of the pain.

"Come with me, R.J.," she said softly. Her voice was close and intimate, choked with passion. "I want you to come with me to my . . ." She stiffened. She couldn't do this. She wanted to take his pain, to take all of his torment, and give him moments of passion that would carry him to consuming pleasures. But she couldn't. He would misunderstand. Afterward, he would think it meant something else. She eased her embrace, and they were no longer so close. "Let's go inside. Let me fix you a drink, honey."

Two hours later, she sat before the fireplace thinking of him. She felt drained.

He had become quiet after coming in from the balcony. Withdrawn behind his wall. They had listened to music and had a drink, but soon he had excused himself and left.

Desire had nearly overwhelmed her. She had wanted him so badly. To heal him. To make him whole with her body. It was all she could do to back away.

God, the things he had told her, the images that must have been pass-ing through his mind. There were no signs of self-pity. Only bitterness and sorrow. Not all of R.J.'s scars were on his face.

She had wanted him since they first met. He was handsome and virile and she had wanted to know purely physical passion with him. That was all, just sensual hours of pleasure. But she couldn't do that now. He was so fragile, so damaged. She couldn't take him in simply a physical, sexual way. Tonight she had wanted to hold him and make him warm. Her every instinct had been to take his hurt from him. To nurture him.

She picked up the telephone and dialed the number of Sydney Hooker.

"I know it's late, Sydney, but I need a big favor. I want to know what's going on in the American embassy. It's R.J. Some general is apparently pissed at him." She listened to a brief protest. "I don't care if what goes on in the embassy isn't any of your business. Please, find out what it's all about, would you?"

After hanging up she sat motionless, staring into the fireplace. Her thoughts were of the young man and his friend Noonan. Their courage and their youth. And the supreme sacrifice both had made for an uncar-ing country.

Her eyes welled up with tears, and she wept.

Fifteen

"anda, I was just going to give the Air Attaché's memo to Major Jefferson," Vivian Rutherford said. "The one directing him to be at his office at ten. There's no mention of why General Elliott wants to see him. The major should at least know what it's about. What can I tell him?"

"I can't say, really, Viv," Wanda Weatherford answered. "I mean I don't know. The general simply said to have the major here at ten this morning."

"Okay, but I wish Major Jefferson knew."

"Maybe he does, Viv."

"Well, thanks anyway. Let's get together for lunch one day soon." Vivian hung up. This was strange. It was very unusual for a staff member to be called to a senior officer's desk without knowing why. She picked up the memo and rose from her chair. She checked the time: 8:35. Major Jefferson had been at his desk only a few minutes. She would take him a coffee with the memo.

As she poured the coffee she thought she ought to warn Major Jefferson about the Air Attaché's cool and impersonal manner. Cool, impersonal, *and* handsome. General Sam Elliott could never have been anything but what he was: a poster-perfect general who had become more handsome with age. His features were sharp, his eyes clear blue and sincere, his graying blond hair combed carelessly in place. Athletic. He was in his early fifties and the secret fantasy of many secretaries in the building. He had once been hers.

She entered Russ's office and placed the coffee in front of him.

"Thanks, Miss Rutherford. I need that."

"You've received a memo from the Air Attaché," she said, holding it out to him.

He took it, glanced at her, and read it.

"I tried to find out why he wants to see you. The attaché's secretary doesn't know. She suggested you might. Do you?"

"No."

"Have you met General Elliott?"

"A quick introduction. He took ten seconds to welcome me on board."

"He's a very aloof person," she said. "Cold. Controlled."

"Anything else?"

"Yes. He will never, ever allow anyone to put a blemish on his record. If there is a potential Air Force problem in this embassy, he will take care of it immediately. Like an executioner. He doesn't believe in working through lots of details; he just makes the problem go away. Any way he can."

Russ stared at the inner-office message. Gerald Graves had warned him that the Air Attaché was endorsing General Eads's charges, but the next step above Eads in the chain of command was Admiral Fleming, and the admiral was not yet back from Washington. Anything as serious as an Article 15 court-martial would be addressed only by the appropriate senior officials, in this case Eads and Fleming. Surely Eads wasn't going to go over

Fleming's head with the admiral due back so soon, and surely the Air Attaché wasn't going to involve himself in this matter. Not *now.*

Or would he?

Promptly at ten Russ entered the Air Attaché's office. The two-star general offered him a chair and asked him to wait a moment until he finished signing "just one more piece of correspondence." After scrawling his signature with a sweeping movement of his pen, he pushed the paper away and turned his attention to the younger officer. "This is a bad situation that's developed between you and General Eads, Major," he said. "But the situation *has* developed. And it is an *Air Force* situation."

That didn't sound good. The Air Attaché apparently wasn't going to wait for Admiral Fleming to take care of this. This was not going to be a Military Affairs action but an Air Force action. Russ looked more closely at the man behind the desk, to better assess his judge.

"Major Jefferson, I've received a report on your recent submission to USAFE of proposals for training routes and bombing ranges. I am not interested in debating the issue. I haven't called you here to discuss the merit or lack of merit in the proposals. I have asked you to come here to meet a problem head-on, the problem you've caused with General Eads."

Russ tried to appear at ease, not wanting to give any indication that he feared judgment.

"The general has submitted his report to me. He describes the situation as serious. He thinks your offenses deserve disciplinary action, and he plans to bring charges against you. General Eads gave you direct orders, and you chose to disregard them. *That* is the problem." Elliott jutted his chin out a bit more. "I wish there was some way to reconcile this matter. It should have been corrected before it reached this point, but you saw to it that we didn't have that opportunity. I will not tolerate things as they are."

The general seemed to carefully consider his next question. "Major Jefferson, do you deny that you deliberately disobeyed orders given by General Eads?"

"No sir."

"You deliberately defied him?"

"I used my own judgment in what I considered to be a critical matter."

"But you understood his orders?"

"Yes sir."

The general's voice was sharp. "Major, you have two choices. First, you may contact your sponsor. Ask him to get you an assignment out of here. I don't care if you get the best deal in this modern Air Force, my only condition is this: it happens immediately. Second, you may stay here and prepare for the charges by General Eads. You will be charged with an Article fifteen, at least, and your career will be over."

Russ returned the steady gaze of the blue eyes, showing no reaction.

"I suggest you contact your sponsor. You have an important one or you wouldn't have been sent here in the first place."

"I have a third choice, General." He remained composed. "I can resign my commission."

"Think it over, Major. You have a very promising future ahead of you if you want it. You have all the credentials and you've paid your dues. A lot of people, whom I respect, think you are one of our brightest young officers. I would like to think they're right, but all I've seen is your arrogance. What's worse, you seem to think you have license to unleash your resentment at anyone unlucky enough to get in your gun sight."

Russ said nothing.

"I respect your combat record, Major Jefferson. I respect what you've been through. But being a MiG killer doesn't give you that license."

The general, expecting a rebuttal, raised an eyebrow. Seeing that Russ had no intention of saying more, he ended the meeting. "But you are exactly right, Major. You certainly may resign your commission, and if that is your choice, I will expedite the paperwork."

The mellow growl of the Alfa was the only sound along Ennismore Gardens on this quiet weekday afternoon. His thoughts were still on the meeting with the Air Attaché as they drove slowly toward Kensington Road.

"Got something special in mind for lunch, R.J.?" Ava asked over the exhaust note.

"No." He tried to snap out of his somber mood. "Whatever you like."

"Okay, drive toward East London. I'll give directions."

"I'll follow you anywhere."

"Promises, promises."

Fifteen minutes later they had driven farther east in London than he had ever been. They had followed the Thames past Tower Bridge, then through the warehouse area of St. Katharine's Dock. He gave her a questioning look. "Have faith, R.J.," she said. "Have faith."

Amid vast docks and warehouses, he felt completely lost. "Okay," he said, surrendering. "Just where are we going?"

"I'm taking you to the oldest pub on the river, the Prospect of Whitby. It's been in the same place five hundred years. It was the pub nearest Execution Dock, where sailors found guilty of crimes on the high seas were hung."

"If you only knew what my morning was like, you would appreciate the irony in this."

She let his comment pass with only a curious glance. "Five hundred years ago it was called the Devil's Tavern, because it was a notorious haunt of thieves. I would've loved to have been there then."

"First the story about the crown jewels of France hidden in Hyde Park, and now this." He glanced over at her. "You could write a guidebook."

"But I find it intriguing, don't you?"

"When you're the guide, yes."

"If I were new in your hometown, wouldn't you share the local folklore with me, R.J.?"

"Yes, I would."

"We're going to the Prospect of Whitby because they have the greatest hot dogs in the world. German sausages, sauerkraut, and hot mustard on homemade buns." She closed her eyes, a look of complete contentment on her face. "And, oh, such wonderful, huge dill pickles."

He loved her enthusiasm over simple things. He carefully nursed the Alfa through a slow, tight turn.

"We'll be there in just a moment, R.J.," she said.

He leaned back in the wooden booth and nodded. "You certainly didn't exaggerate. Wow."

"Hang around me, honey, and I'll show you lots of fabulous places."

"Well, that's . . . that's what I want to talk to you about."

"What? Hot dogs?"

He smiled at her, and then the smile disappeared. "I was called to the Air Attaché's office this morning. He accused me of . . . well, of some very serious things. Told me to go back to my fighter squadrons or face legal charges."

"You did something wrong?"

"I did something that was necessary."

"Honey, misunderstandings can be worked out."

He put his hand on hers. "It's not a misunderstanding. I was given an ultimatum, but I'm not going back to a fighter squadron, and I'm not going to be court-martialed. I'm going to get out of the Air Force, Ava. I'm going to resign my commission. I'll be a civilian shortly, and as good as anybody." It was an attempt at humor, but she didn't smile.

"What do you think you'll do, R.J.?"

"Don't know. Maybe go back to school. A London university. Become a starving writer." He leaned toward her. "The important thing is I'll be here."

"I know you think you're doing a noble thing by this. And it will attract attention from your peers and others because you're a high-profile young officer. I know you made a name for yourself in the war."

He frowned, telling himself again that he had told her too much the night before.

"This honorable act," she continued, "to show *them* that you're above having to accept their judgment, is not going to accomplish what you think it will, R.J. Believe me, it's not."

"You don't understand."

"Yes, I do. I've been there."

He started to protest, but she held up her hand, silencing him. "Believe me, I've been there. The star system was alive and well when I signed with MGM. Luckily I caught a couple of good roles and became a profitable commodity. But that's all I was, a commodity. I became a star, whatever the hell *that* pretentious word means, but still I was treated like a piece of merchandise. I rebelled, R.J. Believe me, I really rebelled. After my third or fourth starring role, I just rebelled right out of Hollywood and the studio. Went to Spain and stayed there. I told them to go straight to hell. I rebelled for ten years, honey."

The waiter came to the table and took their order for another beer and shandy.

"Like you, I had produced. Like you, I believed in the system, but then I saw it was only going to smother me. I only wanted to enjoy my life. I would live according to my own principles, and if they had a problem with that, it wasn't my problem." She gave him a look that said he needed to understand what she was telling him. "You see, R.J., I only wanted to control my own life. I wanted to be happy."

She toyed with her near-empty glass. "An exaggerated notion of self-importance made me think my symbolic act would shake up the entire movie world, or at least those who exercised control over other people. But you know what, honey? They had no trouble at all finding someone to take every role I turned down. They didn't blink twice. I had my way all right, but I only fooled myself into thinking it mattered a damn. The establishment—the government, Air Force, or Hollywood—isn't fazed by anybody who stands up to be counted. No matter how justified we may be, it doesn't matter, honey."

"But you accomplished so much."

"No, R.J., I accomplished nothing. Pretty much a wasted effort, my little rebellion was. And now, almost twenty years later, I don't live the life of luxury or wealth that might have been mine. Nor do I have the eternal gratitude of anyone who benefited from my noble deed. No, I accomplished nothing."

"You don't understand why I'm resigning." He spoke with urgency. "I suppose it is partly because I want to show a few people wearing stars that I don't have to accept their terms, but that isn't the most important reason."

"What is the most important reason?" she asked hesitantly, as if she knew what he was going to say.

"To be here with you. I hadn't expected to choose this time or this place to say this, but . . . I've fallen in love with you."

Sixteen

Sydney Hooker arrived promptly at Carrier's on Camden Passage, but Ava was already there. He saw her sitting near the pale brick wall, under the skylight and vine-covered lattice, and walked directly to the table.

He kissed her cheek and took his chair. The waiter appeared and she ordered coffee; Hooker, tea.

A few minutes later as he sipped his tea, she gave him a disapproving look. "I would bet that everything wrong with England could be traced to tea."

"At least"—he lowered the cup—"we haven't been taken over by that *herbal* crap."

"Okay, Sydney, we've exchanged our customary cheap shots. Now, tell me what you've been able to find out."

"Very well. First of all, your young man is quite a hero." Hooker edged forward in his chair, as if to emphasize what he knew. "He has been a standout since the beginning of his career. A distinguished graduate in pilot training, resulting in an assignment to the newest fighter in the Air Force.

"He went to Vietnam at age twenty-five and flew a hundred combat missions. He returned to the war for his second combat tour four years later. Shot down two enemy MiGs. In all he flew one hundred fifty-two and a half missions over North Vietnam."

"A hundred fifty-two and *a half*?"

"He was shot down while leading one of the biggest raids on Hanoi."

"Where did you get all of this? From the embassy?"

"No, this came from his file at the Military Personnel Center at Randolph Air Force Base in Texas." She raised an eyebrow. "It just so happens that I know a young lady at the center. She spent a summer in London a few years ago. We became . . . well, we became very good friends during that short summer. We've kept in touch."

"I see." Ava smiled knowingly, then became serious. "But what's going on now at the embassy? What have your spies told you?"

"I shouldn't have meddled in this, you know."

"What did you find out?"

"Your young man is in very deep, very hot water. I'm told that he became aware of a problem associated with the F-111s at Upper Heyford. It was an important problem requiring embassy solutions, but proposed solutions had been repeatedly killed at the embassy. So Russ took on the problem. He also took on the task of finding out who had been rejecting the proposals. He even maneuvered me into helping him."

"And?"

"And he ran directly into a general—General Eads—who ordered him to stop. He didn't. He didn't go around the general, he went directly *over* him."

"And that's gotten him into trouble?"

Hooker smiled at her understatement. "You might say so, yes."

"Why would R.J. allow himself to get into trouble? Why didn't he just do as the general wanted?"

"The F-111 is the most important weapon system in NATO. Russ was willing to take on the world to eliminate the problems plaguing the F-111 wing."

"And this Eads character can cause trouble for R.J.?"

"Darling, let me explain," Hooker said patiently. "General Eads is the Deputy Director of the Office of Military Affairs, Russ's superior officer. He didn't order Russ to stop working on the F-111 problem for no reason. I don't know what it might be, but Eads had a reason. Generals always do. General Eads is now in a hurry to court-martial Russ before the Director of Military Operations returns."

"Who is that?"

"Admiral Fleming. He's in Washington. He's also Eads's boss. Fleming is thought to be an obstacle to a court-martial. He is known to be the sort who works things out, rather than destroys careers. Especially careers of promising young fighter pilots. Eads, on the other hand, is not at all reluctant to ruin careers."

"Eads has the final say in this?"

"No, but he has enlisted the support of an even bigger general, the Embassy Air Attaché."

"And this guy can have the final say?"

"Yes, my dear, he can. The Air Attaché outranks Admiral Fleming."

"Oh."

"He's known as a man who eliminates problems quickly, and the quickest solution to this matter is to court-martial Russ. The Air Attaché is less concerned about the merits of this case than he is about having a messy situation. He's determined that the judge in this matter will be he, not a Navy admiral. He will not allow a junior Air Force officer to create a problem at the embassy that will result in a smudge on his own record."

"And they are going to—"

"They are going to exercise their prerogative to draw and quarter your young friend." He sighed, sipping his tea. "And no one at the embassy can stop it."

"And they can do that?" Her eyes flashed with anger. "Just like *that*?"

"Without question, they certainly can, my dear."

"It isn't fair!"

"Darling, it may not be fair, but there is nothing quite as bloody powerful as a general in the military, especially in matters of disciplining junior officers."

"What exactly are they going to do?"

"They are bringing court-martial charges against him."

"Which will ruin his career?"

Hooker nodded as he slowly lit a cigar. "Yes, it most definitely will ruin his career."

"R.J. said he doesn't care about his career now."

"But your young friend isn't thinking clearly. And it is absolutely essential that *one* of you realizes what is happening."

"I understand. His career—"

"No, my dear, you *don't* understand. Not only was Russ Jefferson a distinguished graduate in pilot training and assigned to the newest jet fighter, he also finished number one in his F-4 combat-crew training class. He was tops in his Fighter Weapons School class. He's a *MiG killer*. Do you know what all of that means?"

With an almost imperceptible shrug she said, "He's very good at what he does?"

"No, Ava. Every one of his peers is very good at what he does. Russ is the best of the best. No one is better at what he does. His contemporaries look upon him as tennis players look upon Rod Laver, as chess players look upon Bobby Fischer." Hooker spoke carefully. "It is *very* important that you understand what that means. He is one of those men born to do a certain thing, and if you take it away from him, you do much more than ruin his career. You ruin his *life*."

"Is there any possible way he can get out of this?"

"I'm told he has friends at the Pentagon who are hoping to reassign him, if the Air Attaché is willing. But the general doesn't suffer fools gladly."

In a near-whisper she asked, "Who is this all-powerful man, this Air Attaché?"

"Major General Sam Elliott." Hooker gave her a look of warning. "And, darling, he *isn't* willing."

"Sydney, you must talk to R.J. You know what he's like, how he feels, what he's thinking. You flew in the RAF; he'll listen to you."

"I know how he feels, but I'm not certain he'll listen."

"It's the only chance I have, Sydney. R.J. thinks he must get out of the Air Force, that he must stay in London, and I can't let him do this."

"Why?"

"He thinks he's in love."

"With you?"

"Yes, with me."

"And could it be that you are in love with him, my dear?"

"No. I could have been once, long ago. But no."

"Very well, darling. I shall call him tonight. I'll invite him for golf tomorrow."

"And I must ask one more favor of you, Sydney. Please introduce me to this General Sam Elliott."

Seventeen

Russ watched as Sydney Hooker took a practice swing, stepped up to address the ball, then drove it with a smooth, full swing. The long drive bounced to a stop in the center of the fairway.

"Very nice, Sydney." Hooker's ball had carried twenty yards farther than his own. Russ's caddy picked up his golf bag and adjusted the strap on his shoulder. Russ waited for Hooker to hand his driver to his own caddy. "It's turned into a perfect day for golf," Russ said as they began walking slowly toward his ball.

"It's time we got together again," Hooker said. "But I know you've been busy."

"Yes, the last several days have been busy. Kinda rocky."

"I'm sorry to hear that. It seems that all of England is nothing but rocky lately."

"I suppose that's why bars are so full on Fridays," Russ said with a smile. "The need to talk about the week's problems and events over drinks."

"Yes, that's the ticket."

"In fighter squadrons we went to the club bar every Friday as soon as the last aircraft landed. Happy hour. Only it always lasted several hours."

"Yes. Yes, quite. I often wish I still was a part of that life. I miss it, I tell you." Hooker shook his head. "There's nothing like having a pint with your mate as you describe that perfect maneuver that put you at his six o'clock. But look at me now. I've been spending most recent Friday evenings looking back over a week of approaching ruin for this old country. Depleted coal reserves. Union strikes. Inflation. I sometimes wonder if we're going to make it to the end of the decade."

"Things are really that bad?"

"A friend of mine told me last week that his real income had dropped twenty percent this year. He said that anyone who stays in this country is a bloody idiot." He peered toward the horizon. "This will be our winter of discontent, as the saying goes."

"The U.S. has been having some seasons of discontent as well."

"The war?"

"The war, Watergate, and other things."

"You flew a lot of combat missions, didn't you?"

"Others flew more than I did."

"Someone told me you were quite a hero."

"Someone was wrong."

"Hmm." It was a "but I know better" hmm. "The war. It will become more important and more a part of you as time passes. You will realize it was your life's most defining experience. I saw it happen with our Spitfire lads, and it will happen to you."

"It was important," Russ acknowledged.

"Boswell wrote, 'Every man thinks meanly of himself for not having been a soldier, or not having been at sea.' I believe that to be true."

"I don't know. Maybe."

"You have a great career ahead of you in your Air Force. There aren't many of your peers who have shot down enemy MiGs. You have been anointed, as it were."

This abrupt change in the conversation caught Russ by surprise. How had Hooker known about the MiG kills?

Hooker went on. "You don't realize it yet, but you have the greatest opportunity of your life, the opportunity to live as part of an elite military group *and* to be distinguished within that group." He slowed almost to a stop, took a deep breath, and resumed walking. "Believe me, my young friend, there is *nothing* to compare to that."

"You've done well in civilian life."

"Not in comparison to those who remained in the RAF. Believe me, you will never find anything comparable to the camaraderie, the shared loyalty, that is unique to flight operations in an air force. I can only recommend, Russ, that you give everything careful consideration before giving that opportunity away."

Now he knew. This friendly conversation was a warning.

"I've been told that you may resign your commission."

"Yes, I've decided against a career in this uniform."

"What do you plan to do? Where do you plan to go?"

"I'll stay here in London."

"Didn't you hear what I said a few minutes ago? My friend said anyone who stays in this country is a bloody idiot." Then Hooker said, "It's because of her, isn't it?"

"I beg your pardon?" Russ said defensively.

"It's because of Ava, isn't it?" Russ didn't answer. They were only a few steps from the first ball now. "Ah, fighter pilots," said Hooker. "We never change."

"Meaning?"

"Once a fighter pilot, always a fighter pilot. After all"—he smiled—"it *is* an attitude, isn't it?"

"I've heard that said."

"What a wonderful thing it is, this *fighter pilot* attitude." Hooker watched Russ step closer to the ball and size up his shot. "We are truly a different breed. And what wonderful, bloody fakes. We validate our maleness by daredevil feats in the skies, sometimes dueling with an enemy, staring death in the face. But that isn't enough. Not for us, it isn't."

The older man seemed to be enjoying his analysis. "No, shooting down an enemy is not enough, we must go beyond daredevil feats to prove our manliness. We must seduce every woman we meet. Constantly. At parties. On a train trip. Whenever we aren't proving our manhood in the air, we must do so by overwhelming the resistance of the fairer sex." He became silent as Russ selected his club, took two practice swings, and drove the ball almost to the green.

"Why do you suppose it is that law school professors aren't that way?" Hooker watched the ball until it stopped rolling. "Or bankers?" He didn't wait for an answer. "Think it over, my young friend. Before you chuck it, think it over very carefully."

"You just don't understand."

"Oh, but I do. There was a time several years ago when I would have chucked my seat in the Parliament, my entire career, for her. Believe me, it would have been the wrong thing to do." The admission was followed by a thoughtful silence. "She is a wonderful person, the most loyal and devoted friend in the world." Hooker's eyes were sympathetic, his voice understanding. "But you must ask yourself one question, my friend. Is she in love with you?"

Russ lowered his eyes.

"Enough for an old meddling fool," Hooker said in a harsh tone. "I really don't mean to pry into your business. It's only that I am fond of you both."

"I understand," Russ replied. "I'll be seeing Ava tomorrow night. Her housekeeper has returned from the States, and she's going to cook dinner for us."

"Carmen Vargas?"

"Yes, that's the name."

"Ava doesn't think of Carmen as her housekeeper."

"No? I thought—"

"Carmen is one of her best friends. She's been with her thirty years."

Thirty years? He had been two years old!

Saturday was a workday for Captain Ted Sanders, who paced back and forth in his office, reciting to himself over and over what he had heard ten minutes ago. The Air Attaché had threatened Russ Jefferson with formal charges. Jefferson had thrown it back in General Elliott's face; he would not be available to be charged with anything. He was resigning his commission.

He rubbed his face. *Damn it! This is wrong,* really *wrong.*

No one in this building could relate to Russ Jefferson like he could. He had been on that raid on May 10. He had flown against the targets at the Paul Doumer Bridge and the Yen Vien rail yards that day, his F-105 going in before the strike force to provide SAM suppression. And he knew what it was like for the strike force that day. The F-4s had rolled in on their targets in a literal barrage of anti-aircraft fire. They had flown into a firestorm to deliver their bombs. It was a wonder any of them had returned from that mission, and Russ was one of those who hadn't . . . not for a long time.

And this was wrong, goddamn it, wrong!

He went to his desk and pulled a directory from the drawer. Moments later he was dialing, then through the static of the Autovon he heard a distant phone ringing and an answer. "Torrejón operator? Connect me with the Sixty-third Tactical Fighter Squadron, please." Even though it was Sunday, he had an idea that Scott Mitchell would be in.

He waited. A moment later the hollow ring was answered.

"Sixty-third Ops. Lieutenant Wilson, speaking."

"Lieutenant Wilson, this is Captain Ted Sanders, with the U.S. Embassy. Is Colonel Mitchell available?"

"Just a minute, Captain."

Almost immediately he heard the familiar voice from the conference at Ramstein. "Hey, Ted! How's it goin'?"

"Okay, Colonel. But I've got a problem that I need to talk to you about."

"Sure. What's up?"

"At Ramstein, you told me that you were Russ Jefferson's best friend. Remember? You said you would be the one to crank up the network anytime he needed help."

"That's right. I meant it."

"It's time to start getting some help for him."

"What's happened?"

"All hell broke loose here this week, Colonel. They're going to crucify him."

Eighteen

The phone sounded far off, but it kept ringing. Russ blindly reached toward the receiver. "Hello," he grumbled.

"Russ, General Kreeger."

"Good morning, sir." God, it was still dark. He switched on the bedside lamp and checked his watch. Almost midnight at the Pentagon. The general was working unusual hours.

"What's going on with you and that puzzle palace over there?"

"Nothing very important." He rubbed his eyes. "Routine staff work. Not much else so far, sir."

"Have you had enough of soft embassy life? Ready to get back into the cockpit?"

"I . . . er . . . I don't know, General," he stammered. He wasn't prepared to tell Kreeger of his plans.

"There's an assignment that's right for you. Advanced testing of new laser weapons. Holloman Air Force Base. Alamogordo, New Mexico. Very advanced stuff. Important to the Tactical Air Command. Could move us toward a weapons-delivery method other than rolling in off the perch and diving straight into the teeth of defenses."

"Sounds interesting," Russ said lamely as he tried to organize his thoughts.

"They need a man experienced in the tactical mission. You'd be flying the F-4 in the tests. You'd work for a great man, General Mark Baker."

"I appreciate that you would consider me, General, but I've been thinking of something else. I mean I—"

"I know. Scott Mitchell told me. He wants you in his fighter squadron. Think about it. You have three days. Close of business Wednesday."

"It's not—"

"I know, it's not going to go well with the embassy. I need to explain to someone why we're pulling you out. Who's the senior Air Force officer in there? Who's the Air Attaché?"

"Major General Sam Elliott."

"Elliott? 'Sudden' Sam Elliott?"

"You know him."

"We've been at each other's throats since we were gold-bar lieutenants." Kreeger paused. "There's no question about Sudden Sam cooperating with us. He won't. I'll come up with something. Think it over. You've got three days."

Russ laid the phone down. At one time he would have jumped at the chance to fly in the test program, but not now. He didn't need three days to decide what he was going to do. He was resigning to be with Ava. He threw the bedclothes aside and hurried to the kitchen to make coffee.

Ava filled his mind now. He thought about their Friday lunch at the pub, when he told her he wanted to stay in London. When he told her he loved her. She had seemed to expect his admission, and if she hadn't expected it, she'd now had time to think about it and become adjusted to the idea.

He would wait three days to call General Kreeger. Not because he was uncertain about the testing-program assignment but because there may be something else to call on the general for. He didn't know about General Elliott, but he didn't trust General Eads. He was *not* going to allow his records to contain statements about *pending* charges or *pending* court-martial actions. He was resigning, but he wasn't sacrificing his record! If anyone was going to try to ruin his record, he wanted to call on General Kreeger for help.

So today would be a busy day at the embassy, followed by some important shopping. It was time to focus on his appearance, to buy some stylish clothes. Ava attended high-society affairs, and it would matter how he looked when he accompanied her. She had to be proud to be seen with him.

After a late afternoon of shopping, Russ hurriedly showered and shaved, eager to see Ava. He pulled on his old robe and gathered wrapping paper and ribbon for the gift he'd found. It wasn't expensive, but it would remind her of him. To make sure everything was as it should be, he opened the small box and checked its contents: a sterling-silver cigarette case and lighter, each decorated with miniature Air Force pilot wings. He wrapped the box, then wrote a single line on a small card, which he tucked under the ribbon.

He checked the clock. Time to get dressed. And his nails. Clean and short, but it wouldn't hurt to file them again. Certainly wouldn't want to snag anything silky. He returned to the bathroom to get the nail file, humming a Sinatra tune.

Ava looked at her watch and laughed lightly. "No one can accuse you of keeping them waiting, R.J."

"I got dressed early, there was almost no traffic, and, well, I'm here sooner than I expected," he explained. "Carmen let me in."

"You two introduced yourselves, I gather. Want a drink?"

"Sure. Two G's will be fine."

She laughed again. "Learning my bad habits, I see."

"I like your habits." God, he sounded like a high school freshman with a crush on his teacher. He slipped his arm around her waist, pulled her close, and put his lips to her hair.

"R.J., don't tell me after all this time you're going to make a pass."

"The window's open. You can always scream."

She looked at him with surprise. Those were lines from one of her movies: *Seven Days in May*. From a scene she had with Kirk Douglas. She smiled and stepped away from him. "Do you know the dialogue from all of my movies, R.J.?"

"No. Just certain scenes."

"I'm flattered." She walked barefoot to the bar. She was wearing a low-cut gown of dark rust and gold plaid. There was the clinking of ice against glass and soon she returned with their drinks. As she tucked her feet under her in the big, soft chair, she caught his expression. "You don't have to give me that look, R.J. Only in moderation. I'm following the good doctor's advice pretty goddamned faithfully." She lifted the glass. "Cheers."

"I brought you something." He handed her the gift.

"R.J., you don't have to always be giving me things, honey. It's sweet, but . . ." She unwrapped the gift and opened the small box, removed the silver cigarette case and lighter, and admired them for a long moment. "Oh, R. J., I love them, I just *love* them." He watched her, pleased.

She read the card slowly and her expression became pensive. She placed the gift and card on the table beside her and turned to him. "So, you had a long visit with Sydney yesterday."

"Yes. A round of golf." He tried to sound comfortable in the world of her friends.

Carmen entered the room and announced that dinner was ready.

"I hope you're hungry," said Ava.

"Starving." They went to the table; he held her chair out and then sat across from her. She was beautiful in the soft glow of the candlelight.

"I'm so glad Carmen's back. You're finally having dinner here. Carmen always wants to cook Mexican, but tonight I wanted to have a typical North Carolina meal."

The table was spread with fried chicken, whipped potatoes, gravy, and green beans. "I think this is perfect," he said.

"Wait until you try her buttermilk biscuits. She could win blue ribbons at any county fair."

Dinner was delicious and he said so, repeatedly.

"It's good to see a hearty appetite," she said with a smile. "It's one thing I miss with the privileged types. They never roll up their sleeves and eat like they mean it."

He thought nothing of her contrasting him with the sophisticated, and he enjoyed watching her as she held pieces of chicken with her fingers, picking at the crispy brown crumbs on the platter. She had once told him that she was really, deep down, a simple country girl, and tonight he was nearly convinced that was just what she wanted to be.

"I hope Sydney didn't take up your entire afternoon yesterday. He can talk politics for hours."

"No, he didn't." He hesitated, then said, "You two have been friends for a long time."

"Yes, we became friends years ago when I was here making a film."

"Nothing more than friends?" he asked and immediately regretted it.

Her look had a hint of disapproval, then softened. "No, nothing more. We have never been more than friends. But that's quite a lot, don't you think, R.J.?"

"Yes, that's quite a lot. Sorry, I didn't mean to sound that way. It was stupid." He wanted to hurry to the next thought, to the next sentence, and leave his unforgivably embarrassing question forgotten. "I enjoy listening to Sydney. He's an interesting man."

"Ah, the political science background is coming out, isn't it? You're the first person I've met who just might be able to last through a complete conversation with him."

"I think I'm going to enjoy British politics."

"Oh?"

"I think I'm going to like everything about England."

Her expression became serious. "Do I take it you're still considering resigning from the Air Force?"

"And staying in London. And, like you, I'm going to love living here."

"R.J., you need to think things out carefully."

"I have. I'm finally accustomed to driving on the left. I have no trouble calling the hood of a car its bonnet; fenders, wings; a convertible top, a hood. I know suspenders hold up socks, braces hold up trousers. When I need medicine, I go to the chemist, and when I ask for a biscuit, I get a cookie."

"But you're making assumptions you shouldn't."

"No. I don't think so."

"Your card, R.J." Her voice was soft, patient. "The card with your gift. The things you said are lovely, but if you feel that way and if that's the reason you're getting out of the Air Force, then we must straighten some things out."

He finished his coffee. "We never played the Mancini record the other evening. Why don't I put it on? Nice for dancing."

Before she said anything, he went to the stereo. A moment later the full, rich sounds of instruments filled the room. He approached her and held out his hand. "If you're not particularly Compton's lady, would you honor me with this dance?"

He gently pulled her to him and she came into his arms. He thought she fit exactly right. They moved to "Charades" as one. She was light in his arms, warm against him, and her perfume was intoxicating. He had never been so in love. Too soon the song ended and she stepped back, looking up into his eyes, and then away. "Let's talk, R.J.," she said. She sat on the narrow love seat and he joined her.

"Okay. You're incredibly gorgeous tonight."

"Thank you, but I meant about more serious things."

"Okay, you are seriously gorgeous tonight," he offered.

"These assumptions. The reasons you're getting out of the Air Force . . ."

"Yes?"

"There was a time when I thought love would solve everything. But, you know, honey, it never did."

He was ready to tell her it would be different this time, but he waited.

"When I filmed *The Barefoot Contessa,* there was a scene I thought had been written especially for me. It seemed to express my own views and feelings exactly. The story was about a poor girl who grew up to be a famous woman. The lines were: 'When I was a little girl, like so many others, there was no money to buy shoes for me. And when the war and bombs came, I would bury myself in the dirt of the ruins to be safe. I would lie there, safe in the dirt. I would wiggle my toes and listen to the noise and dream of the day when I would be a great lady with nice shoes. And when I was older and the bombs still came, I would still hide in the dirt, needing someone to love me, to make me safe.' "

He didn't know what to say.

She looked at him fondly, reaching for his hand. "R.J., I've been in love with men who I thought would make me safe. I've been married three times, and each time I was 'in love forever.' But it never worked out that way and I think it was always because the men fell in love with what they thought I was, not what I really was."

"That was then. I'm not wrong now."

"You don't even *know* me."

"Yes, I do," he blurted. "I've known you for a very long time." He didn't care if he sounded irrational. "And you won't have to hide any longer, waiting for someone to make you safe."

"R.J., I've reached an age where I know who I am and what I am. It isn't all I had hoped for, but I can live with it."

"But you don't know how I feel about you. I told you I'm hopelessly in love with you, but that doesn't begin to describe my feelings."

"R.J., don't—"

"I can't make you understand completely. Even I don't understand completely, but I know how I feel." He took both of her hands and held them tightly. "I've flown in extremely dangerous situations, and sometimes it was so intense I'd forget to breathe. That's how I feel when I'm with you."

"You're so young. We—"

"I'm older than my years. Much, much older."

"Be serious, R.J."

"Let's dance again," he said.

"No. We have to talk, work this out."

He stood. "There's nothing to work out. We've talked enough. Can't we just let our feelings take over?"

She came to him, and he put his arms around her. The music enveloped them. For a brief moment she seemed to be doing as he asked, simply enjoying dancing and the music. He was sure she found it pleasurable to have his arms around her.

The song was over now, but still he held her close. Their faces were only inches from each other, and he saw her glistening lips part slightly. He bent to her, watched as she closed her eyes and he kissed her. Their kiss deepened.

When it ended, she leaned back slightly to look at him. Her green eyes sparkled with excitement. She rumpled his hair and smiled at him. He wondered if she was feeling what he was feeling. After so many wealthy and famous men, would she allow him to be the one to make her happy? Could the fates be so kind to him, at last?

Ava touched his cheek and gazed into his eyes. She moved closer to him, putting her arms around his neck, her face nearer to his. "You *are* something special, Major Russell Thomas Jefferson." She pulled his face down to hers and kissed him. She pressed harder against him, opened her mouth wider. Their kiss now had the heat of desire, the heat of an impatient lust.

Suddenly she broke the kiss and lowered her arms. She rested her forehead on his shoulder, her eyes closed. "I'm sorry, R.J.," she said. "I didn't mean to do that."

He was shaken and confused. What happened? Why the sudden change in her?

She stepped away from him. "I'm really quite tired tonight. Would it be terribly rude if I asked you to leave now?"

His expression was inquiring at first, and then it softened. "No, it wouldn't be rude at all." Now he understood. Passions were overheating. He had pressed against her and she must have known he wanted her. Perhaps things were moving too fast.

"Would you mind, terribly?"

"No, I understand." He placed his hands at her sides, holding her at a relaxed arm's length. "Is it all right if I call you tomorrow?"

"Of course."

"Good night," he said, and he kissed her on the cheek.

"Good night, R.J."

He got his coat from the closet, started toward the door, and stopped. He turned to her. "Ava . . ."

"Yes?"

"When I'm not with you, I miss you like crazy."

"I know."

Nineteen

The next day he tried to reach her several times, but there was no answer. On the other hand, his telephone had been constantly busy. The many calls added up to only one conclusion: the word had gotten out about his meeting with the Air Attaché. Although the fighter community was stretched around the globe, it was a small world and news traveled fast.

The first call following General Kreeger's had been from Josh Sims, asking if helping the 20th Wing was putting his job in jeopardy. He assured Josh it wasn't and explained that the proposals were awaiting Admiral Fleming's return on Monday; then they would be hand carried to the Ministry of Defense. Sims was grateful, but he assured Russ that he had never intended to create problems for him at the embassy and he would do anything to help. Let him know, he had said, if there was anything they could do to influence the Air Attaché.

Scott Mitchell had called Sunday morning from Spain. "Aren't you ready to leave the paper shuffling to someone else and strap your ass in an

F-4?" he asked. "Even if you don't want to be in my squadron, that's a pretty outstanding opportunity with the test program at Holloman." Mitchell had caught his slip before he finished the sentence. "Er, ah, General Kreeger just happened to mention it to me the other day," he improvised.

Ted Sanders and Gerald Graves also called Sunday, just to offer encouragement. One of them had sent the word out, and Jefferson suspected Ted.

He knew why he was getting the telephone calls. The relationship between fighter squadron pals was one of the things he had always appreciated most in this life. Sydney Hooker was right—there was no other life in the world that provided as many loyal friends as the life of an aviator in fighter squadrons.

He didn't deceive himself about what awaited him in the outside world. Corporate hierarchy could be as rigidly structured as the military, and younger executives—if they were to advance—were expected to be true reflections of their seniors. Co-optation. One rung at a time up a very long and difficult ladder. But his decision wasn't being made according to some pro-and-con ledger or some list of pluses and minuses. He didn't need a rational basis for this decision.

Ava was an attraction he could not resist. If she could share her world with him, if their lives could be bonded into a lasting . . . no! Never mind *lasting*. If it were only for a while . . . months . . . that their lives were shared, it would exceed anything he had ever dreamed. Only to be with her, to talk to her, to laugh with her.

The usual trio of secretaries wasn't together during their coffee break this morning. Vivian Rutherford had called Joanna Thompson first thing, asking her to meet for coffee. She wanted to know what Joanna knew about last Thursday's meeting between General Eads and the Air Attaché, General Elliott. She hadn't invited Irene. The coffee shop was crowded and the two women sat closely to avoid being overheard.

"I don't know much," said Joanna, "but I do know that Eads will formally submit his charges today. He'll notify Jefferson that it's official. Probably have the major come to his office."

"Any chance that Eads would reconsider?"

"No. He won't stop until he's ruined Jefferson. Destroying careers is nothing new to him. He thinks he can crucify him."

Rutherford replied evenly, "I thought he had stopped that years ago."

"What? Destroying careers?"

"No. Thinking."

"He's such a repulsive bastard." Joanna sat silently a moment, then asked, "May I ask you a personal question, Viv?"

"Of course."

"Did you and the Air Attaché once have a close relationship?"

"No, but not because I didn't want to. Why do you ask?"

"I was under the impression you had. I just thought you might influence him in this matter with Major Jefferson."

"Not a chance. General Elliott would never allow a woman to affect his decisions."

Just after eleven Joanna Thompson called and said, "He wants him, Viv. Now."

There was a note of encouragement in Miss Rutherford's voice as she told Russ that General Eads was waiting for him. She had always been able to take care of her guys in OMA, but not this one. No, not this one. Shaking her head slowly, she returned to her work.

Eads's outer office was empty when Russ entered. "Go right in, Major," Miss Thompson said. "He's waiting for you." He stepped into the office, closing the door behind him.

"I'll be right with you," the general said, gesturing to the chair across from the desk. He finished reading a letter and placed it in a file. The file went to a stack of others on his desk. Hands clasped at his chest, he leaned back in the black leather swivel chair. Russ waited.

"Major, I don't know how our problems are going to work out. I don't know if you're going to be working here much longer or not, and frankly I don't care. But you work here *now,* and before another day passes I am going to straighten you out on one or two matters."

Russ settled into the chair.

"I realize you don't have a lot of admiration for those of us on the *staff* side of things, Major, especially in the diplomatic world. I know there's a lot of talk about this trouble we're having, and I know you're letting it be known that the general officers in this embassy are nothing but bureaucratic bumblers." He leaned forward and his eyes bored into Russ's. "I may not change your mind about that, but I am going to eliminate your excuse for thinking you're all-knowing about what leaders in this Air Force should be doing, and how they should be doing it." His voice became sharp. "In short, Major, I'm going to take away that arrogant, self-righteous attitude of yours."

Russ's cheeks stung. He felt his anger rising.

"I've been rejecting proposals for new F-111 routes and ranges for months, and for good reason. For your benefit, I'm going to say for *crucial* reasons that go far beyond the here and now."

Eads picked up a fountain pen from the desk and unconsciously began twirling it between his fingers. "This is turning into one hell of a world for those of us in Air Force policy formulation, Major. We've lost a war and, in the process, immeasurable financial standing as well as public support. Not a desirable condition." He frowned.

"Until '64, the F-105 was the backbone of our airpower in NATO. Losing our entire F-105 force in Vietnam has put our Western European defenses in a dismally weakened condition. Losing about the same number of F-4s has further reduced our ability to accomplish the NATO mission."

Russ straightened and started to speak, but the general held up his hand, silencing him.

"NATO has one purpose, Major—to protect Western Europe from the communist threat. It has always depended on us to provide that protection. That's a tougher job now. You, of all people, know how weak we are after losing our best fighters in Vietnam. Now we don't have the airpower to defend Western Europe." His eyes were piercing. "But that's only part of the picture, Major Jefferson.

"In two years, a Democrat is going to be elected President of the United States, and even though it may not be George McGovern or anyone quite that dovish, he *will* be cool toward the military. Our already weakened forces will be allowed to decline even further."

The younger man wanted to disagree but decided to listen instead.

"So NATO is left facing the threat and strength of the Soviet Union and the other Warsaw Pact nations with a ground and air strength approximately a fifth of what the communists have. Even though our airstrike forces are at an all-time low, airpower is still the key to successfully defending Europe. As you have noted previously, Major, the F-111 is about the only thing we have to ante up with."

"The essential air weapon."

"And, as of now, they are being placed in England. The first F-111 wing at Upper Heyford. The second at RAF Lakenheath. After that, there will be two more wings."

"All the more reasons for getting adequate areas for training—"

"Can it, Major! You haven't listened to much since you've been here, but you are going to listen to me now. America's not up to honoring many commitments right now. The only war we may be willing to fight is the defense of Europe, and we'd better win *that* one. If we're going to win the next war, Major, we'd better get smarter. To win it, we're going to need every advantage. Every edge we can find.

"The most decisive advantage we can gain is to reduce the early-warning time available to the Soviets. We must shorten the time required by our fighter-bombers to reach their targets. Major, we can only do that by placing our F-111s in France! From France, an F-111 takes twenty-five less minutes to reach its target in Russia—critical minutes that dramatically increase its probability of successful penetration." He paused. "And taking off from France, our fighter-bombers would have adequate fuel to return to their bases, and to fight again."

The room dimmed as the sunlight streaming through the window slowly disappeared. The sky was becoming gray.

"But the politics of this world have allowed France to reject any requests for our fighter squadrons to be based there. There were several reasons for De Gaulle's popularity, but it just may have been mostly due to how he thumbed his nose at the United States, and, now, almost three years after his death, it's still politic. Today's French leaders are also thumbing their noses at us. All of this fierce independence is enjoyed, of course, because the United States and NATO protect France from her enemies."

The sun came out momentarily and then dimmed again. Russ was now keenly following every word.

"American presidents allowed De Gaulle to have his way for too long, and now others follow his example. It is critical that France no longer imposes constraints on NATO, constraints that may be the difference between our success and failure. It's time to confront this ridiculous posture of the French, and I've been preparing for that showdown.

"Something must be done before the other three F-111 wings are put in place. Because the F-111 is so vital in that mission, any political debate will be won on the argument favoring its implementation. Nothing else is as critical to NATO. It is the case for the F-111 that must put a stop to French restrictions. The wing at Upper Heyford must be the *only* F-111 wing in England. The other three *must* be in France. There is only one way we can get them there: compelling and irrefutable evidence that there is no airspace for their training in England."

He stood and walked to the window, where he stared outside as he talked. "For now, our political argument with the French is going to have prevailing military reasons. In order to have the F-111 in NATO, the Western European nations will have to pressure France to provide bases. After we have F-111s on French soil, Major, I'll be the first to help the wing at Upper Heyford. I'll fight like hell to give the Twentieth Wing everything it needs.

"But there's another war we must anticipate. The war for oil. The present oil crisis is clear warning. So was the Olympic bloodbath in Munich." He turned from the window and faced Russ. "Mark my words, the day will come when we will have to fly strike missions to the Mideast from the soil of friendly nations, as we did from Thailand in the Vietnam War. Our strike forces will have to fly over the sovereign boundaries of friendly nations to reach the enemy, just as we flew over Laos and Cambodia to get to North Vietnam."

Russ listened carefully.

"Right now, some of our friends won't allow us to fly over them to reach enemy targets." His voice was now a low warning. "We can't accept that, Major."

The general returned to his chair. "I'm not a ring knocker from the academy. I'm not a highly decorated fighter pilot, but I do have twenty-five years experience in fighting the cold war. I know how to fight other kinds of wars with both our friends and enemies. I may not fight the kind of battles for which combat medals are awarded, but my battles mean just as much in the war against communism."

Russ's tendency to be clever and sarcastic had disappeared. He showed no impatience, no insolence.

"I fight my wars, Major," the general said, "just as hard as you. I will see to it that pressure is put on the French and that there is a sound, undeniable basis for that pressure. You have probably ruined my first attempt to do that, but I'll find a way."

He stood, leaning forward on his desk. "You see, I will do everything I possibly can to see that our pilots never have to be handicapped again as they were in Vietnam." He looked to the door and nodded. "Good day, Major."

Twenty

In spite of what General Eads had said, Russ was determined to finish his work. He had promised that he would see this through, and he would. He called Admiral Fleming's office and was told that the admiral had been delayed, that he would not be back until the following week. He told his secretary he would pick up the Upper Heyford proposals today. Then he made a second call.

The jovial voice of Squadron Leader Ian Palmer greeted him. "Well, hello, old chap. Are you calling to ask me to take the car back?"

"No, I'm very pleased with the car," Russ said with a chuckle. Then in a serious voice he said, "I'm in a bind, Ian. I can't get final approval of the proposals for the F-111 training routes and bombing ranges because the admiral is away this week, but I can't afford to lose time. I need you to review and approve the proposals now. The package is ready. Will you be in your office this afternoon?"

"Well, a bit unorthodox without embassy final approval. But, yes, of course."

"Good, I can have them there by two."

"Very well. I'll have a pass ready for you at the security desk. They can direct you to my office."

"Thanks, Ian. You don't know how much I appreciate this."

"No problem, old chap. Only one condition."

"Oh, what's that?"

"Please come in the Alfa. I want to see her once more."

Russ thanked Palmer again and hung up, his mind now returning to Ava. He dialed.

No answer. Finally he hung up. He wondered where she was. It seemed forever since he had seen her. He called her twice more before leaving for the ministry, but again there was no answer.

The doctor's unintelligible grunts and facial contortions alone described his findings as he reviewed Ava's test results. He rubbed his cheek and ran his hand through his hair as he read. Then he tossed the file onto his desk, his gray eyes trained on her.

"Well?" She tilted her head quizzically.

"Just as modern computers do, the brain requires outside sources of power. Blood carries oxygen and other elements that produce vital electrical impulses, and interruptions in this power source have disastrous consequences."

"Interruptions?"

"Yes, caused by obstructions interfering with the flow of blood to the brain." He leaned forward, both elbows on the desk. "These blood vessels are subject to atherosclerosis with subsequent narrowing of the passageway for blood flow. Obstruction may also be caused by a clot in the narrowed artery. Either way, as soon as the blood's supply of oxygen to the brain declines below a critical level, the brain is rapidly damaged." He wrinkled his brow and paused. "If blood flow is not quickly restored, the brain tissue dies, unable to regenerate."

"My brain has never been my greatest asset," she said, and smiled.

He frowned at her. "The attack you experienced indicated reduced blood flow in the vertebral artery. Loss of vision, with dizziness, double vision, vertigo. Difficulty in speaking. Loss of consciousness. You've experienced each of those symptoms, haven't you?"

"That about covers it."

"Medication does not provide sufficient treatment in this case. Cerebral angiography revealed lesions that must be removed to reduce both the probability and severity of future strokes. Surgery is required to open up the major arteries, to lessen the threat of arteriosclerosis."

"And if I don't?"

"The chances of a stroke that may paralyze you increase dramatically. Or one that could possibly kill you."

"Doctor, you're my kind of guy." The slight smile and dimples reappeared. "You lay it right on the line, don't you?"

He had never heard that particular American expression, but he understood. "I only want you to understand how serious this is. To know the truth."

She looked at her hands for a moment. They were tightly clutching her gloves. "How long will I be in the hospital if I consent to this surgery?"

"Ten to fourteen days. Following that, another thirty days to recover."

"I can't do it, Doctor. I have to leave London. My career."

"Career! My dear young lady, do you understand what I said? Career, indeed! You may not live long enough to pursue your career."

"Is it really so certain?"

"No. Certainty is not part of the equation. It could be two months, two years. Twenty years. I can't say with certainty *when* it will happen, which means, of course, that I can't say with certainty when it will *not* happen. But I can assure you with certainty that if you don't allow proper treatment, it *will* happen."

"Sorry, Doctor. I just can't consider surgery at this time."

"There is a misconception that strokes occur randomly, without warning. That isn't true. There are often warnings that can help you avert a disabling or even fatal stroke, and you have had a very clear one." He paused. "Miss Gardner, we are talking about your life."

"How I live my life is far more important to me than the number of years I live."

"You must have the surgery, or you could die. Don't you understand?"

"We all have to die, Doctor. I think it's the quality of life, not the time of death, that counts."

"I must insist you give this more thought. You must—"

She was no longer listening. If she were in the hospital, R.J. would never leave London. He would stay throughout the months of recovery. She pulled her gloves on. No, she must leave London.

Russ sat at his desk, eyes closed, pinching the bridge of his nose. He shook his head and picked up the phone. His attempts to reach Ava had been futile. He was absolutely desperate to talk to her, desperate to discuss their plans together. He had to keep trying. Now he listened to the soft double purr of her phone ringing.

"Hello." The husky silkiness of her voice caressed him.

"Hello! I thought I'd never catch you."

"I'm sorry, R.J. I've been terribly busy."

"I've been trying to reach you all day. It's been an eternity." He tried a relaxed laugh, but it came out dry and nervous.

"I do apologize. You remember the script I've been reading? A couple of big-time producers are here, and we've been negotiating a contract." She paused. "I'm sorry I didn't tell you. They wrote me a month ago, arranging these meetings. I had simply forgotten, when suddenly here they were. We've been terribly busy discussing terms for the movie."

"Do you think you'll reach an agreement?" He had no earthly idea what else to say.

"These guys are pretty hard-nosed, but I think we may have a deal. It'll take one or two more meetings, though."

"When can I see you?"

"Oh, I don't know, R.J. It's a real bitch, baby. I have to meet with them again tomorrow evening. They're coming here. I'm going to try to raise the price of poker. If they bump me back, we'll close the deal."

"How about tonight?"

"No, R.J. I don't think so."

"I need to see you. It seems forever since I saw you last."

"I'm sorry, but I really can't tonight. I've been having that dizziness again, and I have a bit of a headache tonight." She was silent for a moment, then offered, "Come by tomorrow night. The producers are going to arrive at seven-thirty for dinner. Come by about six-thirty. I'll dress early and we can talk a few minutes."

They said good-bye and he turned to look out the window. It was disquieting. A small warning bell he had been hearing for two days sent a louder signal that something was going wrong. Very wrong. She hadn't been unkind. She hadn't been unfriendly. It was just that she hadn't really been *anything*. She had only been busy.

Knock it off, he told himself. *You'll see her tomorrow night. And you don't own her.*

A light knock at his office door turned him around. "Yes?"

Miss Rutherford stood in the doorway. "Got a minute, Major?"

"Of course. Come in."

"I won't take long—"

"Take all the time you need. I'm not going anywhere tonight."

"Major, I know everything seems to have gone wrong since you've been here."

"It's had its moments." He gave her a crooked grin.

"I know. I only want you to know that I think you've done the right
thing."

"Well, thank you, Miss Rutherford."

"It's been a very long time since anyone has shaken this place up. And
these career bureaucrats needed it."

"I don't know that I have served any good purpose, Miss Rutherford.
I'm really not qualified to question anyone at this business."

"Well, I think you've been terrific." He raised an eyebrow in surprise.
"I know you've gone through all of this alone," she continued. "So if you
ever need someone to talk to, someone just to listen, let me know. I'm a
pretty good sounding board."

He nodded, realizing her desire to help him was genuine. "I will," he
promised.

"I must say, Major Jefferson, you've been more than an encouragement to the rest of us. Destroying Eads's composure by calling him a penguin was really inspiring."

"For the sake of accuracy, Miss Rutherford, let the record show that I
did not destroy the general, verbally or otherwise, and the penguin thing
wasn't even original."

She smiled. "Doesn't matter, Major. That's the stuff that legends are
made of."

The hours dragged painfully that night. The next day too seemed to go on
and on, but finally it was time to go to Ava.

He arrived at six-thirty and found preparations for her guests busily
under way. Carmen hurried here and there, checking every detail, making
certain everything would be perfect for the dinner meeting. Caviar and
other delicacies were arranged on a small table, and the bar was set up.

Wearing a long black dress, Ava appeared from the bedroom. No matter how many times he saw her, the effect during the first few moments

was always the same: he could hardly get his breath. She was a perfect vision of glamour, but more than that, she was made up of remarkable qualities; so honestly direct and with a charming simplicity. Vivacious and alive. He adored her.

"Good evening, R.J." She smiled at him.

"God, you are beautiful" was all he could say.

"Honey, cut the crap. Even when I *was* beautiful, I didn't like to be told I was. But now? I'm just another fifty-something-year-old broad."

"Don't try to shock me with that talk. It doesn't work anymore, and no matter what you say, you are gorgeous in that dress." Before she could protest again, he looked about the room and said, "It looks like everything is ready for the dinner party."

"I hope so. Honey, I'm sorry I can't ask you to stay, but this is strictly business, negotiations between the studio and my agent." She laughed. "Well, that's not quite true. I always get involved, calling the producers thieves and other obscene names you wouldn't like to hear me say."

"I'm sure you'll be a perfect lady."

"Honey, you really *do* see me through rose-colored glasses, don't you?"

"I had no idea you were seriously considering a script. You've said nothing about it."

"I suppose I forgot. They've been talking to me for months. They start filming in less than two months, shortly after the first of the year."

"Is it a good role?"

"What would I know? I choose roles for all the wrong reasons. Once, because the filming was on the Mexican coast and I was in the mood for waterskiing. Sometimes, just because I'm bored." She laughed. "No one could be worse than me at choosing parts."

"Why this one?"

"The loot, honey, the loot." She studied the hors d'oeuvres. "When I'm in need of money, I just take a deep breath, hold my nose, and jump in."

"Then you really don't want to do it?"

"It's just a job. Chuck Heston is in it, and I don't like him. It's one of these disaster films. This one is going to be an earthquake. But, unlike Jeanette MacDonald in *San Francisco,* this leading lady is *not* going to stand in the ruins and sing at the top of her goddamn lungs."

She stepped over to a small table and rearranged two dishes. He checked his watch. His precious hour was passing too quickly.

"It'll be nice in California," she said, turning back to him. "Right now, London is so depressing, so dark and dreary. This may be a winter when having hot water for a bath will be an occasional luxury."

She went to check the bar. He followed her. "I need to spend some time with you," he said. "You know that, don't you?"

"R.J., I wish we could." She examined a bottle of scotch. "But if I agree to do this film, it's going to get hectic. I'll have to fly to Hollywood right away to sign contracts, go through preproduction, promotion, a million other things."

"How long will that take? Three, four weeks?"

Her look told him that he just didn't understand all that was involved in her work. "No," she said patiently. "It will be much longer than that before things are finished."

"You'll be back for Christmas, won't you?" He had hoped to spend her birthday with her alone, on Christmas Eve.

"As I said, they start shooting right after the first of the year. I won't be back at Christmas, R.J. I'll be away several months. Half of California will have to fall apart for this shoot."

"But I must be with you. I *have* to see you."

"No, honey. That's not true. You have to think about your own life. Your career. Your future."

"You *are* my future!"

"No, R.J., I'm not," she corrected him gently. "I'm just an ex-sex symbol, a little battered and bruised from being knocked around."

"Don't talk that way."

"But it's the truth. You look at me, but you see a romantic illusion,

R.J. You see me as I once was, when you wrote to me for an autographed photo. Even though you're looking at me, you aren't seeing me."

"That isn't true."

"Oh, but I'm afraid it is. I have crow's feet at the corners of my eyes, wrinkles in my neck, and bags under my eyes. I've smoked too much, drank too much; it all shows."

She reached out to him, running her hand through his hair and ruffling it fondly. "Remember when you told me that when you were a small boy you read about foreign lands and ancient cities, dreaming about them and imagining what they looked like? You said you've seen some of them and they have been disappointments, looking nothing like you had imagined."

He nodded.

"R.J., when you see me the way I am instead of the way you have always imagined me, you will be very disappointed. I'm not Julie in *Show Boat.*"

"Please, don't—"

"I'm just a dame with headaches and dizzy spells. Now, does that sound like someone you want to spend your life with?" She paused a moment, took his hand, and said, "I think not."

He began to argue, but she didn't allow him to. "Please excuse me, R.J. I must get things ready for tonight. It's almost time for my guests."

"I *will* see you . . . talk to you tomorrow, won't I?"

"No, R.J., no." The look in her eyes was emphatic. "I've got my own life to take care of right now. We'll see each other again, someday." She smiled warmly. "And then I won't rush you off, honey. We'll have dinner together."

"Someday?"

"Yes." She smiled. "And I will offer you two things: a very good steak, medium rare, and an honest relationship—which is extremely rare."

He stepped toward her, reached to touch her face, then stopped. "I'm good for you, Ava. You drink less when we're together. I can see to it that you take care of yourself, take your medicines. I'll watch over you."

"No," she said sadly. "Please go, now." She kissed his cheek. "Good-bye, R.J."

He tried to speak but he couldn't. His mind was reeling. *Good-bye?*

"We'll see each other again, but I have my work to tend to now, and you must take care of your own future."

He stood unmoving. His temples pounded.

"Good-bye, R.J."

He stared into her soft eyes for a moment and felt blood rushing to his head. It was as though he had been stabbed in the chest. For several moments he could not speak. Words were beyond him. He could only struggle to resume normal breathing. Then he turned abruptly and left.

Quickly he stepped through the cold, light rain to the sports car, the click of his heels the only sound along the empty street.

He slid into the bucket seat and stared into the rain-glittered night. He was enveloped by an oppressive sense of isolation. Desolate, lonely isolation.

He turned the headlights on and the rain slanted across the white beams. He could no longer deny reality. He had thought she would be his happiness, but he should have known better. He would never again depend on another to bring meaning to his life.

Contentment. Satisfaction. For him, these things had only been found in the one thing he did better than anyone, and it required him to depend only on himself. Only himself. It had always been that way.

He would shut out the pain. Just as he shut out the deadly violence of ground fire and anti-aircraft fire during his dive-bombing runs . . . just as he shut out the pain and fear of torture in Hanoi, he would shut out the pain of heartbreak.

Twin pools of light flooded the street in front of the car as it pulled slowly away from Ennismore Gardens.

From her window she had looked down on the street and the sports car, watching the curl of gray smoke rising from its exhaust. It was done, as it had to be, for he had lost himself in his fantasies of her. She would miss him. He had a certain decency that was both rare and refreshing in her world, but he had a promising career, and she couldn't allow him to give up a life that would be his salvation from the haunting experiences of the war. His world, not hers, would heal his wounds.

A sadness weighed heavily in her chest. R.J. was a good person, had been there for her when she needed someone. In some ways he was one of the most desirable men—the almost boyish face, and yet such courage in a horrible war. In some fanciful way she wished they could have made love just once, but it would have complicated things beyond recovery, all because he thought he was in love with her.

When she saw the Alfa's red taillights disappear, she sighed, turned from the window, and started toward her bedroom. "Carmen, put all of this away now, or invite your friends over. Do with it as you wish." Her voice was flat. "My makeup's a mess. I've got to repair some of the damage before General Elliott gets here."

An hour later a limousine drove serenely through the night, its black body gleaming with reflected light. General Elliott sat erectly in his Air Force formal tuxedo uniform. He had long played the role of the hero escorting the most desirable women, but even Sudden Sam was overwhelmed by the presence of his companion this evening.

The actress was perfectly comfortable seated beside the general, her long black dress and fur the perfect costume for this scene. She was dressed for a performance, prepared to play a role.

There was, she decided, no need to waste time. Looking straight ahead, she said, "Thank you for escorting me to the reception tonight, General. I had almost decided not to go until I met you."

"Please call me Sam."

She continued as though she hadn't heard him. "The Bedford reception is one of the most important social affairs of the year. Are you familiar with it, General Elliott?"

"Oh, yes."

"I'm surprised. Not many Americans are. Have you attended before?"

"No. No, I haven't."

"Members of the Royal Family will be there. The Prime Minister. The most influential MPs. Of course, everyone in the highest social circles." She let the words register. "Quite a little mix, even for a Texan, isn't it, General?"

He didn't know quite what to say. "Yes, it certainly is."

This was the moment. If she continued into negotiations now, there would be no turning back. The door would be closed on any possible future with R.J. But she had decided. She turned to him. "You know, this gathering tonight could make or break a person, regardless of their standing or wealth. Regardless of title."

She would give him time to guess where she was taking this conversation, and how she knew he was from Texas. The point wasn't lost: *she knew.*

"I know many of these people personally." Her gaze made him understand that he should listen carefully. "And I know they have made many successful careers. They've destroyed many too."

He wasn't listening politely now; he was all ears.

Her words were carefully chosen. Measured. "I understand that you're a very ambitious man, General, but you've gone about as far as one can go in the United States Air Force without very important political assistance. Is that true?"

"I don't know if one can say that," he postured.

"It's *true,* isn't it, General?"

Her tone made it clear that this was an important conversation, too important for him to be playing ego games. "Yes," he said softly. "Yes, it is."

"Political assistance from leaders of the United Kingdom would be important to your career, wouldn't it? Assistance rarely awarded by very important Brits in government, the military, and finance?"

"What are you saying?"

"I'm asking if such support from the highest British levels would uniquely *distinguish* your embassy record."

"Of course it would." Her directness had unbalanced him.

"As I said, I know these people personally, General. I can get favors from them. They can bestow every important British honor this side of knighthood—the highest levels of political endorsements possible. And on rare occasions, when requested, they can provide letters commending an Air Force general." Then she asked, "Interested?"

Now he understood her purpose for being with him this evening. "Yes, I'm interested." He took a deep breath and paused a sober moment. "Of course, there will be a price to pay."

"Of course," she answered, her beautiful smile reappearing. "Are you ready to make a deal, Sam?"

Twenty-one

W hat is this?" said Russ. "An execution at dawn? The process for an Article Fifteen court-martial is pretty clear about certain things, and one is that I have the right of representation. I haven't had time to even talk to a lawyer."

Gerald Graves stood beside the desk, his own surprise and confusion apparent. "I don't understand. I've never heard of this being done before. Ever."

"An *informal hearing.*"

"May I see the memo, Russ?" Graves picked up the paper from the desk.

"That's what it says: an informal hearing. And it instructs Eads and Raymond Holt to be there."

Gerald silently read the memorandum. "This is really strange," he said curiously. "What is Elliott doing?"

Russ had planned to call General Kreeger as soon as possible, but the time difference meant he had to wait until early afternoon London time.

And now *this* had happened! General Elliott holding his own hearing before he had time to do anything! A fixed trial! He had left Ava's last night determined to get his assignment, but Elliott's memo had been delivered to him first thing this morning. He hadn't time to call General Kreeger to get his assignment . . . and he hadn't had time to get a lawyer.

Russ entered the small conference room on the second floor and paused. Centered in the room was a long polished table with leather chairs along each side, a captain's chair at the end. Two men were sitting at the table. On the wall opposite the captain's chair was a rear-projection screen flanked by American and British flags.

He closed the door behind him, and the two men looked up. General Eads's eyes met his briefly, showing scant interest, then returned to his yellow legal pad. Raymond Holt nodded and smiled weakly, uncertainly.

"Hello, Raymond," Russ said. "Haven't seen you since that night at the Graves's." He took a chair across from them, checking his watch. Time for the meeting to begin. He tried to relax. Wouldn't do to appear anxious or worried. Did he still have the ability to appear calm in the face of danger? He wasn't sure. Just then the door opened and he rose with the other two officers to stand at attention.

"Please be seated, gentlemen," said General Elliott as he approached the captain's chair. A woman carrying a stenographer's notebook followed him. She quietly took a chair two down from Russ.

Elliott adjusted to a comfortable position, his eyes moving from Russ to Eads and then to Russ again. The overhead lights reflected brightly on the two silver stars on each epaulette and the wings on his chest. He leaned back, his features set, as though he was preparing to begin an unpleasant task. Russ held the eye contact as long as he could, finally blinking and glancing at Eads, who appeared calm and confident. Holt shifted uncomfortably.

"Good morning, gentlemen," Elliott began. "I think we're ready to proceed—"

"Sir, if I can interrupt a moment—" Russ started to express his grievance about his lack of opportunity to obtain counsel.

"No, Major. You'll have your chance to speak later."

"But—"

"Major Jefferson, for now you will just answer my questions. Later you will have an opportunity to make a statement, if you wish."

Russ stopped in disbelief.

"This meeting is not an official hearing, nor is it a formal part of a disciplinary process," General Elliott said flatly. "But I've asked Captain Holt to be here to make sure we don't violate anyone's rights or step on any provision of the United States Code of Military Justice." He turned to the accused. "Major, do you know Captain Holt?"

"Yes sir, we've met." It seemed a lifetime since the Graveses' party.

"This meeting," continued General Elliott, "is being held for one purpose: to provide me with an understanding of where we are in this unfortunate situation. If I can determine that the *problem*"—he looked at Russ—"has been resolved, I will dismiss this entire matter." He paused as if weighing his words. "If, however, it turns out that nothing has been resolved and that charges are still to be filed, I will set a date and time to begin formal court-martial proceedings."

Eads nodded as though he agreed.

Elliott's voice was smooth. "Although this is an informal meeting, minutes will be kept as a record. Miss Weatherford, if you will note today's date and time, the place of this meeting, and the name of each officer in attendance, we will begin."

The woman smiled primly as she nodded to the general. Holt tugged at his shirt collar. Eads leaned back in his chair, elbows on the armrests, fingers intertwined across his chest. He waited patiently as if he already knew what the outcome of this meeting would be and was satisfied with what he knew.

General Elliott went on. "Major Jefferson, in a previous meeting, you and I discussed the charges being brought against you by General Eads.

I advised you of what the charges were, and I told you at that time the minimum legal action could be an Article Fifteen court-martial. Is that correct?"

"Yes sir, that's correct."

"I have no interest in taking legal action against an officer who, by his own choice, is resigning his commission. Especially one who has distinguished himself in combat. I understand you are considering taking such an action. Have you decided? Is it now your intention to resign your commission from the United States Air Force?"

"No, sir, it is not."

Eads looked at Russ in surprise, the grip of his interlaced fingers tightening. Elliott had told him Jefferson planned to resign. Moreover, he had been told that an important MP had said that the major was going to get out. How could the information he had gotten be so wrong?

General Elliott, concealing any reaction, nodded thoughtfully. "I see," he said. "It's certainly your prerogative. Since you aren't resigning your commission, have you requested orders reassigning you from the embassy?"

"No, but—"

"Any orders in your pipeline, Major?"

"I've not been officially notified of anything, sir." Russ thought of all the phone calls.

"You *haven't* an assignment."

"No sir, but I—"

"I would say, then, that you remain assigned to the Current Operations Directorate of this embassy under the supervision of General Eads, until you receive PCS orders assigning you somewhere else." He turned to Eads. "General, it appears that Major Jefferson is still under your charge. Do you still wish to bring formal court-martial charges against him?"

"I certainly do, sir."

"Would you reconsider? Are you willing to consider that Major Jefferson's actions were the unfortunate result of misunderstandings? Are you willing to resolve this by, let's say, a written reprimand and the major's

assurance that he will do nothing that has even the appearance of insubordination?"

"No sir, I'm not."

"Think it over, please. You would still have the opportunity to give
him an unsatisfactory officer-efficiency report if he causes any problems.
Worst case, if there are further problems, you could always resort to
court-martial action at a later time."

"General, there have been no misunderstandings," Eads insisted. "I
have given Major Jefferson legal orders, which he clearly understood. He
has made a conscious decision to disobey my orders. He did so repeatedly. This officer's violations of authority are so extreme and frequent,
there is no other choice but to court-martial him."

The room became silent. Russ felt his stomach tighten. It was going to
happen. He had never believed it possible, but the career he had worked
so hard for, that had meant so much, was going to be taken from him.
Others—not he—were going to conclude his career. An Article 15 was a
death knell. He was being held accountable for his attitude of these recent
months, months of not caring about a career. That had been someone
else, someone lost in an unreal world. That was over now. He *wanted* this
career. He *had* to fly now more than ever before. And just as he was returning to his senses from that strange, unexplainable condition he had
experienced, his career was being taken from him. He felt sick.

The Air Attaché leaned forward. "Major, do you have anything to say
in your defense?"

Throat dry, Russ managed to say, "No sir." There was no purpose in
saying anything now. This was a kangaroo court and his only hope was in
a formal appeal. He could hear the woman's pencil scribbling her shorthand, creating a record of his irrevocable confession of weakness.

General Elliott was expressionless. "I see. Then I suppose it's time to
decide if there is to be a court-martial proceeding."

Eads smiled. Russ clenched his jaws.

"Gentlemen, this has been an unfortunate occurrence. A highly decorated fighter pilot, recently released from a prisoner-of-war camp, is accused of insubordination by his commanding officer. This sort of thing can bring great harm to the Air Force's role in this embassy, can tarnish the Air Force image irreparably. Very unfortunate."

Raymond Holt looked at Russ like a bystander witnessing a lynching.

"This is a critical time in the history of the United States Air Force, gentlemen." Elliott frowned at the other men and began tapping his finger on the table. "There has never been a time when the public's perception of the Air Force has been as negative as it is today. The public's view is that the best-equipped, best-trained Air Force in the world couldn't win a war against a Third World, third-rate military foe. The leadership of the Air Force is particularly in disfavor, seen as fat cats more concerned about pleasing wealthy industrialists than developing an effective fighting force.

"And, of course, every story that reflects badly on the Air Force is given one hell of a lot of space in newspapers and one hell of a lot of time on television news." The general stopped tapping his finger, as if he had reached a conclusion. "We can't afford mistakes in high-profile matters, gentlemen, and we are dealing with a potentially very big story here. The court-martial of a war hero will be front-page headlines. Can't act on assumptions that reporters could punch holes through. Can't take disciplinary action if there are substantial uncertainties, substantial areas of gray."

Elliott straightened in his chair, lifting his chin and taking a deep breath.

"I've made my decision, gentlemen. There *appears* to have been insubordination on the part of a junior officer in this embassy. There *appears* to have been disregard of orders given by his superior officer. If it were so, court-martial charges would be appropriate. But if there has only been the *appearance* of insubordination, due to misunderstandings or bad judgment, such a damaging legal action would be a miscarriage." He turned toward Eads, his voice growing stronger. "It is my opinion that there has not been deliberate, willful disobedience in this matter. It is my opinion that misunderstandings, confusion, miscommunications, and unfortunate coincidences have resulted in a regrettable situation, which can be corrected. Gentlemen, there will be no further action in this matter." He rose from his chair and left the room.

Eads sunk into his chair, his face frozen in disbelief and dismay. Holt's mouth fell open in astonishment. The secretary scribbled her shorthand.

No one understood.

Word spread quickly. The certainty of General Elliott and General Eads successfully pursuing an Article 15 against Major Jefferson had been accepted by everyone; there were no doubters. Now no one could believe the news. Elliott had dismissed the charges in a pre-hearing! No one understood.

The first thing Russ did after the meeting was call Washington. General Kreeger still wasn't in. He would be in the office 0900 Washington time. Russ would have to wait.

By that afternoon Russ had made his request. General Kreeger had approved it. Two o'clock London time, nine o'clock Pentagon time. Things were being taken care of.

Yes, General Kreeger had said, the flight-test assignment at Holloman was his if he wanted it. The general would cut through all the red tape. Orders would be at the London embassy by Monday.

At this very moment General Kreeger was telling his executive officer to authorize orders assigning Major Russell T. Jefferson to the Weapons Test Center. Long-distance lines would be humming soon as the Pentagon directed the Military Personnel Center at Randolph Air Force Base to prepare the orders. The personnel center would wire them to London. Any hesitation along any step of the process would be immediately ended by the knowledge that a four-star general was the authorizing official.

What normally took weeks would be done in three days. But four-star generals could do that.

Twenty-two

I 've worked in this embassy fifteen years, and I've never seen any-thing like it," said Joanna Thompson as she peered at her friends over her coffee cup. "Never."

"What happened?" Irene looked first at Joanna and then at Vivian. "Everyone knew that Elliott and Eads were going to court-martial Major Jefferson. It was all planned. Eads was in the driver's seat. So, what hap-pened?"

They were at the corner table in the third-floor coffee shop. The three secretaries couldn't wait to get together this morning, to combine what each had been able to find out. Everything following the Air Attaché's meeting the week before was confusing. Everything was contradicted. Now, at their Monday morning coffee break, they were putting the pieces together after a weekend filled with rumors.

Irene lit her cigarette, clicked off her lighter, and blew a plume of smoke toward the ceiling. "I saw the minutes of the meeting. After a few minutes of discussion, General Elliott simply declared there was no basis for an Article Fifteen court-martial. It appeared to be simply an arbitrary decision by the Air Attaché not to bring charges against Major Jefferson."

"But Eads had put together an unbelievable file to hang the major with," Joanna hurried to say. "He stacked the facts the way he wanted, but he built one hell of a case."

"He can take it with him," said Irene, giggling.

"I heard about that late Thursday," said Vivian. "But I had no idea about General Eads. God, that was the blockbuster."

"The next day was when it happened," Joanna said. "Elliott sent Eads a notice of reassignment late Friday, without so much as a courtesy call. It arrived just before close of business."

"Is it true?" asked Irene. "Is Eads being sent someplace in Utah?"

"Yes," said Joanna. "He's being assigned to some insignificant job at Ogden Air Force Base. It hit our office like a bomb."

"The Logistics Command," said Irene, tapping ashes from her cigarette. "My God, that's latrine duty. He's being screwed over."

"Eads . . . fired. It couldn't possibly happen to a more deserving person." Joanna looked at the others wonderingly. "God, I thought I'd never see the day. I feel so liberated."

"And Jefferson?" Irene looked to Vivian. "I heard he's getting some kind of terrific assignment. Is that true, Viv?"

Vivian nodded. "Orders came by Teletype. The personnel office is processing them right now."

"Where's he going, Viv? Is it really something special?"

"Apparently. It's a high-level test program at Holloman Air Force Base."

"Cool," said Irene.

"Fifteen years in this place and I never saw anything like it," mused Joanna Thompson. "Irene, give me a cigarette."

Cleaning out his desk was a quick and simple task, as there wasn't enough in it to fill his briefcase. Two and a half months, he thought. Not long enough to accumulate much stuff.

"May I come in, Major?" Vivian stuck her head through the doorway, her hair gleaming in the brightness of the fluorescent lights.

"Of course, Miss Rutherford." With a smile he stood and gestured to a chair.

She sat down, crossed her legs, and looked at him for a moment before speaking. "I see you're almost ready."

"Not much to do, actually. I'll come in tomorrow, pick up my records, and sign out."

Her hesitant smile betrayed both admiration and regret. "So, it's off to bigger and better things."

"Who knows? I only know it will be different." He shrugged. "I may be begging you to take me back in two months."

"I doubt that." Her eyes were warm, her smile wide. "But if you do, I just may take you back, Major."

"I need you to do something for me. Would you forward my personal mail to this address?" He handed her a sheet of paper. "I've done the change-of-address thing, but I'm sure some of it will slip through the cracks."

"Major, I must admit I hate to see you leave."

"You've been my best ally," he said. "Thanks for everything."

"This may be the last time I have a chance to say this, so I'll say it now. You were right, you know. You were right to do what you did. It was courageous, and you earned the respect of everyone in this old building."

"I haven't done anything to make a big deal about."

"The secretaries in this organization see it differently. An informal poll at the coffee shop made you our man of the year. It was unanimous."

"I'm honored," he said, smiling.

"Have you heard about General Eads?"

"No. What about him?"

"Before all the dust settled last week, he received unexpected orders at the last minute Friday. To some administrative job at Ogden Air Force Base, Utah. Logistics Command." She smiled. "That's about as obscure as it gets."

"Unexpected orders? You mean like—"

"Like swift and sudden punishment, Major."

"General Eads fired? Exiled? How did that happen?"

"Very mysteriously." She stood and looked at him a moment. "I'll say good-bye tomorrow."

He watched as she left, then he sat down again behind the desk. It defied reason. Charges against him dropped. Eads exiled! Banished! He shook his head, picked up the telephone, and dialed the number again. He listened to Ava's phone ring eight times. Nine. Ten. He lowered the receiver to its base. Where in the hell was she?

He closed the briefcase and pulled on his coat. Only a few people that he wanted to see before he left. He would see Gerald Graves and Admiral Fleming tomorrow and say good-bye then. And Ted. It would be easier to keep visits short tomorrow.

As he buttoned his uniform coat, he thought about Ava. He had called her time and time again. He had gone to her flat each day, sometimes twice and three times, and there was never an answer. Thursday, Friday, and Saturday, the doorman Roberts would only say that she was away a great deal and, yes, he would tell Miss Gardner that the gentleman had called. Yesterday Roberts had not even been there. No one. No messages.

The telephone buzzed. The flashing light told him it was an intercom call. He fastened the last button and answered.

"Hello, Major." It was Ted Sanders. "Got a minute?"

"As a matter of fact, I was just leaving. But I can stop by your office on the way out."

"Great. I'll have coffee poured."

Russ took the elevator to the basement, still thinking of Ava. He had last seen her Tuesday night, six days ago. Had she left for Hollywood over the weekend? He entered the door at the end of the hallway and walked into the open-bay offices of the Air Attaché's staff.

"How's it going, Major?" Sanders stood waiting for him.

"Okay, Ted. Everything's okay."

"I hear you're getting out of Dodge. Going to test advanced toys at Holloman. That's some pretty cosmic stuff they're doing."

"So they say." Russ sat in the offered chair. As Sanders had promised, a steaming cup of coffee was there for him. "Smart bombs. They're making them smarter than the pilots."

"That's not hard to do," Sanders said with a smile. "Badly needed technology. Better than having to drop them at the target doorstep." He returned to his chair. "I spoke to Palmer today, and he said the British Defense Ministry is expediting its review of the proposals for the F-111 training routes and ranges. He said there would be no problem getting them approved."

"Quick work. They got the package only a few days ago."

"Palmer said he was afraid that if he didn't get it done quickly, he might be sent to some godforsaken place like Ogden, Utah."

Russ laughed, visualizing the gregarious RAF officer, but also wondering how Palmer had heard about the Eads matter. "Good man," he said.

"Yep. I've also notified the guys at Upper Heyford. They went bananas. The fighter wing is finally going to have the opportunity to train properly. Major, you did one hell of a job getting it approved for them."

"Couldn't have done it without you. I just hope you didn't get your tail feathers singed by the fireworks."

"I'm fine. No sweat."

"Well, keep your head down for a while. There could still be some collateral damage coming out of this."

A smile crinkled the captain's face. "Word got around fast about Eads."

Russ looked evenly at Sanders as he took a sip of coffee.

"Yep, amazing." Sanders shook his head slowly. "The word spread to USAFE, Tactical Air Command Headquarters, and the Pentagon very quickly. Lotsa interest in Eads's handling of the F-111 training problems." He paused briefly. "And what he was doing to you."

"It couldn't have been spread by a young navigator captain in an embassy and a lieutenant colonel in Spain, could it?" Russ gave him an accusing look.

Sanders shrugged. "General Elliott was the surprise! No one could believe what Sudden Sam did. No one ever dreamed that he, of all people, would pull such a reversal. He did a real hatchet job on Eads!" Still Russ sat quietly. "Elliott sure as hell found the dead end of all dead end assignments, didn't he? A pencil-pushing job keeping inventory of logistics items in Ogden, Utah." He nodded slowly. "Sure does satisfy my sense of poetic justice."

"Justice takes strange turns sometimes."

"Seldom as strange as this. Everyone's asking what in the hell turned Elliott around?" Sanders immediately corrected himself. "No, it wasn't *what* turned him around, 'cause we know it had nothing to do with the facts of the case. He'd court-martial his own brother to keep his paperwork neat. Nope, the question is, *who* turned him around?"

"I have no idea." And he didn't. General Kreeger had admitted he couldn't.

"Well, somebody flat-out got his attention. Somebody who knew exactly how to deal with the mighty Air Attaché."

"We'll probably never know," said Russ as he stood. "Thanks for the coffee, Ted. I've gotta go."

Ted stuck out his hand. "Major, it's been one hell of a pleasure working with you."

Russ took the elevator to the first floor and followed the wide hallway to the front of the building. He put his cap on, pulled on his raincoat, then he stepped out into the gray day.

Crossing the damp marble surface to the steps, he was turning up the collar of his raincoat when he saw Eads coming up. At the top step, Eads's eyes met Russ's. Frozen in midstride, he paused for a moment. His hardened eyes revealed fury.

Sensing that he should say something to the general, Russ hesitated, then pushed the feeling aside. He stepped past the thin man, looking straight ahead. Courtesies weren't important now, but neither did he want to further disparage the man. Some of the things Eads had said to him had been convincing and had given him a new perspective on matters in Europe and the Middle East. Something to think about. But not now. He hurried down the wide steps and to his car.

There would be no further discussion. Everything that needed saying had been said.

Five minutes later Russ steered the Alfa out of the embassy garage. Buses and taxis crowded every intersection, even from minor side streets, and traffic was further complicated by pedestrians, for the rain had stopped. His impatience mounted as he made his way through the streets, and then he was finally turning onto Ennismore Gardens. He parked in front of her steps and hurried to the door.

The building was closed and silent. Russ used the door knocker and waited. There was no response, not even Roberts was there. He waited and knocked again. Still nothing.

He stepped back out onto the sidewalk and looked up at the windows of her second-story flat. Where was she? There was only one possible answer. She was in Los Angeles and she had avoided his calls and had avoided seeing him before leaving. He returned to the door and rapped the brass knocker again. He knew it was no use, but he knocked once more, and then turned and walked slowly to his car.

Time for reality. She was gone. It was over.

Now they would go their separate ways. He would return to his world of tactical fighters, reentering through several weeks of recurrency training in the F-4. Could he regain his former skills? Could he be aggressive again, pushing to the edge of the envelope, taking his fighter to its limits?

Of the many questions tumbling in his mind, only one could not be pushed away. Only one carried the burden of sorrow and heartache. Where was she?

Twenty-three

Los Angeles International Airport was crowded. Streams of travelers with luggage stood and watched, curious to see why the large group of newsmen and photographers had amassed in a small area near gate 38's double doorway.

As flight 208's arrival from London was announced, the newsmen watched two well-dressed men they recognized as studio executives walk through the gate and toward the plane. Then the execs reappeared, but not alone.

Ava Gardner, her smile wide and dazzling, walked with them toward the assembly of reporters. She was bathed in white as the television light bars and cameras came alive. The newsmen watched her approach with an eagerness and excitement they seldom showed. More travelers stopped to see.

The news of Ava's arrival had gotten out because the studio execs wanted it out. They couldn't arrange her meeting with the media soon enough. In their view there was never too much publicity for a project, and when they had an opportunity they used it for all it was worth. Movies, even big-budget movies, weren't doing well, and they needed publicity. Cameras and microphones were ready. Even now Ava Gardner could attract the media like only Elizabeth Taylor and one or two others could.

One of the execs stepped to the small podium and the bank of microphones. He told the reporters of the studio's great pride in having one of its greatest stars return to make an important film. It would be one of their most anticipated releases in years, he told them. Ava watched, smiling. The exec finished his remarks and checked his watch. Plenty of time for the six o'clock news. He extended his hand toward the actress, inviting her to the microphones. He kissed her cheek and stepped aside.

The reporters began.

"How does it feel to be back in the United States, Ava?" asked the KABC reporter.

"Wonderful, as always."

"What do you enjoy most about being back?"

"Why, honey, stopping to talk with you boys after being on an airplane ten hours." She smiled and winked at the questioner.

"Still have a chip on your shoulder toward Hollywood, Ava?" He was one of the older ones. Channel 5.

"Hi, Mac. Now, you know I never did. I love Hollywood."

"Are you excited about making this film, Ava?" he asked.

"Of course. It's going to be a wonderful film. And what girl wouldn't be thrilled to work with Charlton Heston?"

"Is it true that you demanded twice what the studio first offered? Are they paying you twice what they wanted to?" It was a loaded question asked by a fat, sweating man with an unpleasant voice, a loose tie, and soiled collar.

"Maybe you should ask them." Her smile remained, but not as wide.

"Is it true that you demanded that this film be made in England?" the same reporter asked.

"Seen an earthquake in London recently?" She gazed levelly at him.

"Do you have other films planned after this one, Ava?" This reporter's tone was friendly.

"Hello, Charlie. You still working?" Her smile was wide again. "Honey, you know me better than that."

"Will you visit your family in North Carolina while you're here?"

"I sure hope so. I'm dying for some grits."

"Dan Robbins, *Valley News,* Miss Gardner. Do you still enjoy bull-fights?" The young reporter was standing near the rear of the group.

"No, nor bullfighters," she said playfully.

"You gonna see Frank?" It was the sweating fat man with the unpleasant voice again.

"I don't know. He's a dear man. I'd love to see him."

"How's your health, Ava? BBC reported you were recently hospitalized."

"I'm fine, Charlie. I just had a bit of flu."

"Is it true that this trip interrupted a romantic interlude, Miss Gardner?" Dan Robbins asked politely.

"No. No romance, Dan."

"There were rumors that a real romance was blooming between you and an American Air Force officer."

"Really? Well, you know how rumors are."

"There were photographs of you."

"There was no romance."

"You were just friends?"

"Just friends. But that's quite a lot, don't you think, Dan?"

The older reporter spoke again. "It's good to see you here again, Ava. We've missed you. Welcome back."

"Thank you, Mac. We all have to return to where we belong, sooner or later, don't we?"

Twenty-four

Time had not begun to heal Russ. His return to the United States had not begun to ease his loneliness for her. He longed for her touch, the scent of her perfume. Her smile. Her voice.

He had watched on the BBC the press conference of her arrival in L.A. He had seen television interviews. Her return to Hollywood was an event. The reporters couldn't get enough of her. He followed accounts of the filming of her movie, and he couldn't have felt more distant from her.

Before reporting to his new assignment with the test center at Holloman Air Force Base, he would have to learn to fly the F-4 fighter jet again with the F-4 training squadron at Luke Air Force Base, near Phoenix. Now the soft greenery and gentle rains of England were far away. The embassy's hushed corridors and offices were no longer a part of his life. His world now was the dry, cracked desert, and he struggled to put the memories of London away, out of his mind, and to reenter the violent world of tactical fighter combat.

After two years, he was in the cockpit again.

His skills had become dull, his instincts slow; response time sluggish; his situational awareness was nonexistent. The F-4 training squadron at Luke was his gateway back to flying fighters, his place to regain old skills, and now he worked at recovering his abilities in the high, clear skies above the brown, baked terrain.

Step by step he was returning to his world, but it was more difficult than he had expected. Air combat. Dogfights. High-G maneuvers against other maneuvering F-4s, taking them into close and dangerous encounters. Slashing at one another at blinding speeds. Turning as tightly as possible to gain an advantage, riding the brink of blacking out. Taking his fighter to its limits, to the edge of the envelope. It was like learning to win a knife fight in a telephone booth.

It was, he knew, more than regaining a lost skill. It was healing. Growing strong and whole again.

"Perfect day for flying," said Walter McDonald as he entered the squadron's personal-equipment room.

Russ looked up as he zipped on his G suit. "Yeah, it is."

"Always good flying weather this time of year in Arizona," McDonald said. "Late February. Early March. Another month or so and we'll be having those scorchers." The squadron exec officer was on cheerful terms with the world. He was qualified in the F-4, but his primary duty was making sure the squadron's paperwork got done.

"Hopefully, it won't take that long for me to get checked out," Russ mumbled.

"I wanted to catch you before your flight. Wanted to give you this. Thought it might be important. It's postmarked L.A." McDonald handed him a large manila envelope. "Mighty pretty handwriting."

Russ looked at it and saw the L.A. postmark. He shook his head. "I've got to go out to my airplane in just a sec, Walter. Leave this for me at the duty desk, would you?" He handed the envelope back.

After finishing the final adjustments of the G suit, he picked up his flight helmet and gave his oxygen mask a quick check: 100 percent oxygen. Pressure breathing and no leaks; it was okay. He had to concentrate on this flight. He couldn't think about anything else right now. Not the envelope. Not anything.

Today's flight would be the toughest yet, and he would have to nail it if he was going to succeed in this checkout program. And success was too damned important to allow anything to keep him from it.

He picked up his gear and started out to the airplane.

The two F-4s slashed across the pewter-gray desert skies, leaving behind a booming echo of thunder. Russ looked hard through the fighter's windscreen, searching. They were out there somewhere—just beyond visual detection were two other F-4s hunting for him. The enemy. He blinked sweat from his eyes.

A calm voice from ahead crackled through the UHF radios. "Waco Flight, this is Austin Flight. Fight's on. Fight's on."

Russ acknowledged, trying to sound equally calm. "Roger, Austin Flight. Waco copies. Fight's on." He tried to sound confident, but he felt as if he was going to lose his breakfast. "Fight's on," he repeated.

Russ slowly took off his G suit and draped it on the hook in his locker, then pulled the silver chain over his head and hung his identification tags over the same hook.

He slouched on the bench in front of the lockers. He was exhausted. Five engagements. Each one had wrung him out a little more than the previous one; now he felt totally wiped. He had forgotten how tiring these missions were. He used to . . . well, that was *then.* He was badly out of shape after two years. He looked around self-consciously, hoping no one had seen him slumped on the bench. He straightened and took a deep breath. God, he was zapped.

He made his way to the washroom, pushed his sleeves up, and turned on the cold water. Splashes of water on his face helped.

Walter McDonald entered; seeing Russ, he paused and said, "I hear you did real good up there today. Glad things are going well for you."

"Thanks, Walter." Russ dried his face and hands with a paper towel.

"Gotta go debrief. See you later."

"Sure. See ya." Just before Russ reached the door, Walter called, "Oh, by the way, I left that mail at the duty desk for you."

"Thanks."

Four F-4 Phantoms had been in the fight. Eight men. Now they gathered with Russ in the briefing room. Maps, briefing aids depicting cockpit layouts, weapons, bombing ranges, and lineup cards covered the walls of the small room. The eight men were the pilots and weapons-systems officers of Austin and Waco Flights. Don Burnett had flown as Russ's wingman, and he was the primary instructor pilot for the mission. Russ's backseater had been Tom Moore.

Burnett stood at a blackboard, diagramming each individual attack in the order they had been set up. During the next half hour each attack was reconstructed and Burnett described the flow of details. Hands and F-4 models were used to illustrate the relationships of the four fighters throughout the dynamics of air-combat maneuvers. The other pilots described their viewpoints. Pieces of puzzles. A matrix of decisions. A dynamic sequence of moves and countermoves.

The others were helping him find himself. They were giving him the benefit of their experience, skill, and attitude. They knew how important this was to a MiG killer. They were helping him recover. Helping him heal.

"A damn fine ride overall, Russ," Burnett summarized.

Moore patted him on the back. "Enjoyed flying with you, Major. I'm looking forward to the next one."

Then it was over. He thanked the men and left the briefing room. He felt better about his progress now; some of the barnacles were coming off. Maybe, just maybe, he thought, he was going to hack the program. Tonight he would celebrate. Go into Phoenix to a good steak house. But first he wanted to see what had come in the mail.

He went by the distribution boxes and picked up the manila envelope. He looked at it thoughtfully, tapped it against an open palm, then walked slowly to the coffee bar.

A lone enlisted man was cleaning the area. The day missions were over and the pilots scheduled for the night flights were at their briefings. The airman finished wiping off the coffee bar, nodded to him, and left. Russ removed his mug decorated with the squadron insignia from the ornate board behind the bar, poured a cup of old, strong coffee, and settled into one of the deep lounge chairs.

He took a deep breath and looked at the envelope for a long moment. He wasn't sure he was ready to read a letter from Ava. God, the hurt had been bad those first weeks when he had been unable to think about anything but her. But he knew he had to read it. He opened the envelope carefully, slowly removing the small sheet of green stationery.

There you are, back in your gallant fighter squadron. There are many dragons remaining to be slain on your great crusade and so many damsels in distress, just waiting for you to rescue them.

I do admire you, R.J.

An incredible sense of her presence overcame him. These weren't words on paper. They were her words, spoken to him. He could hear her. Her soft voice, like a husky whisper, was at his ear.

I know everything is going well for you. You are back where you belong, where you are meant to be.

As for me, well, I'm probably where I belong also. This is such an inexcusably bad movie that it's probably just right for me. Two more months of shooting this godawful thing and then I will return to my little flat in Ennismore Gardens.

The very words made him want to be there more than anywhere else in the world. London. Her flat. He reread the words, just to hear her voice again. To be with her. But it would never be. She had seen to that.

And now for the real purpose of this letter. Thank you so much for the birthday present. Although I'm only an uneducated country girl, I do so love poetry and the book has the most beautiful poems, some reminding me of you, my very good friend.

The surprise was, of course, that you knew my birthday was on Christmas Eve. That was so wonderful of you.

He thought of November, only three months ago, when he had planned her birthday. He had imagined a special day for that London Christmas Eve, the two of them enjoying all the city had to offer, all the traditional things belonging to Christmas in London. He had been determined to give her the best birthday she had ever known.

I have enclosed something for you. But first, a confession. The black-and-white autographed photos sent out by the studio in 1952 weren't actually signed by me. I know you have never imagined such a piece of fakery would come from Hollywood. You will find this time—unlike that previous bit of deception—the picture is signed by my own hand.

Take good care of yourself and fly your fighters safely.

He removed the photograph from the envelope, a large color print of her. It wasn't from her MGM days. It was recent. On its wide, white border, she had signed:

To Russell Thomas Jefferson
My most precious chum, my R.J.
Love, Ava

He was held hostage by her image. Just holding her letter, the sight of her written words and her photograph, stabbed him with a surge of desire and regret. He closed his eyes to the sensations, then looked again at the photograph. She was in Los Angeles, only a five- or six-hour drive. She was so near and he wanted to go to her. But he knew how impossible that was, how impossible she had made it.

It had been his dream, not hers.

He smiled grimly and very carefully replaced the picture and the letter in the envelope.

He wanted to get away, off to himself. The Alfa waited outside, its tonneau cover in place, protecting the cockpit from blowing dirt and sand. He removed the cover, got in, and started the engine. He slowly idled across the base, past the security guards at the main gates. He braked to a stop at the intersection of the base exit and the highway.

Which way to go? He sat at the stop sign for a moment more, then suddenly jammed his foot on the accelerator. The engine screamed and tires squealed as he abruptly turned right, to the west and away from Phoenix. He accelerated rapidly, executing racing changes through the gears, toward the desert.

Soon he was driving fast along the straight black ribbon, dry desert air whipping his hair. The sun was disappearing, the bright orange and yellow blaze across the western sky changing rapidly to a subdued pink and purple, the desert changing to a blur of mauve shadows. Soon it would be night, and cold. His expression was intense as he fought the sense of being out of place, the vague sense of being cheated. Of loss. His thoughts of her were painful and pointless; the desire to turn his car toward Los Angeles was overwhelming.

He turned from the highway onto a state road, following it into a low mountain range landscaped with giant saguaros. The road twisted and undulated from the desert floor as it climbed up into the mountains, treacherous and narrow with nothing but desert sand at its edge. He used all of the road, speeding toward the sharp turns, swinging widely as he touched his brakes, and gearing down just before clipping the apex of each turn, then accelerating dangerously out of the turns to unforgiving speeds. But not even the cold night air of the mountains and the adrenaline rush of danger could drive away her haunting image.

Days passed, then weeks. Training flights became more demanding, but former skills returned, decisions became instinctive again, and Russ was once again proficient in the complex environment of aerial dogfights. He was once again one of the best. He had recovered. He had healed.

"Damn fine mission, Major." Tom Moore lifted his coffee mug toward Russ in a salute. "They tried every dirty trick in their book, and you still hosed 'em. You're a damned good stick."

"High praise," said Don Burnett. "It's a rarity for Moore to compliment a frontseater. But he's right. This was your last flight with us, and it was classic textbook."

Russ rubbed his face, trying to erase the lines left by the oxygen mask. His hair was sweaty and matted; dark perspiration stains marked his flight suit. It had been a wringing flight, but he felt terrific. "Thanks, both of you. I appreciate it."

Moore unzipped the legs of his G suit and grinned. "We knew you'd make it, Major. You just had a little rust to get rid of."

"One hell of a lot of rust. I appreciate your patience."

"Our pleasure, Russ." Burnett's voice was flat now, his expression serious. "Wish all of the others had made it out of the Hanoi Hilton. Gotten back in the air."

There was a brief silence. No need to speak their thoughts. Each man knew.

Moore finished removing his G suit and slung it over his shoulder. "Congratulations again, Major. I've gotta go to a safety briefing. See you guys later."

"Good man," said Russ, watching Moore disappear through the doorway.

"The best. If they need a super backseater at the Weapons Test Center—"

Suddenly Walter McDonald stuck his head through the door and said, "There's a phone call for you, Russ. General Kreeger on line two."

Russ hurried to the duty officer's desk, picked up the telephone, and punched the blinking second button. "Good afternoon, General."

"Hello, Russ. I understand that you finished the course this morning, and I'm told you did all right."

"I won a few fights."

"I need to see you."

"Well, of course, sir." He hesitated, confused. "How? Where are you, sir?"

"Here at Luke. One-day conference. Right now I'm at base ops. We'll be taking off shortly for Washington. Can you hurry on down?"

"Yes, sir. I'll be there in ten minutes."

The Alfa growled solidly as he drove slowly to the other end of the flight line. It would be good to see the general. It had been more than a year since they had spoken other than by telephone.

The low, sprawling building next to the control tower was ahead. He parked and pushed the seat back forward to protect the seat from the sun. Within moments he was in base ops and the duty officer directed him to the small office where the general waited.

Their greeting was brief. "Doesn't look like you're traveling by fighter," Russ mused, referring to Kreeger's class-A uniform.

"Nope. Traveling in comfort and style." Kreeger clamped a short cigar in the corner of his mouth. "First-class accommodations on a scat-back Lear jet."

"Nice way to motor."

"Sorry to get you down here in such a hurry, Russ, but we have some bad weather coming in back east and we need to get ahead of it. When you're here in Arizona you forget that the rest of the world has bad weather to cope with."

"It's been perfect. Didn't lose a single flight day during my entire course."

"I'm glad you took the Holloman assignment. It's vitally important that we have proper flight tests of the smart bombs. Need our best people."

"I'm looking forward to it, sir."

"Now I have a favor to ask of you."

"Calling in your IOUs, General?" He smiled. "If so, I may have to cover my chits in installments."

"Just a small favor. But an important one. Important to the United States Air Force."

Russ's smile vanished. The general didn't use phrases like that lightly.

"Things have changed over the last few years with our people. The attitude of our young people. And it isn't good. Our young officers are the most obvious examples of this change, but it extends beyond them. We're a very dispirited fighting force, Russ."

"Sir?" He was surprised to hear such words from this man.

"You haven't been around our fighter wings and squadrons for a while, and you wouldn't have seen it with the old pros you've been working with here. But the young guys coming in aren't taken by the idea of being fighter jocks. Not like you and your peers have always been. They aren't pumped full of panther piss and JP-4 anymore. They're lukewarm about all of it, just as soon be flying for TWA or American, playing grab-ass with the stews and making big bucks." He tapped the cigar ash into a tray. "Even the guys who came in and got their combat tour during the last couple of years of the war aren't filled with the patriotic reasons for wearing G suits and flying fast jets. Their attitude's different. Today they're skeptical, cynical. The war did a number on our young people, and it's showing up in our new fighting men."

Russ waited for the general to continue.

"So, we're trying to do something about it. Don't know what all should be done, but we're starting with basics. We're making our leadership courses in pilot and navigator training a little more motivational. Turning up the focus on tradition. At best, it'll take time to overcome the nightmare of the last few years."

"We have good men at the wing and squadron command level. They can turn it around, sir."

"Yeah. And that's what I need to talk to you about."

A lieutenant stuck his head in the room. "Sorry to interrupt, General," he said. "But we'll be starting engines in about ten minutes."

Kreeger looked at his watch. "Let me get to the point. We need certain men to generate this renewed dedication, Russ. You and men like you."

"Well, of course, sir, but what can I do?"

"Whether you realize it or not, those of you who shot down MiGs, who came out of the POW experience and still wear wings and fly fighter jets, are the only ones these young men will listen to. And I need you to talk to them."

"Sir, I'm not—"

"Yes, you are." Kreeger relit his cigar. "You, Steve Richie, Chuck DeBellevue, Rick Fowler, and some of the other young lions are going to have to do this. Senior officers—Chappie James and Robin Olds—will do their part, but it's you younger guys that the new pilots and WSOs must hear."

Russ gave Kreeger a thoughtful look, then said, "General, are you interested in a quid pro quo?"

"A what?"

"A deal. I'll do something for you and you do something for me."

Kreeger drew on the cigar and peered at Russ through the smoke. He liked what he heard, an outrageous demand by a cocky young fighter pilot, and now it sounded like the old Russ Jefferson. "What's on the table, Major?" he asked gruffly. "I may be willing to bargain."

"Sir, it's General Eads. General William Eads."

"The one in London? At the embassy?"

"Yes sir. He got a raw deal, General. He had every reason in the world to hammer me, to bring me up on Article Fifteen charges. Dumping him in a dead-end job at Ogden was a bum deal. He deserves better."

"So, the quid pro quo is that if I am to get you to speak to groups of young officers, I have to find something better for this Eads character."

"Yes sir. That's about it."

He was pleased with the younger man's manipulation, but he didn't allow it to show. "Hmm, okay. You've got it."

"Thanks, General. And someone should listen to what Eads has to say about the balance of power in NATO, as well as his views on the Middle East. He has some opinions worth listening to."

"Okay, you've got your deal. Now, you've got a couple of weeks to get squared away at Holloman. I need you to go to the Air University."

"Now?"

"Within three or four weeks. There's a Squadron Officer School class in its last phase. I want you to talk to them."

"Yes sir."

"This is important, Russ. I'll try not to take you away from your flight-test duties any more than necessary, but we must get these kids' spirits rekindled, their blood stirred . . ."

Jefferson remembered Scott Mitchell using those same words that day at the Columbia Club in London.

Twenty-five

F ive hundred uniformed men rose to their feet clapping as Russ concluded his speech.

He stood at the podium, near the front center of the large stage, under bright lights. The audience's response surprised him and, in a way, embarrassed him. He frowned slightly, taken aback by the loud, unending applause.

The moderator, a faculty member of the Air University, appeared from offstage and stood beside Russ, gesturing the audience to take their seats again. "Gentlemen, we will have a few minutes for questions. There will be a microphone on each side of the auditorium. Be brief, and Major Jefferson will try to get to each of you."

As the microphones were being put in place, Russ looked out over the audience. He felt uncertain, unprepared for this. Five years earlier he had sat in this same auditorium, eager to question guest speakers, to challenge their views. So long ago. If that younger Russ Jefferson saw him now, would he recognize himself?

At the microphone on the left now was a tall man with golden hair. The first question. "Major Jefferson, what do you think our next war will be like?" he asked, and then his cynicism surfaced. "Will future wars be like Korea and Vietnam? Wars that can't be won?"

Russ took a half-step forward. "I don't know." He paused. "In World War II airpower was unleashed without limits, to strike and destroy strategic targets. Very different from the wars that followed; limited wars that have been politically controlled. Future wars may be even more limited. Influenced even more by political factors. We may be deployed to hot spots in the Middle East, Asia, Europe. We may be continually shuffled from one to another, and required to operate under the worst possible conditions."

He thought of what Eads had said to him in the embassy. "Historically, we have become allies with other nations through treaties and regional organizations such as SEATO and NATO. We knew who our allies were. But future wars may bring an uncertainty when it comes to allies. Some may not be willing to make the sacrifices required for democracy and liberty. They may not even allow us to overfly their country as we strike against our common foe. International politics of oil and economics may change alliances in unexpected ways." He shrugged. "I don't know."

A young officer spoke into the other microphone. "Major, what if we don't believe in the war we're asked to fight? What if we have zero trust in our president and commander-in-chief?"

It was the same question that had tortured him for more than two years. The breach of trust. Why had politicians sent him to bomb Hanoi when they had already lost the war? He couldn't answer. He wasn't the right person to answer this question. Then he heard her. The voice he had first heard from the screen. Ava spoke to him, her voice warm and soft, and real. *You are back where you belong, where you are meant to be. . . .* She was guiding him. After a moment's hesitation, the words came to him. Confident, certain words.

"Those of us who wear this uniform may not always agree with the politicians or their strategies for our wars, and we may not always understand the political objectives." He gazed directly into the young officer's eyes. "There may be times when we even disagree with each other about strategic decisions and tactics. But we *do* understand our mission. We *always* understand our mission. It's a simple one: to fly and fight."

Light applause rippled across the crowd. "If you can't morally carry out the president's orders," he continued, "get out of the uniform. If you simply want to fly planes, then you should work for an airline company or join a flying club." His words were flat, rapid. "But if you're among those who choose to wear this uniform, these silver wings, there's no place for frauds. If you fly the fighters, you must be prepared to make personal sacrifices. Our way of life requires that commitment. This isn't a job or a profession. It's a way of life."

The officer asked another question, a natural follow-up. "Major, what enables you personally to make that commitment?"

An important question. There was but one answer to it. "The men who preceded us. The men who flew Spads in France. P-47s in the Pacific. F-86s over the Yalu." His eyes swept over the audience. "And most certainly the guys who flew their F-105s into Hanoi. They enable me to make that commitment. They are always in that cockpit with you. Some are famous, with names such as Eddie Rickenbacker, Hap Arnold. Some are not so famous, with names such as Noonan. They have made their personal sacrifices, and they're with you. Always."

The audience was standing again, applauding louder than before. He saw it now. It was visible. The young officers stood straighter, their eyes bright with purpose, proudly holding their heads high.

As the applause continued, he could hear her voice again. *You are where you are meant to be . . . my Sir Lancelot . . . slaying dragons . . . doing what you are meant to do . . . where you belong.*

He left the stage.

Epilogue

General Russell Jefferson looked out the large window at the lengthening shadows of the winter afternoon. The soft glare from the window highlighted the gray at his temples. Deep lines creased his forehead and crinkled at the corner of his right eye, the result of years squinting at the sun through fighter canopies. The scars at his left eye kept other lines from forming there.

It would be dark within an hour.

Mrs. Emory entered his office. "If you're through with these, sir, I'll put them away," she said, nodding toward the files in front of him. "Is there anything else before I leave, General?"

"No, I'll go through the rest of these tonight." The Commander of the Air Force Fighter Weapons Center was behind on his paperwork because he had flown an F-15 mission today.

Mrs. Emory returned to her outer office and he could hear her closing and locking drawers. She was putting on her coat when the telephone rang. A moment later she came to his door and said, "Telephone, General. England."

He picked up the phone, curious who could be calling from England. "General Jefferson speaking."

"This is Sydney Hooker, General Jefferson. Do you remember me?"

"Sydney! Of course! It's been years. How are you?"

"Not so good, old man. I'm sorry to call you under these circumstances."

"What is it, Sydney?"

"Very bad news, my boy." He paused briefly. "Ava died today."

Russ was silent. Then, "I'm sorry, Sydney."

"She died this morning. She had been quite ill."

"Was it a stroke?"

"No. Two strokes had left her partly disabled, but no, it was pneumonia."

"Oh."

"I talked to her two days ago. She said she could hear the water in her lungs."

"I'm so sorry."

"She had given up. Had quit fighting."

"That doesn't sound like her."

"Well, since the last stroke . . . you haven't talked to her recently, have you?"

"No. Not in a long time."

"It's too bad how we lose contact with those who mean so much to us, isn't it?"

"I don't think I ever meant that much to Ava, Sydney."

"I beg your pardon?"

"I was a brief episode. Nothing more."

"You must be joking."

"No, not at all."

"Do you mean you don't know what she did for you?"

"She stopped seeing me."

"To save your career. Possibly more."

"I don't understand."

"General, when you were to be court-martialed, Ava insisted that I find out what the facts were at the embassy. When I told her it was improper for me to pry into the business of the United States government, she gave me to know I would do it or else. Well, I did." He paused at the memory. "I learned that the principal authority in your case was the Air Attaché. I told her that."

"General Sam Elliott."

"Yes, I think that was the bloke. She made me introduce them. Ava somehow forced him to dismiss charges against you and to discipline the officer who was bringing those charges against you."

"She what?"

"Don't ask me how. Lord knows what she may have done. Whatever it was, she did it."

"I never knew."

"There is something else you didn't know, General. Ava knew there was more than your career in jeopardy, General. There was your life. She was not going to let you be blinded by your infatuation. For that reason she left London that winter."

"She wanted to make a film."

"Rubbish. It wasn't the film. You would have stayed in London if she had been here. And she left in spite of everything."

"What do you mean, 'in spite of everything'?"

"The doctor told her she must have surgery to prevent future strokes. She refused, because that meant that she would be in London and you would have stayed with her. She left so you would return to your career. She may have risked her life, General."

Russ didn't know what to say.

"I never knew anyone like her," said Sydney. "I can't imagine life without her."

Russ could no longer speak. He couldn't think. Long, silent moments passed.

"Good-bye, Russell."

He tried to say thank you, but he couldn't. He mumbled, "Good . . . good-bye."

He rose from his desk, crossed the office, took his uniform coat off the hanger, and went outside. The desert air was cool. He walked toward the officers' club, only a block away.

He remembered other days, other walks. A Friday afternoon when he had wandered aimlessly onto Ennismore Gardens and the rich, colorful foliage of the trees lining it. Another autumn day and the paths of Hyde Park lined with flowers of gold and yellow, and the soft haze over the park's Serpentine Lake. Her arm in his.

He entered the officers' club and went directly to the bar. Apart from the noise of the television, it was quiet. There was also noisy laughter from the stag bar downstairs. It was the informal bar where flight suits were always the uniform of the day, where war stories and hilarious accounts of misdeeds flourished, and young fighter aviators could be rowdy.

Charley, the bartender, looked up in surprise. "General! Haven't seen you in a long time." In a gesture of welcome he wiped the shining bar where his customer took a stool.

"Hello, Charley, how are you?"

"Just fine, sir. What can I get you?"

"I'll have a double G. Gordon's gin with tonic."

The bartender left to mix the drink. Jefferson stared at the mirror behind the bar. Glass shelves filled with bottles were mounted against the mirror, and their reflections created a kaleidoscope of pattern, color, and light.

Charley returned and placed the drink on a napkin in front of him. "Is the television irritating you, General?" He started to turn it off.

"Leave it on, Charley. The network news is coming on soon. I want to see it."

"Sure," said the bartender, and he went to the other side of the bar where another customer was taking a seat.

Russ sipped his drink and remembered. So long ago and yet the images were so clear. The afternoon at the Crown Inn in Chiddingfold, the expressions on the faces of the old men as she sat on the bar singing to them. Dining at the Dorchester after seeing *The King and I*.

And suddenly it had been over.

It had been all over except for the cuff-link story, of course. Cindy and Greg Powers had simply been unable to keep their experience to themselves, and soon the cuff-link-found-by-the-bed tale had reached legendary proportions. For years pilots had occasionally looked at him with *that* look—profound admiration—as a result.

The newscast began and he watched the commercials without interest. The day's lead story, a lengthy report, was on the economy. Then her picture appeared on the screen and he listened as the anchorman said:

American film star Ava Gardner died of pneumonia in her apartment this morning following a lengthy illness. Miss Gardner, MGM's top box-office star for fifteen years, soared to stardom in such films as Show Boat, The Snows of Kilimanjaro, The Barefoot Contessa, *and many others. In 1953 she was nominated for an Academy Award for her role in* Mogambo. *Ernest Hemingway once said she was the only actress he wanted to play the female roles in his stories. At the height of her career and after her stormy marriage to Frank Sinatra, Miss Gardner left Hollywood to live in Spain. She had been living in London since 1968. She was found this morning by her housekeeper. Funeral services will be held in North Carolina on January 29th.*

Miss Gardner died just one month after her sixty-seventh birthday.

Her picture filled the screen behind the announcer, who, looking levelly into the camera, solemnly said:

"Ava Gardner was once called 'the world's most beautiful animal.' "

The photograph stayed on the screen for a long moment. She was so beautiful. And she fascinated him now just as she had when he was twelve years old, sitting in a darkened Charlotte theater. He lifted his glass, toasting the image on the screen. The photograph faded into black.

He would fly an F-15 to Seymour-Johnson Air Force Base. It would be less than an hour's drive from the base to Smithfield and her funeral.

The plains of the midlands were behind him now. Ahead was the flat delta and the wide, brown ribbon of the Mississippi River, winding and meandering its way to the Gulf. Soon the green mountains of Tennessee would be in view. And then North Carolina.

Russ checked in with the FAA. "Nashville Center, Disco one, flight level two-nine. Seymour-Johnson."

"Roger, Disco One. Nashville Center copies. Maintain heading and altitude."

He shifted his weight in the seat and adjusted his oxygen mask. The F-15 cruised between scattered clouds. There were some buildups to the south, nothing to worry about. He ran an instrument check. Everything normal.

In just over an hour he would be in North Carolina. Small towns, dirt roads, and tobacco fields. Where little girls once ran around barefoot half the year and loved the feel of soft mud and dirt under their feet, stream water between their toes.

Three thousand people had silently filed through the Underwood Funeral Home that day, sometimes whispering as they caught sight of the spray with the card signed "With my love, Frank." The funeral parlor was quiet now that the period for public viewing was over. A woman moved slowly from one floral arrangement to another, removing the cards from each wreath and spray. It was a southern custom for thank-you notes to mention particulars, so she jotted a brief description on the back of each card she removed. She was perhaps seventy, a handsome woman, with iron-gray hair cut short. She performed her task without pause, for this outer room was filled with flowers and there were many cards to collect.

A movement caught her eye, and she looked up to see a man slowly approaching the casket. He was slender and wore an Air Force uniform. His dark hair was flecked with gray at the temples. His face was angular, his features well defined. He stopped at the casket and stood perfectly still.

The woman placed the handful of cards on a chair and went quietly to the front of the funeral home into the brightly lit office of the funeral director. He was sitting at his desk and stood up when she entered.

"Mr. Underwood," she said softly but firmly, "we were very definite about the hours available to the public."

"Yes, ma'am. Nine to six. Today only."

"Well, a man just entered the viewing room."

"Yes, ma'am. He said he was a friend of Ava's."

"Oh, really? I don't know him."

"That's what he said, Miss Myra," Underwood said apologetically. "Also, he was a high-ranking Air Force officer."

The woman returned to the outer room. She stopped at the doorway, just as the dark-haired man leaned over the casket and placed something inside. He stood very still, gazing down thoughtfully. Without looking left or right he turned and walked away, stopping only to sign the guest book. He put the pen down and then disappeared through the doorway.

The woman went to the casket. They had taken precautions before the public had been allowed to view the body—soft, dark purple ropes connected to brass standards restraining visitors well beyond reach of the casket. They had feared that some would want to touch, or to place things in the casket. And now this solitary man had done just that, and the woman was angry. He wasn't a family friend; she knew that much. She went over to the casket and saw immediately what he had placed there.

The small gold object lay on the satin, partially hidden by a fold. She picked it up and looked closer. An ordinary cuff link. She held it and looked at the door through which the man had left.

A gold cuff link.

How very curious. She went to the register to see who this man was.

The next day skies were heavy and gray. It had been raining at first light, and a mist filled the air. The Sunset Memorial Park was just off Highway 70 coming into town, surrounded by modest houses and trailers. Trees with naked limbs lined the streets and dotted the cemetery grounds. A green pavilion covered a grave site.

The pavilion was in place to shelter the family and close friends who now gathered. Fifty or so relatives and friends had arrived, most of them still standing outside the canopy, in twos or threes, speaking softly to one another. Twenty feet away a larger crowd was gathered, held back by the yellow rope cordoning off the family plot. Some stood reverently and were respectfully quiet. Most in this crowd, however, were dressed not in funeral attire but as tourists, and they whispered excitedly to one another as they craned their necks to see if any Hollywood stars were in attendance.

Myra was about to enter the pavilion when she looked over at the crowd. Standing at the yellow rope, and seemingly unaware of the crush of people around him, was the dark-haired officer from yesterday. He was wearing a raincoat over his uniform.

The mist was becoming a drizzle, and the family was now moving to the sheltered grave site. Russ buttoned his raincoat and opened his umbrella. It was beginning to rain harder.

The family was now gathered under the pavilion. The minister took his place before them, his open Bible at his chest. Everyone huddled under umbrellas. The service began.

Russ thought for a moment that the scene was strangely reminiscent of the opening scene from one of her best movies, *The Barefoot Contessa*, in which a large crowd is gathered in the rain at a cemetery, at the funeral of a beautiful actress. Ava had portrayed a dancer from the wrong side of town who had become a movie star.

He was grateful for his stolen moment with her last night. It had been a private, reflective time, unlike standing with this large crowd of onlookers today. The rain now drummed on his umbrella.

The service ended after the brief eulogy. He watched as family members and close friends put roses on the cherrywood coffin and offered one another comforting words. Many in the large crowd started moving away, for it was too wet to stand out there any longer. Russ remained at the rope, thoughts of her holding him to this place.

He wasn't sure how long he stood there, but only a few of the curious remained clustered nearby when he became aware of a woman walking toward him. She was attractive, with gray, short hair, wearing a dark coat and scarf. He recognized her from the funeral home the night before.

"Hello," she said softly as she neared him. "Did I see you last night?"

"Yes," he said.

Now she stood very near him. "My name is Myra Pearce. I'm Ava's sister. You *are* Russ Jefferson, aren't you? Major Russell Jefferson?"

"Yes. How did you know?"

"The guest book. You signed it. Your name was familiar."

"How?"

"Oh, Ava talked about you a lot. There was only one Russell *Thomas* Jefferson."

"It was a very long time ago."

"Would you go to the car with me, Major? Oh, I'm sure you're more than a major now, aren't you? I don't know about military ranks."

"That's okay."

"The car isn't far," she said.

"Of course."

They walked through the wet grass, and she motioned to the row of cars behind the hearse. "It's right over here, Major. I'm sorry. What is your rank now?"

"General."

"Oh, she would have liked that."

They were at the funeral home limousine. She opened the back door and removed a small paper bag from the floor. "During the past few months, Ava was recording her autobiography. As she worked on it, there were certain items she identified that she wanted given to particular persons. She wanted you to have this." She handed the paper bag to him.

It was light, and he could feel a box inside the bag. "Are you sure?"

"Yes, General. Ava wasn't the most organized person in the world, but in the end she got some things in order and left quite specific instructions." Her expression of certainty reminded him of her sister.

"Thank you."

"I hope it means as much to you as it did to her."

"I'm sure it will."

The rain became heavier, drumming harder on their umbrellas. "We should go now," she said. "It's only going to get worse."

"Yes. It's time to go." He reached to take her hand. "Thank you."

She held his hand firmly. "You're more than welcome, General."

He moved away from her, holding the paper bag carefully under the umbrella to keep it dry. He sauntered slowly, not ready to leave. He wanted to be in this place a while longer. No one was at the pavilion now other than cemetery workmen. The casket had been lowered into its grave, and the men were beginning their work. Soon they would have everything removed and the only indication of what had taken place today would be the fresh dirt. He walked to the grave site, stepping under the pavilion and folding his umbrella.

It was a family plot. One large monument said simply GARDNER. A few feet away, almost covered with flowers, was her small marker. It was a temporary marker of metal, and it was inscribed AVA LAVINIA. He hoped they would leave the pavilion in place longer. He didn't like to think of the dirt around her becoming mud.

Carefully he removed the box from the bag. The top was held closed by Scotch tape. He tore the tape with a fingernail and opened the box. It was the doll. The Detherage original. That remarkable likeness of her in that scene from *Show Boat*. As he held the doll closer, he could almost feel her presence.

He forgot it was raining.